Silence Under a Stone

Norma MacMaster

Doubleday Ireland

TRANSWORLD IRELAND
Penguin Random House Ireland, Morrison Chambers,
32 Nassau Street, Dublin 2, Ireland
www.transworldireland.ie

Transworld Ireland is part of the Penguin Random House group of companies
whose addresses can be found at global.penguinrandomhouse.com

First published in the UK and Ireland in 2018
by Doubleday Ireland
an imprint of Transworld Publishers

A CIP catalogue record for this book
is available from the British Library.

ISBN 9781781620441

Typeset in 11/15 pt Minion by Jouve (UK), Milton Keynes
Printed and bound in Great Britain by Clays Ltd, Bungay, Suffolk

Penguin Random House is committed to a sustainable
future for our business, our readers and our planet. This book
is made from Forest Stewardship Council® certified paper.

1 3 5 7 9 10 8 6 4 2

For Gwyneth, with love

To the memory of Vernon Grattan MacMaster (1939–2016),
my beloved husband and faithful encourager

All the . . . little orthodoxies . . . contending for our souls.

George Orwell

CHAPTER 1

The Cairn, 1924

'Move over there, child, like a good boy, till I get this hem fixed.'

I tugged at the strong thread I was using to patch my husband's trousers. Our son, not much more than a baby really, was twisting himself around the iron legs of my sewing machine, in my way as I worked the treadle.

He undid himself slowly. 'When is she coming?'

I stopped the wheel and looked down at the pale freckled face. He was anxious these days ever since his father had said we must have a woman to help in the house.

'She'll be coming tomorrow.'

'And will she be here long?'

'Until Father says.'

He stood up. He was small for his age, still in need of caresses and cuddles.

'Where will she sleep?'

'In her own house.'

He clung to me now as I undid the swatch of cloth and snipped off the thread. 'I don't want her to come.'

'I know. But your father says.'

I folded the sewing machine away. 'Come on, James. We

have to collect the eggs and feed the hens before he comes in from the fields.'

At once he was ready, although his lip quivered.

That night when I was putting him to bed he was still anxious so I chose 'Daniel and the Lions' for his scripture portion. It was a longer text than usual, and while I read I held him close as I thought of another scripture that warned of 'bad seed'. My mind wandered out to the high-waving meadows and the hillocky acres of oats, and I knew that if ever bad seed was sown out there, we'd have no bud, no meal, nothing come harvest. Rebuking myself, I knelt to hear the child's trustful prayers, thin lisping tones that begged protection on us all: me, his father and Sailor the dog. Then I smoothed his bed covers, kissed him, and as I tiptoed out to the landing, I heard the back door shut with a bang.

I hurried down just as the clock chimed for a quarter past seven. Thomas was in very early and would be looking for his dinner. I picked up my apron from the hook by the kitchen door and watched him while he slowly undid the whangs of his boots and set them on the rung under the table, his broad back bent as he stretched, and the worn grey overalls needing a stitch.

'We finished the near meadow sooner than I thought.' He straightened himself. 'And the oats will be going in next week.'

I put down a plate of cabbage and a bit of bacon saved from Sunday. 'That's good.'

He tore at the meat eagerly, chewing and whistling through his moustache, and at last said, 'I hope the boy's asleep.' I was tempted that minute to speak again of my fears, but he added, with a smart slap on the table, 'His whims and fancies must never be pandered to if he's ever to be a man.'

He talked some more then about the planting and the good men he had working, while I waited, mopping and wiping in silence behind him. Then, scraping up the last of his dinner, he pulled off the overalls and headed to the scullery. I heard water splashing and the mumbled snatch of a hymn and I knew he was drawing the razor over his face.

'There's a meeting in the church tonight.' His words, thick and mangled, came echoing back to where I stood by the empty plate, my hands twisted up in my apron and a hollowed-out place filling my stomach. 'You'll be in bed the time I get home?'

'I will.'

It was very chilly that evening. The clocks had gone forward, and there was a miserable coldness lingering on in the house even with winter passed.

CHAPTER 2

Sunnyside Residential Home, spring 1982

Well, that's just a bit of my story and there's no chill where I'm housed now. I eke out my days here with care, spend them carefully one at a time, like pennies in this one little room where all the straggles and strays of my life are gathered up neat as a ball of wool; the eighty-two years of them drawn taut to a single hard knot that weighs me down like a stone.

From my window I look out on smooth parkland bright with daffodils; the snowdrops and crocuses are finished and the snow that brought its own comforting blanket is now softening the earth; there's even a glimmer of sunshine. Nearby I see the gardener trundling a wheelbarrow down a path. Every day he comes to dig and rake and hoe, and since I have so few visitors, I've come to consider him a friend. Now he's kneeling down beside a flower bed and begins to sow seed – it's seed without blight, no doubt, shaken from little green packets. I sit back and watch him with some satisfaction as he goes on tending these lawns with their giant ferns and ladylike willows, all so unlike The Cairn, where laurels shoved themselves rudely out of the damp near the parlour window and wild poppies and scutch grass awaited the snick-snack of the scythe. I feel relaxed today, content enough to be lodged here with only, on occasion, a passing wish to be free the way I was before the weakness overtook me: this terrible shortness of breath that can level me, remind me that it can't be too long till I meet my Maker. But that thought's for another day.

I read an article recently that said the way to iron out creases in your head was to write down the happenings of your life, the good and the bad, not that I have that many creases to smooth out any more, just some tangled snarls of shocking bad feeling that cling to me, sticking like cobwebs. So I write things down in this little book, a present last Christmas from Molly McKinley, a member of Ballymount Presbyterian. I didn't think I'd use it for more than sticking in a few pictures cut out of a magazine the way we do here during what they call OT, but when I gave it some thought, I was deterred from abusing its prettiness by fixing 'houses' and 'ladies' and 'flowers' on the smooth and delicate pages, each enscrolled with a text of scripture, so boldly I wrote 'Harriet Campbell's Life' on the cover. Of course, I realize it won't be me who'll write the ending and I must be content in the knowledge that 'all things work together for good to them that love God'.

I was born in 1900 in the back lands south of what was to become the Border, and for over thirty years have been truly afraid to tell the story I'm about to set down. But it has to be brought out, its doings excised like poison from a boil, and so I'll disclose as much of it as I can. I don't live in The Cairn now, of course, which I'm not sorry about because that big house was always unfriendly and cold, a great lump of granite thrown down by the Campbells in a weeping wet valley where the sun seldom shone, a house bald and bleak as the things that went on in it.

There are so many things I don't like to think about now, but I've learned to rein in my mind, wild steed that it is; harness the troublous scenes that come one on top of the other, folding themselves over and over like the jumps on a paddock. And at night, *when the curtains are drawn, dark memories gather like drumming black beetles and my heart beats faster and faster making me pray that God will strengthen me according to his Word. The Bible was always a great comfort in my younger days, but I'm not as religious as that any more, yet Molly McKinley goes on calling with the Scripture Union notes and tells me she still plays the harmonium in Ballymount Presbyterian – such a terrible place for me at one time, with people accusing and cold as last Sunday's mutton. So I think it's a credit to Molly to keep on coming although we have nothing to talk about now.*

Away near the big white gate to the road the gardener's still busy sowing and planting and a breeze is gently ruffling the willows, scattering the birds. I like the goldfinches best; they used to feed on the grass at the back of The Cairn, and I remember the time that Thomas, my husband, wanted to snare them with birdlime, which was cruel enough and yet there was cruelty in him of another sort.

There's a rap on my door now and I turn round: it's Bernadette, the rosy-cheeked girl who looks after me, coming like clockwork with another tray.

'How are you doing, missus?'

I shift in my chair and tell her I'm fine, fine enough.

She settles the tray in front of me and tells me to eat up, that the 'egg in a cup' will make me strong. A breezy young one, she bustles about, closing a window, humping up a cushion.

'Any visitors today?'

Idle chat. I ignore the question for she knows very well that Cissie Lynch was here this morning, dear Cissie, my Roman Catholic friend and neighbour of many years. I sigh, pick up the spoon and look around me: someone else must have come while I was nodding off for there are mignonettes there in the vase that I didn't see until now. Perhaps they were left by Sarah, who calls now and then, treating me always as if I'm half simple, with her 'Can I wash your face? Can I comb your hair? Can I knit you something?' Oh, I'm not as forgetful as people suppose nor as confused either, yet even so I do admit that a kind of a fog, what we used to call a haar, is beginning to creep over me on occasion so that if it wasn't for this window showing me snow one day and violets another, I mightn't even know the time of the year. For in this Home days can lose names, and time bloom and sway like weed in still water. I have too much time, and that's a problem, for my thoughts aren't always the best: like burned-out cinders they still hold some heat, and fiery sparks can erupt in their gritty blackness.

Bernadette is still here, staying longer than she needs to, pitying, hovering, arranging.

'Oh, I nearly forgot to say,' she tells me. 'That lovely son of yours called again this morning, missus, but you were down in the art room doing OT, and he wouldn't have you disturbed. Left you those flowers, he did.' She straightens them up in the vase. 'You're so lucky to have him, you know. They say he was very devoted to you all through the years.'

'Hm.'

'Many's a one,' she persists, 'is just left here with no one at all.'

'Well, he knows his scripture, my dear.' That's that and I turn my face to the wall.

She makes no response but, examining her teeth and hair in my mirror, tells me I should try to be cheerful, if only for him, because I'll get used to it all. And I mutter, 'A person can get used to anything.' But I don't believe what I say. I watch as she undoes the tie on her apron and wipes her damp face with a cloth. How could I explain? How could I hurt this innocent Roman Catholic girl by beginning to recite my history, none of it her fault?

'*Your minister's here too, waiting to see you, and that'll be nice, but I suppose there's no place like home after all, is there?*'

She watches me eat, then turns to pick up the shawl which I've laid at the end of my bed. Purple and embroidered with peacocks, this flowing silk shawl was a gift from my son long years ago and I give a sharp cry as she lumps it up in her hands. 'Put that down at once.' She reddens, picks up the tray and, as the door closes behind her, I take a deep breath, sit up straight and wonder at the intensity of pain that shoots through me, on fire all over again. I take that shawl into my hands, hold its fine weave to my cheek. In all this time it has lost none of its wine-flowing softness; it remains unblemished save for a smudge on the corner down near the tassels. I linger entrapped in a moment of far-off sunshine that's edged with grey before folding the garment gently and thrusting it firmly into the back of a drawer.

Just then the Reverend Boyd, successor to the late Reverend McGoldrick, raps on my door. He's a nice enough man and comes often to see me. Unfailingly he comments on the weather and enquires after my health. I always tell him, of course, that I'm grand, always grand, for there's nothing he could do about the knots of sorrow-filled anger forever threading through me. He asks again about 'family', and I tell him again that there's no one but James, my son. He says nothing to that, so I say it once more for him. 'James,' I say and I watch the name flutter idly in the air like a leaf, detached, just another word like grass or box . . . or blade.

As we sit, Reverend Boyd and I, the sun creeps down along the floor, marking out time, covering the squares on the lino. It's very quiet in the afternoon: only a man in a clerical collar and me in what Thomas used to call the half-asleep time, this languor that can fall across the middle of any afternoon. I feel very tired all of a sudden, drop my chin and sit silent, filled with drowsiness. My thoughts are running to a blur, and I hope to goodness I don't say them out loud for he'd surely think me demented.

When I raise my head, he's still there, patient, silent, waiting like Sailor the old dog we had long ago at home; waiting for me to come back, waiting perhaps to hear from my lips what he must surely have heard already from the people in Ballymount Church.

At last he rises to his feet, 'May I come again?'

I nod acquiescence for I find his company agreeable and soothing in its peaceful spaciousness, inviting conversation and disclosures, yet making no demands. As he puts on his coat, I look past him to the treetops wagging their heads at the end of the garden and know that I'll tell him nothing – not today anyway, some other time maybe.

But when he's gone, I sense a new spirit in me: something like a prayer he's left behind, a kind of hope, a wispy shred of assurance, and I go on sitting by the window, my crooked fingers not fidgeting now but resting in my lap. The gardener has finished his work, and in the late-afternoon sunshine the grass is so green I can almost feel its dewy softness; the still darker leaves of the forsythia by the window twinkle with leftover raindrops bright with promise, and I know a marvellous quickening of my spirit. Tomorrow, if I'm spared, I'll write some more.

CHAPTER 3

It seems like yesterday that I was wed. It was a balmy spring day in 1916 and, along with my own flutterings, I remember the rumbles of trouble and strife that were coming from Dublin. My mother often took the *Anglo Celt* and she read out some hair-raising stories from folk who'd managed to leave the city. But, like distant thunder at the end of hay-making, Dublin was too far away to bother us much; France was closer. And cruel it was to know that so many of our lads from Ballymount – Wauhobs and McIntoshes, Wilsons and Fishers, the cream of the flock – went on fighting for King and Country in Europe's Great War while underhand ruffians in Dublin were going behind their backs. Oh, the terrible things that were going on as I left my childhood home, an innocent bride.

I was just turned sixteen when I married Thomas, and he was heading for thirty-one. Looking at the one photo of the wedding, I came to see what a slight young person I was at that time: my forehead high, long dark hair plaited in little coils over my ears, my face full of trust and hope. I had my pick of fellows then, though there weren't too many left on account of the war. Every Sabbath after service, I'd see them hanging around the gravestones, and I'd think how handsome they looked, all cleaned up and tidy, their hair sleeked smooth with Brylcreem. I'd been in the Ballymount School with them all and had more than a bit of an eye for Johnny Williamson, but sadly Johnny was one of the first to be killed in France – him and Georgie, my brother.

There had only been myself and George in the family, and even though older than me, he and I used to play together when the work was done, making wee boats of paper to float on the stream or looking to see where the birds were nesting. But Georgie was wilful and bold, and as soon as he turned eighteen, he enlisted to fight for the king, wouldn't be stopped, and that went hard on me and my parents.

Yet after he'd gone, I continued at home, carefree enough in spite of the skirmishing beyond in the fields and the rumours that Mr Carson's volunteers were patrolling the lanes. Regardless of all, I'd fall asleep every night lulled by the Woodford River that flowed by the end of our lane on its way to the loughs in Fermanagh, the magical land where we went for our outing at Christmas and again to the 'walks' on the Twelfth.

But I remembered that terrible day when I was sent out on my own to look for a heifer strayed in the storm. I was a young one of no more than fourteen years at the time, but Father was laid up with pains and Mother had to be by. So off I went with an ashplant. The wind tore at my coat as I battled through bucketing rain; branches of trees were everywhere down but I struggled on, and I'll never forget meeting wee Harry Watts, the telegraph boy, beating his way to our house. Forgetting the heifer, I turned at once and went back with him and later we both held our breath as Father opened the envelope: 'We regret to inform you . . .' And that's how poor Georgie went to his Maker while serving the king. I remember no more of that night.

Georgie's death had a bad effect on us all, but it was my father who took to his bed and died not long after.

I do believe it was then that a line was drawn under my childhood, for thereafter my mother, in need of more help, took me from school although I'd barely begun the Seventh Book. I would always be sad to think how, just after my fourteenth birthday, I was told to put learning behind me and how Mother paid me no heed when I wept, just bade me put on an apron and set up the churn. (How quickly I had to grow up, how quickly become a woman, how quickly a wife.)

I felt very lonesome myself for a while after that, but during those months I noticed that my mother was getting very friendly with Thomas Campbell. Thomas was a long, burly man even then, much older than the ones who hung round the gravestones, and he used to come over to talk to her when the service was ended. I'd listen as they talked about fairs and bullocks and the sowing, never dreaming that it was me they had in mind at the back of it all. I was much in awe of him then, big hefty man that he was with feet like ploughshares and a face open to the wind, raw and laughing as he handed around his bags of boiled sweets. Very often he called to the house to return a saw he'd borrowed or to give Mother a sack of windfalls, but one evening in June, when we could do no more with the hay, I happened to be walking the road with a can of buttermilk for a neighbour. I was taking my time, just ambling along, when I heard the squeal of tyres on the road behind me. Startled, I jumped to move out of the way but there, all set to dismount from his bicycle, was Thomas Campbell himself, out of his overalls and all dressed up. He continued to sit on the saddle with his two great feet splayed on the ground before him. 'Where are you off to, girl?' He held out the bag of sweets. I was quite taken aback, abashed to be spoken to thus all by myself.

'I'm going to McKinleys'.'

'Put your can up here on the handlebars and I'll give you a lift across to their place. That's too heavy a job on a warm evening like this after your day in the hay.'

Well, when you're a young one of only fifteen years you can feel fine and fluttery on a summer's evening, so I paid no heed to the bite of the crossbar, felt giddy in truth as we wheeled through lanes that were scented with honeysuckle, and the faraway sky slowly turning dark blue. Then all at once we stopped, so sudden I thought I'd go over the handlebars, but he dropped the bike in the ditch and, grabbing me roughly as if I'd annoyed him, he put his hand down the front of my frock. I felt hot and weak, and when I protested, he just laughed and put his mouth over mine; and so it was there in those dewy-sweet grasses of summer that I first felt the bristling moustache and his breath falling over me, sticky and warm. Then he laughed again, threw his leg over the bar of his bicycle and said he'd be seeing me.

Next day, still ruffled and very put out, I recounted it all to Cissie. I was full of shame but she just laughed – 'Oh, you'll have to grow up now, didn't you know?' – and she twirled the strings of her bonnet. 'That's the way of life, my girl: more to it than folderols and skipping ropes. Besides,' and she gave me a hug, 'you can be glad he's one of your own.'

But after that I was very afraid of Thomas Campbell and had sinking feelings whenever he came by our house with apples or such. Of a sudden he seemed to be everywhere: even in church he sat right in front of our pew so that I could count the stripes on his broad serge back, see the creases in his red-burned neck and the hair slicked to one side to hide the patch that was bald. Or I'd find him in the kitchen along with my mother, a porringer of buttermilk clenched in his fist and the two of them talking earnestly together. Then I'd feel I must shy away at once, but Mother would call me briskly to come forward and greet 'Mr Campbell', as she insisted on calling him. And on seeing me stand by the table, awkward, reluctant to move a step further, he'd reach for the bag of boiled sweets he always kept in his pocket and, with a grin like the slipe on a mower, he'd hold it out to me.

And so our courtship began, driven by mother and Church, but it felt no more like romance than 'Hey diddle diddle, the cat and the fiddle . . .' although he was always very attentive. He took me to dances in his smart little pony trap and provided a rug of fine plaid to spread over my knees, visited our house more often than before, walked with me in the darkening lanes, and the kissing went on; yet I knew in my heart that, behind all the niceties of talk and behaviour, something more ponderous lay ahead, something as grave as an oath on a Bible. In due course arrangements were made for our marriage. I protested at first, not wanting to settle, for a liveliness still ran in my veins and a longing, but I yielded for peace, with my mother pleading that Thomas Campbell was a good catch, what with him being a farmer of substance, a Presbyterian and an Orangeman. She emphasized too how it would be such an easy house to walk into, with his parents passed over and his only relation a distant cousin living somewhere beyond in Scotland.

And so our wedding took place in Ballymount Church, me in a nice white frock quickly run up by Mother. Thomas, stiff and unsmiling in a navy-blue suit, stood by me, and Sam Hanna, an elder, stood in for my father. I felt like crying there in the church, and the posy of daisies shook in my hand, yet I held myself tight as I said the required words in a marriage service that was down to the bone like always, simple and dree, quickly over. With scarcely a thought I had promised to obey my new husband, to serve and assist him all my days as a pious and faithful wife, and if I shivered that day as I stood being kissed at the door of the church, it wasn't because of the wind that whipped around the hills. Thomas Campbell was a good man and righteous, but I knew even then that there wasn't much more than a promise in our attachment.

The women of the church provided the wedding breakfast, and no sooner was it over than my husband was helping me over the puddles around The Cairn, his two-storey farmhouse, grey and empty and waiting. I sniffed back a few tears as we entered, but he bolstered me up and said that before too long, he'd be hiring Owenie Brady to carry us off in his hackney car to the seaside on honeymoon.

So, sure enough, the very next day, as soon as the milking was done, Owenie Brady drove us over to Laytown. Arrived at the strand, I clambered quickly out of the car, looked around me and threw off my shoes. The sky was so clear that day, the air so thin, and I ran off at once, barefoot and laughing like any child, way out to the faraway tide. And I marvelled at how all my fears dropped away and, knowing again the freedom of the meadows and lanes I'd strayed in with Cissie, I drew my frock up to my knees, paddled and splashed in the little white waves. Excited, I waved back to Thomas, but he was far away now, almost a dot, sitting unmoved on the bank where I'd left him, his trousers rolled up, his white feet splayed on the grass. I was skipping through water, my skirt in my hands, but my dancing slowed down as I recalled the past night: how my new husband had lingered below in the kitchen till, trembling, I'd got into the bed, and how, even in the dark, I'd been shy of his nearness, frightened by his great looming strangeness beside me; and then, when his sudden frenzy left off, how he'd risen so quickly and gone. And I lay bewildered, empty and bruised, in the cold grey dawn, my body an alien thing. I stayed there for a while, nursing my hurts, and heard him grumbling away to himself below in the kitchen. But I needed to wash, and even as the water trickled through my fingers into the basin I recalled how Mother had told me I'd soon get used to being a wife.

But it was chilly now and the waves were getting bigger, so I went back to Thomas and found him asleep. He roused himself quickly and shared out the cold potatoes and beef he'd brought, and we ate together on a bank at the Nanny River, admired the seaweed that swirled and the wind that sang in the telegraph wires. I wanted to mention the night before, hoped he'd have some little word to say about that, but the time passed on and Owenie was back with his car to carry us home: the cows wouldn't wait.

Still, in the following flattened-out early days of our marriage, I gradually grew used to all his wee ways. He was nice enough, and I did believe he tried to be kind. I supposed too that in many ways we were fairly well matched, like the good team he ploughed with, him doing the heavy work and me the poultry and calves. And of course we worshipped together: Sabbath by Sabbath we sat side by side in Ballymount Church, four pews from the front. Here I delighted to hear myself called Mrs Campbell (the first Mrs Campbell and her husband being long deceased), and I'd smile across the aisle, nodding to this one and that. I was one of them now, an obedient wife, careful in Sabbath observance and, God willing, might soon be a mother.

Round The Cairn there was always plenty of labour, but this was no trouble for I'd been brought up to work very hard, and so the days and the weeks passed swiftly away as I settled into my new life. Aside from the poultry and calves, I was kept busy with sewing, mending and scrubbing, and on Saturday nights I brushed down Thomas's suit for Meeting and set out his best leather boots. Quickly I learned all his needs: how he liked his razor and strop laid out at the side of the basin, his overalls washed every Monday and his porridge hot and not too thick. On occasion, when time permitted, I'd call to see Mother, lonely now with Father passed and her two children gone.

But in winter, when night fell and the range was stoked up, I'd sometimes look across at Thomas stretched on the horse-hair sofa under the tilley lamp and think how nice it would be if he'd come and sit by me. Yet I was slowly learning that he wasn't a feeling man: he always had to be reading the paper or changing the battery in the wireless or something like that, and I pretended not to notice the times he was sullen and contrary for he was God-fearing, devout in his practice, and who was I to trespass on a righteous mind. Every night without fail before we'd retire, he'd take down the Bible and call me to the table, where we'd read together in the arc of the lamp, but even as he read with a voice like the burr of a saw my thoughts would stray from the bold-printed pages to the cloth's lacy white edges and I'd fall to the wonder of dreaming. I was high-spirited and playful still, and the sameness of month piled on month began to weary me, and the days to fall dark, like great herringbone coats heavy with rain. And slowly I realized that for my husband there was only The Cairn and Ballymount, Ballymount and The Cairn. Still, I chided myself daily for being ungrateful, minded of the hymn we sang so often in Meeting:

The daily round and common task
Should furnish all we need to ask.
Room to deny ourselves,
A road to bring us nearer unto God.

And I longed for a child, but as month after month went by,
I wept, bewildered by failure.

CHAPTER 4

We were much alone over those early years of our marriage: never had many callers, unlike at home, where our door had always stood open with this one and that stopping by for a bit of a chat. Sometimes my mother, ever full of praise for Thomas, called on us whenever she got a lift in a cart, and it was hard for me to hear the two of them above in the parlour, him praising her for the way she'd brought me up and her admiring his devotion to the Church and the Orange Order. Sometimes Cissie called to get a read of the *Celt* on her way from Mass, or it could be Johnny Long to collect the milk churns for the creamery, but on the whole there were few visitors, and I wouldn't count Sam Hanna, the elder, and a tailor by trade, who came once a month, just doing his duty: making sure there was nothing amiss with us or if we happened to be absent from Meeting for any reason, wanting to know why. Twice in the year Reverend McGoldrick himself came, having given us notice. This was an important visitation, and in the parlour I'd take down the china tea set, a wedding present from Mother, and on a table dressed with an embroidered cloth I'd set out some of my gingerbread. Thomas would pull around the chairs then, and when tea was over the three of us would pass an hour in wholesome converse and prayer.

And so the months passed, all heavy and toilsome: a

Christmas would no sooner be over than the ploughing would begin; and then the harrowing with myself dropping seed in the potato drills, a sacking apron round my waist. Secretly I often felt sorry for myself, thinking of summer lanes and lost freedoms, but I spoke nothing of this to Thomas, not wishing to disappoint or annoy him.

After the days of summer, the time I liked best was the winter nights. Those pure black, silent hours, not a stir from outside except for the foothering of the wind in the fir trees at the head of the lane and the gate to the paddock creaking. Sometimes the briar rose would scrape at the window and cause me to startle, but other than that there'd be not a sound save for the tap of my needles and the tick of the clock and the gentle purr of the tilley.

I always sat close to the range with my knitting those times, while Thomas, forever diligent, rootled away at something or other. Often, when he'd finished his tricking and mending, he'd take down the ledger which was kept in the corner press along with the Bible, and if I dared say as much as a word while he examined its columns, he'd frown and tell me to hush. The accounts had to be right to the last halfpenny, and he'd study and fret and look at me over his glasses, wanting to know about the '1oz. of fine wool purchased in McAdoo's Drapery on the 4th of May last' or the 'Fancy Goods @ 6d' bought in the same establishment. It was bred in us both to be careful in all our ways, to practise a wholesome thrift, and so I'd meekly endure his reproach and make no response save to rattle my needles a bit and whip up my wool.

But one wild wintry night when the wind was whistling and whining and the trees in the lane were creaking, ready to break, there came a rapping at the back door. I looked over at Thomas.

He rose in annoyance, pushed the ledger to the back of the press and gave me a nod, so out I went, and there, framed in the light of the scullery lamp, was Sam Hanna himself, his oilskins dripping and black with rain. He was a thin stripe of a man with deep-set eyes well sunk in his head and a face like a fox's, sharpish, the way you'd think he was always hunting for something. I looked at him standing on the doorstep, wringing his cap like a bar of soap. 'What in the name of goodness has you here, Mr Hanna, on such a night?'

'Let me in out of the rain and I'll tell you.'

He brushed past me then as if I was no more than a sack of oats and made straight to Thomas. 'Here's something, Brother, that'll make you sit up.'

I took a look at my husband, who was slouching low in his chair, eyes furrowed deep, jowls set, and not a word of welcome on his lips. I could see how annoyed he was at having his calculations interrupted, and I hoped for some news that'd take him out of himself, lighten his mood.

Sam Hanna drew himself up then, the lanky length of him dripping all over my floor. 'I was at a meeting of Kirk Session this night.' At this Thomas sat up in his chair, while I, flurried and fretting, tugged and pulled at the strings of my apron, uncertain whether to keep it on or take it off. The words 'Kirk Session' could drop like a boulder in people's hearts: draw them up to take measure of their sins and misdemeanours, make them ponder denials of duty and even cause them to examine their loves. In those times the eyes of the elders were everywhere. So we sat waiting that night, for hours it seemed, in a hush that hung like the web of a stocking, making me afraid to tug any more at the strings of my pinny. And Hanna just stood there, in the middle of the kitchen floor, blowing his nose and wiping his eyes until I longed to shake the news out of him.

'Well, what is it?' Thomas could wait no longer.

'Kirk Session is calling you, Brother, to submit yourself for election.'

Like in a mist then, I watched my husband gather himself up and reach for his glasses as Hanna passed him a paper. Then over and back, my poor man strode, his boots scraping the floor as he went. He read over the contents, looked to the ceiling, read again, while Hanna, his wee narrow face in a screw of delight, waited for what he would say. At length Thomas laid down the paper and I, greatly relieved, heard him laugh, a long deep laugh like a gurgling sheuch after rain.

'So they want me to be an elder, do they?' He tapped his knee with the folded paper. 'Well, the Lord be praised! Oh, I'll do my bit for Ballymount. You can tell them I will indeed.' And the two of them stood there a minute, slapping each other's backs.

Folding away my apron, I put on the kettle and was just about to set out a bit of fadge when Thomas turned to me and, taking me by the shoulders, looked into my face, his blue eyes like flints. 'Now, my good woman, what do you have to say to that!' I put down the plates and, with hands clasped together, said I was pleased, so be it God's will, and that I'd be his helpmate to share, if only a little, in the godly burden he'd been called to assume. He stood quiet then, thoughtful and smiling, his great hands gentling me, and forgetting all his moments of contrariness I felt a wonderful tremor of yearning run through me, but he only reached for the Bible and, before we took tea, the three of us sat down together to hear God's Word and give thanks. Later that night, as I watched the tail light of Hanna's bike wobble across the yard, I knew myself flooded with joy:

Thomas would make a fine ruling elder, righteous and astute in all his dealings, and I would help him.

We sat together a while longer than usual in the kitchen that night, Thomas cracking his knuckles and me pretending to count stitches, both of us caught in a kind of holy excitement. Oh, I knew there'd be plenty of work ahead, starting with the book learning, which I knew he wouldn't relish, and until old age put a stop, there'd be Meetings of Session and Bible Studies along with pastoral visitations and the spiritual oversight of the Lord's flock in Ballymount. Thomas's whole life would be dedicated to the Church. My own father had been an elder, and an Orangeman too, in his day, and I'd sometimes heard my mother complain that being an elder was like taking on another job of work; but I prayed that I myself wouldn't grumble: I'd do 'all things without murmurings and disputing', for such was the work of God's kingdom.

So after that, when winter nights fell I was no longer dull and listless for I put in the hours reviewing the *Shorter Catechism* with Thomas: all the questions, and the answers too along with their scriptural proofs. We also studied the 'Six Great Ends of the Church', and I rehearsed him hour after hour in the *Creeds* and in the required sections of the *Westminster Confession of Faith*. The *Confession* was like a deep and guttery sheuch to me, but we had to go through it so meticulously that I'd retain much of it myself. One bit in particular would be engraved on my mind for ever, as though etched upon stone: 'The Lord Jesus is the only head of the Church, and the pope is Antichrist and the son of perdition.' In all of these teachings Thomas would be examined by the elders both before his election and again at his ordination in Ballymount.

It was towards the end of the following April, when I sat in the pew and looked at him standing alone at the front of the church, his face flushed, Adam's apple working and his big farmer's hands wringing themselves, that I knew a rush of pity, even love. Question after question about his Christian faith was put to him by the minister and elders, and his voice rang out sure and true in response. Then came the final question, as I'd known it would: 'Do you accept that the *Westminster Confession* is founded on and agreeable to the scriptures and, as such, do you subscribe it as a confession of your own faith?' I held my breath, but he gave such a resounding 'Yes' that even deaf old Isaac McWhirter in the back seat heard it and jumped up crying, 'Praise the Lord!' The ceremony concluded with Reverend McGoldrick and the other elders giving Thomas 'the right hand of fellowship', and then I watched with pride as the little group left the church for the vestry: Reverend McGoldrick, the teaching elder, went first, followed by the ruling elders and, with them, my own husband, his head up and his shoulders straight in a wondrous new dignity. I knew it only remained for him now to ratify his acceptance of the *Confession* with his signature and 'the Lord's will would be done'. In the packed church there lingered a sweltering surge of emotion with a few of the congregation falling to their knees and fervently calling out long amens.

At home that night in the kitchen, all anxiety of the consecration over, Thomas put his arms around me and drew me close. As he kissed the back of my neck, I flushed with pleasure and nuzzled into the warm earthiness of his chest, but without a word he suddenly stepped away from me, went to the corner press and heaved down the *Family Bible*. Drawing me to sit with him under the lamp, he undid the metal clasps and opened up the great book. Now it was seldom we used that particular

Bible with its embossed leather cover and gilt tooling, so I held my breath, wondering and watching, as deftly he leafed through the pages. When he came to the place he was seeking, he laid the violet marker-ribbon across the sacred text and, looking to me with burning eyes, he began to read. Slowly and gravely he read so that each word fell like a stone dropped down a well: ' "A bishop then must be blameless, the husband of one wife, vigilant, sober, of good behaviour, given to hospitality, apt to teach; not given to wine, no striker, not greedy of filthy lucre; but patient, not a brawler, not covetous –" ' he paused here for a moment and reached for my hand ' "– one that ruleth well his own house, having the children in subjection with all gravity; for if a man knows not how to rule his own house, how shall he take care of the church of God? First Timothy 3:2–6." '

He closed the book at that, and, with a deep sigh for I didn't know what, he looked at me straight. 'Harriet, you understand that this is how it must be with us?' And all in a dither I said yes, and of course that's how it would surely be, for I knew that hour, knew in my heart how it would be. But that night my poor Thomas was kinder than ever before, and taking my hand he held the lamp for me as together we passed up the stairs and later he refrained from casting me roughly aside to the empty dark as he often did. So it was on that solemn night, the night of his installation as elder, that I knew sweet love.

CHAPTER 5

The following morning I rose up early and blithe and, thinking I'd almost forgotten how, I sang as I worked; even Thomas noticed. Leaving his porridge aside, he came out to me in the scullery, where I was scalding the churn, and he patted my head. 'You could be like this more often, I think.' And I knew I could, oh wished we would, and indeed for a good while after we were softer with each other, fitted better. And I went on longing, and Mother went on asking, but month after month passed by and I hadn't conceived so that many a time alone in the sweet-smelling hay of the haggart I brokenly wept at my failure. But February came and then March with its storms, and in April the ewes dropped their lambs in the pastures, and, glory of glories, I saw that I hadn't bled. Excited, I ran to tell Thomas the news. He was out in the stable mending a harness, and on hearing he laid down the packing needle and held me as never before, in a deep and silent embrace. Then we went indoors to offer our prayers.

For weeks towards the end of my term, I took to bed, and as I lay with the little life kicking inside me, I could see the bulge in the plaster over my head, a small white parachute about to open and drop. I'd hoped Thomas would have had this seen to before my lying-in, but he was busy he said and I tried to believe him although I knew full well that the harvest was long gathered in and Thanksgiving Festivals over. Around me, the wardrobes and tallboys of burnished mahogany reminded me of my 'place', and my husband's stern forebears stared out from their gilt frames: his mother wearing a plaid shawl, the father behind her, tall and loping, a cane in his hand. I had of course planned to brighten things up in our bedroom: maybe put up a nice sprigged wallpaper with delicate sprays and shoots of green; hang falls of snowy muslin from ceiling to floor and somehow coax in the sun. When I'd told this to Thomas, he promised to see what could be done, anything to keep me happy, he said, so he'd send to the town for wallpaper samples, get swatches of cloth from the draper, but there hadn't been time.

In those dismal days, waiting and lonely, I lay longing often for the home of my childhood: the low pink house with its rambling white rose and my own little room, its walls quite bare save for the text in the velveteen frame about the wages of sin. Finding no comfort for my weighted-down body, I sighed into the pillow now and longed for someone to talk to. On occasion, if there was a cart going into the town, Mother herself would get a lift to The Cairn and come and sit with her basket of knitting for she knew I'd be lonesome with Thomas so busy and me confined, not even getting to church any more, for I couldn't be seen there heavy with child.

When at last the pains started, grew frequent and hard, the midwife fluttered around, attending, busy as a bluebottle, sometimes stopping to rest on the low nursing chair, to take up needlework or read a paper; sometimes the doctor called, but my husband, in the way of men, betook himself to nearby cattle fairs for the duration of my labour.

For three long days, under the gaze of the Campbells, I

soldiered alone in that bedroom, and on the 14th day of January 1921 I gave birth to our beautiful child. Exhausted and happy, lying proud in a web of joy overflowing, I gazed in something like awe at my baby, so perfectly formed. Cuddling him close, I traced with my finger his tiny wrinkled features, smiled at the perplexed little forehead and wonderingly saw how, with a will all his own, he'd at once begun to nuzzle my breast. We'd christen him James after my late father but also Thomas as befitted a Campbell.

I longed for Thomas to come, but it was evening before I heard his step on the stairs. When he entered the room, the curtains were drawn and the lamp lit; a fire smouldered in the grate, and he found me there the way he'd want: neat as a pin and tidy, cradling my little bundle, the blood and mess all gone and the echoes of screaming well faded. He strutted then, was proud as a rooster and, showing a tenderness I hadn't known to be in him, he kissed my damp forehead. 'Well done, my girl! He looks a strong one.' That's what he said, adding what a great thing it was for a man to father a son, and he'd be making a thanksgiving offering to Ballymount Church of one hundred pounds. He looked some more at his son's tiny face all crinkled in sleep, and then he knelt by the bed to pray. I looked at him hunkering there, his great spades of hands spread open on the patched quilt, his head bowed, lips moving, and I thought what a decent and sober man he was, what an upright father he'd make.

During those long and exquisite weeks that followed the birth, unshackled from tasks in the house and the yard, I did little but tend to my baby: watched him week by week, his uncurling, his opening still more to the light like a tight little bud unfolding.

Then one day he smiled at me, and in that moment my heart was both broken and mended, for I saw again that this child, our gift from God, was blessed with a will of his own. Once in a while Thomas would stop by the cradle, and although I coaxed him to pick up his son for a cuddle, he never would; I think he was fearful of letting the wispy life fall from his calloused hands. But when I wanted to keep the wean in our bed at night, he put down his foot: he'd agreed to plenty but wouldn't have that, and so I spent many's a chilly hour swathed in a wrap on the nursing chair, while the little one suckled.

Of course I grew restless at times during those hours, and one night in May, while Thomas lay sleeping, I took my wee man, at four months old, to the orchard, where barefoot and breathless I gathered him close in my woollen shawl. All round us the soughing of apple and pear and the dewy grass wetting my feet, and I showed him the stars that hung in the darkening blue of the sky, lighting up the hummocky fields, and I whispered into his ear, 'All these, my son, are yours, the land of your forebears: "Every beast of the forest – and the cattle upon a thousand hills."' And I smiled long at the sleeping face before gathering my nightdress around me and slipping back quickly into the house before Thomas could stir.

As the child grew, 'waxed strong in spirit', he was brimful of life, healthy and playful, and of course I gladly responded, although Thomas could disapprove and sometimes he'd snap, 'Can't you be quiet! Is there nothing for you to be at?' But I couldn't be quiet with such a bonny gay child, and so my singing and laughter continued to curl through the house, lighting up all the darkness left by the Campbells, whose faith, I yet gladly agreed, was our son's birthright and Ballymount Presbyterian his spiritual home.

And so those early peaceful weeks ran on, smooth as the water on top of the mill race, until there came a May evening when Thomas came home earlier and brisker than usual, his hefty body seeming to fill up the kitchen, where I was crooning to the child asleep in his cot by the range.

'Oh, look at him, Thomas. Isn't he a dote?'

I looked up eagerly into my husband's face, wanting to include him, but he sat down wordlessly, heavily, and with a grunt began to undo his laces. 'I was talking to the Reverend McGoldrick last night at the Meeting of Session.' He looked at me now in the righteous way he'd lately adopted. 'And he wanted to know about baptism.' I watched him as, puffing and red-faced, he struggled out of his boots, and for a minute I could think of nothing to say. I recalled how Mother had laughed when she recalled my own baptism: 'Sitting up on a cushion in the parlour you were, looking as cute as a button when Reverend McGoldrick came to baptize you.'

My own baptism had thus been discreet and private, but that was then and things had changed, and when Mr McGoldrick recently said from the pulpit that he'd no longer be doing house baptisms, I knew we'd have to bring our child to the church, though I'd have preferred it all to happen at home. Moreover I had to admit in my secret heart that I was jealous, some might say most unhealthily jealous, for where James was concerned I'd brook no rival ever, not even the Church of Almighty God.

Yet here was Thomas, impatient and waiting. But what an upheaval this would be, for I hadn't yet taken my child past the orchard let alone to a public gathering. I was always shy of attention myself, and James made strange with any neighbours who called to the house, even with Cissie; and Sabbath by Sabbath, in those early weeks, Mother had come to care for her grandson, releasing myself and Thomas for Meeting. Now, all at once, I was faced with the whole congregation of Ballymount gathered, the elders and the women all gaping and bobbing.

So I pleaded, 'Not yet, Thomas. Not for another wee while. Not till he's weaned.'

Mute, I listened as he tippled water into a basin, and a burning rose up in my face and a singing started in my ears. I wouldn't yield to him like this – I wouldn't be bullied – yet in a minute he was back beside me, hands still dripping, 'You know right well the child's not ours to do what we like with.' Boldly I shrugged and gave him my back, but he just took a step to the table, where I'd set out the things for his dinner.

Bending over the cradle, I hummed my annoyance into a wordless tune which was how my parents had taught me to deal with anger. 'A soft answer turneth away wrath' they'd said to me as a child, and when I became a wife, Mother was quick to remind me of the Bible's instruction: 'Let the woman learn in silence with all subjection,' adding that it was for my own good. But these were hard words that I often wrestled with, and I wrestled now as, in bitten-back silence, I rearranged the blanket it had taken me nine months to crochet: all those tiny coloured squares I'd worked, crimson and blue and green, filling each one with dreams for this child, my child, who as the psalm says was 'formed in my inward parts'.

But now his father, the elder, was speaking again: 'You know well it behoves us, good wife, to consecrate our child to the Lord while he's yet unblemished, lead him to grow into both witness and active service in Ballymount Church.' His voice fell stout as a stone and hard, and he pressed his big hands together, nodding to himself as he spoke: ' "Train up a child in the way he should go; even when he is old he will not depart from it." ' And he rapped on the cradle with his knuckles, rapped so hard I feared he'd wake the baby. Quietly raging, I tucked in the blanket, and my spirit burned, rose up in me like fire: I would never allow this helpless sleeping mite to be shaped like a pot by his father or yet handed over, just at its beck, to Ballymount, and if it was sinful of me to think like this, well so be it.

But, leaving aside all talk of baptism now, Thomas was throwing his boots in under his chair and, taking up the knife and the fork I'd laid out, was chucking at his lips in that irritating way he had. 'Now, my good woman, what have you here in the pot for my supper tonight?' Well, I just stared at his face then, wanting to see if I understood, but all I knew was a whiskery blank and words dropping out like pieces of lead. 'I'll tell you something, my girl,' and he leaned in to his plate, 'it was pure famishing work out there this day, cleaning the drains, and Hanna was only saying . . .' But I listened no more, just gathered James up in my arms and flung out of the room.

CHAPTER 6

The morning of the baptism Thomas got out the trap, and I was gratified to see it shine like a burnished chestnut, its upholstery sprightly red. I looked at him as he stood in the wan sunlight adjusting the pony's harness: he was long in the jaw, his hair almost gone, and I thought him homely enough even though Mother considered him handsome. Now he was clicking the whip against the side of his boot. 'Hurry up there, woman. It wouldn't do to be late.'

I wrapped James closer and hastily adjusted my hat in the scullery mirror. Though I'd hidden away all my fears, my whims and fancies, I was in no hurry at all for this service, but Thomas was already whipping up the pony, 'Hup! Hup!' and chuckling to himself, 'We'll look well rolling in through the gates of Ballymount in this.'

It was cool enough that morning, so I drew my coat tightly around and spread the rug over me and the little one, who now and then stirred at my breast. As we trotted along, I smiled to see his tiny lips move in voiceless discourse; we were so snug together, and I clung to him closely, greedily, as we turned up the lane to the church.

At the door we were met by Sam Hanna himself. He came marching over the gravel, his cap in his hand. 'Aha! Thomas! And you too, missus! We're right proud of you this day.' He wiped the spit from the sides of his mouth. 'Not a baptism since Betty Wallace's boy, and that's a few months ago now.'

Thomas laughed. 'Oh, but sure every mickle makes a muckle, as they say.'

In silence I settled James in my arms and undid him from the lengths of his christening robe, a Campbell heirloom, as my husband tapped me on the head with his forefinger. 'But it's all the work of this wee woman here.' And they winked at each other, a slow kind of a wink that reminded me of a snail coming under a door. I turned angrily away and straightened myself up, haughty a bit, for I knew I looked nice in my neat grey costume, a fresh-picked rose pinned on the collar.

The congregation, its numbers diminished of course by the war, was now slowly arriving in traps and carts: Williamsons and Stewarts, McCullaghs and Wilsons, some of them grieving their dead soldier sons, and I felt alone as I stood by the door waiting for Thomas to stable the pony. Sarah Williamson came over to greet me. She'd put on a bit of condition since I'd seen her last, and the blue taffeta costume was tight to bursting, but she was simple and kind. 'Mrs Campbell! My dear Mrs Campbell, let me see this wee man who's come to join us.' She pulled back the shawl, 'Oh, isn't he the fine strong child and, the Lord be praised, born into a righteous home.' I gladdened at that, wanted to stay and engage her in chat for I was starved for women's company, but Thomas was soon at my elbow, and with a stiff nod to Sarah he guided me firmly through the people in the porch and up the blue-carpeted aisle to the Campbell pew, which was almost under the pulpit.

It was past midsummer, and as the morning wore on the flower-filled church grew heavy and warm in spite of the white cool wash on the walls. I felt hot and nervous in the high boxy pew. James was heavy in my arms, and looking at the sweet little innocent face I brooded again on what we were about to do to him without his leave or say-so. In a minute he'd be taken from me and, like an offering, presented to God in Ballymount Presbyterian, and I tightened as I'd done that day when he lay in the cradle asleep in the kitchen with his father scolding about baptism. Sometimes that church felt tight as a corset, and sometimes I longed to be free, longed to run in the daisy-filled meadows even as we moaned out the Psalms. But, duty-bound, I smartly laced up my spirit, drew a deep breath. I was after all Presbyterian born and bred, and, come what may, James would have to be joined so that one day he'd sit tall in the pew of his own accord and feed on God's Word. And I packed my wicked thoughts away, reminded myself they were not of the Spirit; Holy Writ and the Church alone were my teachers and not my own wilful wild roamings.

As we waited, I looked around, drew comfort from the rough bare walls unadorned by picture, cross or colour, comfort too from the pulpit, fount of our teaching, all plush in red velvet with the Good Book already in place. Once or twice Thomas fidgeted beside me and wiped his face down; sometimes he craned his neck to see who was coming in late, but mostly he sat composed and upright as befitted his calling.

Finally a hush fell over the gathered people. Reverend McGoldrick was emerging from the vestry, climbing the pulpit stairs, panting quietly, and with a deep sigh he summoned us to worship. At once a great quietness, gaunt as a bush in December, fell upon the assembled people: no coughing now or boot-scraping as, like a mighty bird with feathers ruffling, we bent to pray. I glanced briefly at Thomas, so placid in worship, his screwed-up sun-reddened face almost hidden in his hands, then I too, in the company of God's people, bowed my head.

Led by the minister, all of us silently named our sins, begged forgiveness and implored mercy, while our petitions and intercessions wound and twisted like kites on their way to heaven. We prayed long and fervently, approached the Mercy Seat with such fear and trembling that a couple of times I wandered off to my own dream place, a place instinct with birdsong and the fragrance of flowers, just me and my child on a far-off day in some high-waving meadow.

Mercifully the little one slept on in my arms during that lengthy hour of preaching, while the sweat trickled down my back and the minister's words went round and round so fast I feared they might send me into a faint. Johnny Long, who had a bad chest, coughed in the back, and a small child whined out loud saying she wanted to go home. But she was hushed; she couldn't go yet for the minister was still preaching. Heatedly now he was speaking of 'lurking challenges', 'smitings' and 'ensnarings'. ' "We are hard-pressed on every side, yet not crushed," ' he told us, ' "we are perplexed, but not in despair; persecuted, but not forsaken; struck down, but not destroyed." ' I sat up straight at this for I knew it was Ulster the minister was talking about, and the terrible threats from villains in the south who wanted to continue to fight for their independence. And we knew right well what that meant for Presbyterians. The minister now thumped the cushion under the Bible so that its tassels shook and the dust flew up, little innocent motes caught in a straying sunbeam, ' "The Lord also shall roar out of Zion, and utter his voice from Jerusalem; and the heavens and earth shall shake: but the Lord will be the hope of this people, and the strength of the children of Israel." ' With my feeling of faintness now washed quite away, I sat like a ramrod by Thomas for it was surely the Roman Church the minister was hinting at here again now, and we were sore afraid of its false teachings, its consuming power over all. Quickly I bent and kissed my little one's head, smelled his warm baby smell. We'd keep James safe for ever. Here with us he'd grow strong in his spirit and, enlightened by the simple purity of God's Word, would know nothing ever of grotesque Masses or Confessions and Hail Marys.

But there was nothing at all to fear that morning as we, God's people, prepared to admit our son to the sacrament of baptism, where he'd be washed with water in the name of the Father, the Son and the Holy Ghost. Sealed and engrafted into Christ, he'd engage to be the Lord's just as the Catechism said. Soon the sermon would end, and Thomas and I would be called to stand before the people and surrender our child to God and the Church family, where James would be reared in the Christian faith, trained to be true and just in all his dealings. I'd keep all the sacred vows I was about to make even while knowing deep in my secret places that, Church family or not, my son would always be mine, first and last.

Sunshine, dappled with leafy reflections, fell over the font as the minister took the child from my arms, and I saw the water cascading silver: so it was done. I was strangely graced that minute with a sense, as if from angels, that our child, with all his sins forgiven, was marked out now by the Father for great things in His name. God willing, I silently prayed, he would grow in stature and in grace, prove himself godly and steadfast.

As we trotted home in the trap with our newly born child, Thomas and I were quiet in ourselves. It was a beautiful day, that day of his baptism, the hedges heavy with hawthorn, fuchsia and honeysuckle, young sycamores waving above us and the elder holding out its caps of white lace, which I thought I might brew to a tincture for Thomas's cough. Content as a cat in a cradle, I drifted away, dreaming pleasantly of the long quiet Sabbath hours ahead when no work would be done, not even a dinner would be cooked, for I'd a cold collation already laid out in the scullery safe, prepared since yesterday. And I gazed down at the little one stirring awake again in my arms, he was so beautiful and so dear. Tears sprang to my eyes. He was mine and I'd guard him for ever.

We were just a mile or so from The Cairn when I noticed Thomas smartly whipping up the pony.

'We'll begin with him soon, Harriet.'

The suddenness of his voice startled me. 'I don't get your meaning, Thomas?'

'We made our promises this morning.'

I continued silent, surprised, as we went on jiggling over the bumpy road.

'We'll rear him up well, you know.' And he flicked the whip lightly over the pony's flanks. 'He'll go faithfully to Sabbath School and Meeting, as well as to Ballymount's National School.'

'Indeed he will, Thomas.' And trying to lighten his mood, I added, 'Maybe we'll make an Orangeman and an elder of him just like his father!'

But he didn't so much as smile at that, just kept laying the reins on the pony, and James, who was hungry now, started to whinge and whine.

'Oh, will you give him a touch of the sugar-tit, woman, for peace sake.' And he clicked his tongue against his teeth. 'And another thing: he'll learn to keep the Sabbath quiet.'

He intended this as a joke of course, but as I drew the sweet sucker out of my bag, I couldn't help thinking what a truly hard man my husband was proving to be.

CHAPTER 7

In those early days Mother proved to be of great help, and a sturdy bond formed between herself and her grandson. I relied on her too for a daily supply of her flavoursome bread, which she'd send on a cart when she couldn't get over herself, but one day the loaf didn't arrive. Poor Mother had taken a 'turn' in the night and, although the doctor told us her passing was peaceful, her death came as a terrible shock. She would visit no more, would be a loss in more ways than one for her visits had always a calming effect on our home, but we had to get on.

Now it was a little less than two years after James's baptism when Thomas came in one night from a Meeting of Session barely able to hide his excitement.

'Put down your bucket at once, like a good girl, and listen to this!'

He pulled out a chair and threw his cap on to the window-sill. I'd been out in the shed scooping up turf mould to brighten the fire, but I dropped all now and sat down, silently praying for good news, something to keep him in cheer.

'The news is –' and he clapped his hands '– I've been commissioned to represent Ballymount at the Church's General Assembly in Belfast.'

'Well, Thomas, that's a wonderful honour and so deserving.'

I smiled at him as I picked up my bucket again and began to root at the range: 'But isn't Assembly only a few weeks away?'

'Aye, the first week in June.'

He set down his Session book on the table and stood looking thoughtful while I gazed into the glowing turf.

'But won't that mean you'll have to be gone a few days?'

'Well, of course I'll have to be gone. Belfast's not at the foot of the lane! Mr McGoldrick's taking his car and we'll travel together. And, if you want to know, but maybe you don't,' and he gave me a funny look, 'I'll be lodged with an elderly spinster who opens her home to folk for the week of Assembly.' He chafed his hands and gave me a wink. 'So I'll be well out of harm's way.'

I paid no heed to this smart remark for I didn't know how to take it, but I was proud for him and glad too for I often thought that if only he got a rest, he'd be softer, easier in himself. He put on his cap again, frowning as he pushed it to the back of his head. 'Dang but! I just thought of it now: the hay will be down that week in June for I've a man coming in with a mower!' He snorted and shook his head. 'Those high-up people in big city churches never give thought to the farmers. They should hold the Assembly in May or better still in November when the land's quiet!' I offered some soothing words about getting help from the neighbours, but he calmed down quickly enough, didn't complain much longer in the face of the honour bestowed. Still and all, he had trouble enough finding someone to deal with the work in his absence, especially the handling of cattle, but eventually, with the help of Sam Hanna, all was arranged.

On the last day in May and holding James (now two and a bit) by the hand, I stood on the step at the front door. I didn't know how I was feeling, but the sky seemed looser than usual, the air pleasantly thin. I waved Thomas and Mr McGoldrick off and James waved too, but as the car disappeared through the gate at the head of the lane the wee lad started to wail. 'Hush,' I told him. 'Father's just gone for a drive with the minister. He'll be home again soon.' And, stepping out of the shadow into the garden, I picked him up and dandling him I chanted, 'To market, to market, to buy a fat pig, home again, home again, jiggety jig.' He joined in at the end himself, and we laughed together and the sun poured down.

What a wonderful week that was, just the two of us. I played with him much of the time, and Cissie joined in when she called, and it was truly startling to hear our laughter run all over the house, rattling the floorboards, filling the holes. Sometimes we spent whole afternoons down by the river, a favourite place, and I made for him little boats out of catkins, knotted daisy chains too. Once he picked up one of these chains and after struggling to drape it around my neck, he took my face in his little hands and gave me a slobbery kiss. And the sun was sending its yellow shimmering shafts through the trees, their leaves all aquiver.

When it rained, we played in the kitchen so that it too was transformed: bricks and balls and whistles taking the place of Thomas's chair and elders' visits. Here, the wee fellow sat on my knee and I read, though he understood nothing at all, I was sure: Bible stories and nursery rhymes and gentle tales about little ones dealing with falsehoods or 'falling away', and I knew how pleased Thomas would be.

On days when I needed a cabbage or such, we'd go to the vegetable plot together and I'd point out the onions and the drill that hid the potatoes, and I'd let him examine the snails in their shells. But when we passed the laburnum that swung with its golden chains by the gate to the lane, I warned him never to touch it, that or the yew that stood dark near the kitchen window. He was a placid child, bright and eager to learn, and even then I knew he'd do well in school when the time came but I put that thought quickly away. There'd be more than enough of partings.

Before bed, as he sat on my knee, I'd pray with him: 'Now I lay me down to sleep, I pray the Lord my soul to keep; and if I die before I wake, I pray the Lord my soul to take.' The words were too big for such a wee boy, and his little eyes wanted to close, but when the prayer was done I'd lift him gently into our own big bed, where he'd lie like a bird, asleep in the pillows. Not much later I'd join him there and, as the barn owl screeched in the distant woods and the blackbird still sang, I'd hold his small body in the curve of my own, feel his swift little breaths, wonder what he was dreaming.

As the days ran out, I grew nervous of Thomas's return mostly because I knew I'd neglected my household duties: there were floors not swept, and his shirts that I'd washed a week ago still lay in a crumpled heap at the end of the sofa. So the day before he was due, a Saturday, I bustled about doing this and that, while James still thought I should play and was cranky and had to be coaxed that night to go back to his own little bed. I worried of course that he'd tell his father, would blurt it all out . . . but I eased my mind knowing that Thomas would never pay heed to baby prattle.

CHAPTER 8

Some months after Thomas's outing, we were just finishing up after the milking one evening and I was getting round to putting the dinner on the table. James had fallen asleep on the sofa and I remember thinking how precious to me was this idle hour, for our days were long, the work hard. I felt tired and Thomas was in a narky humour. Since James's birth he had become more and more dictatorial in manner, almost as if his rightful place as head of the house was threatened by a wee thing barely out of the cradle. And I never dared tell him about the play and the fun that went on in his absence.

I had to be very careful when the dark mood fell upon him, so I just went quietly about my tasks, putting out plates and potatoes. But, black as a shadow, he came up behind me that evening. I was scooping out the last bit of stew in the pot when he took a sharp hold of my plait (for that's how I did my hair in those days) and he pulled my head round so that the hairs at my neck stung and he said in an urgent throaty voice, 'Harriet, will you come upstairs with me now?' and I said no I wouldn't for I didn't like the way he approached me, besides I had the wean to attend to. So he let me go at that with a little push which had no tenderness in it and he threw himself down to the dinner, eating in silence. Guiltily, I sat down beside him, knowing full well I was neglecting my wifely duties – 'Wives, submit yourselves unto your own husbands, as unto the Lord (Ephesians 5: 22)' – but I had a house to keep along with poultry and calves and, above all else, I had a child to raise, to nurture daily and lead conscientiously in the ways we'd promised at his baptism.

That little incident must have been the merest shadow of the beginning, for not so long afterwards Thomas came at me again while I was clipping the hedge along the potato plantation. It was gloomy that afternoon and James was playing with pebbles under the sycamore when I heard his father's voice coming to me across the empty drills, a voice I was learning to stiffen at. But he sounded genial and good-natured that day, laughing as he quoted from scripture, '"He who finds a wife finds what is good and receives favour from the Lord."' I smiled back at him then, on guard, wary, but also glad that he was in such fine form. I laid down the shears as he came up to me and I tensed when he began to stroke my shoulders. 'Harriet,' and his voice was as smooth as a ribbon, 'Harriet, I sometimes wonder if you realize quite how tired you are?'

I started to protest, but his voice ran on, increasing in volume and urgency: 'You're worn out, dear wife, by all the toil that's your woman's lot.' He nodded towards the tree. 'And for a start, that child takes up too much of your time.' He paused and turned me to face him, his eyes hard as marbles. 'We don't come together as often as we should.' He cleared his throat. 'Our duty is not being addressed upstairs in the way that behoves a man and his wife.' I hung my head for he sounded almost piteous, but things were as they were and as a dutiful mother I had to devote myself fully to our God-given child, for whom I felt solely responsible, and I didn't yet know what else could be done.

But in a minute he was telling me what more could be done: we could get help, he commanded; he was stern and cold now, no longer calling me 'dear'. We could find a girl to take over some of my tasks, and then I'd have time to do the things a woman should be doing. Oh, there were many things he thought I could be doing. I pulled away from him crossly. 'I need no help from any girl, Thomas.' My voice was so sharp it surprised me. 'Just give us a bit more time. Everything will settle down, and there'll be much more time for each other. I promise.' I said all this with great emphasis, and when he stayed silent I went to fetch James thinking to bring him to his father's embrace, but Thomas had already gone.

I knew full well where my fault lay, and I was coming to see that Thomas was jealous of all the hours I spent with the child while he himself was behind the plough or on top of the thresher. So I vowed in that minute that I'd strive to meet his needs: I'd work harder and faster at my chores and I'd make time for my husband while still preserving the cream of my days for James. This I would do but I'd do it alone and would suffer no assistance from any paid help. I was full of pride then. Young, untried mother and wife, I couldn't easily brook interference in my stewardship of the house, where it was my lot to make a home. But neither did I see what it meant to a man to live in the shade of his son. No, I couldn't see that or the lengths he would go to, seeking to douse what burned in him. And Thomas himself was silent on this.

In the following weeks, despite my best efforts to keep him happy and in spite of my repeated insistence that I could manage everything myself if I tried a bit harder, he still overrode my objections. He was such a strong man, stubborn and persevering. I'd watched him pull calves out of their mothers, his muscles bulging and sinews straining, and I'd been told that in all the disputations in Kirk Session, whenever Tom Campbell spoke out, the minister and elders took heed. But now it was me, his own wife, he was speaking out at and I cowered.

'What's up with you at all?' he'd demand over and over. 'Your womanly duties I needn't spell out, but every other farm employs an extra hand for the work in the house.' His tongue could be bitter, and with scolds like this he gradually wore me down so that in the end, unable to endure his scalding taunts any longer, I agreed to have help but on the sole condition that it'd be for the house alone and nothing whatsoever to do with the child, who was much too young to be left in the care of just anyone.

CHAPTER 9

I held off until James had turned three when, feeling bludg-
eoned and bullied, I reluctantly began to look for a maid. I
advertised in the local paper: 'Mature Protestant woman
wanted, etc.' Of course we hoped we'd get a Presbyterian, but I
was shy of being so openly choosy. When not a single Protestant answered the ad I secretly began to hope we'd find no one
at all but Thomas said we must keep on looking.

He was right of course, and in the end we had to take what
we got, finally settling on Anna May Reilly, a childless widow
who lived in a cottage the other side of the town. She was a
Roman of course but was known for hard work along with
devotion to religious practice. This meant, I supposed, she was
always running to the chapel and belonging to what Cissie
called the 'Legion of Mary'. What a foreign land all this was to
me, strictly reared as I'd been in the light of God's Word, foreign as well to my husband, whose stubborn persistence was
puzzling until I gave it some thought. I believed he considered
himself strong enough to protect us: a bulwark, no matter who
joined our household, for wasn't he an elder and knew his own
competence?

Anyway, he knew that our Catholic neighbours were all very
decent and this woman might suit us well, furthermore adding
that when we couldn't get one of our own, a Catholic maid

would be better than a heathen one. And the thought struck me then that, elder or not, he'd have employed the Witch of Endor herself if he had to, in order to have his way with me, get between me and the boy.

So one morning soon after that I reluctantly sent a message by the postman to this Anna May asking her to come out here to meet us. She was due at seven o'clock that evening and was late. This was the first black mark against her for I was always one for keeping good time. But in truth I resented her before she ever arrived, sensed an intrusion, an altering of ways, and hated to think what the outcome might be. I had such a bad feeling about it all from the start, but in those times silence was the way of women with strong husbands, so I held my peace then, and today I'd give anything, anything at all, to have done otherwise.

I looked over at Thomas at the kitchen table that evening and I burned with resentment, for he just sat there engrossed in his tea, stirring in sugar, buttering bread, indifferent to what was happening around him. He just chewed away as we awaited her arrival, for he'd a great appetite, while I sat in the corner, lost as a dropped stitch. I looked at James at play with his bricks on the mat. He was trying to build a tall tower, which kept toppling down; over and over he tried so, teasing a little, I went to gather him into my arms, but he was too old for that any more and he pulled away from his mammy. He was getting to be such a big boy now with his own little mind, but I knew he was very uneasy.

Now it must have been nearly half past the hour when I heard the dog barking. Thomas stopped eating then and wagged his fork to alert me, so with James now hanging out of my skirt, I went to the scullery window and saw her coming across the yard. She was in a pair of wee gutties, straggling and streeling in the kind of swayback stoop she had.

I let her in, and she shuffled after me into the kitchen, where my husband nodded and went on with his tea while James clung to me tightly. I looked at her shabby old astrakhan coat, which I'd seen on a stall in our church sale and saw a pathetic, poor thing, with lanky hair and glasses in chicken-wire frames. She'd have been around thirty-five then, I supposed. We greeted each other briefly, but Thomas never lifted his head from his plate. She reached out at once to James, who backed off against her approach. 'Ah, look at himself! The wee man! Isn't he the grand wee fellow?' I recoiled as her spittle fell on my face, and the child turned his head away but she prattled on: 'Well, tell me now, missus, what is it you'd want me to do?' I took a deep breath. We were well enough off as it was, my husband's stomach trouble daily improved, I was strong and healthy and growing in confidence as mistress of his house. No, I could think of nothing I wanted from her except that she'd go. But she was persistent: 'I've plenty of experience and I'm a good worker.' It was clear she needed employment.

'We'll see,' I demurred and James hid behind me, cautiously watching.

'You'd need to be here by six thirty each morning for the milking and stay in the evening till the lamps, if needed, are trimmed and the dinner vessels washed up.'

'Oh, that'd suit me well.'

Indeed, I had to admit, she seemed possessed of a very biddable nature, complying with all I demanded, and I sensed that Thomas was happy.

'Mostly you'd be free to go home by eight. And we'd pay you ten shillings a week.'

Satisfied also with that, she started to ooze at James again: 'And what about this wee man here? Wouldn't you want a hand with him too?' She leaned down and looked at James, making little sucky noises. 'I'm very good with children.' I saw Thomas look up at this and grin that extraordinary grin of his that went to his back teeth, but I took James firmly by the hand. 'You'll have nothing at all to do with the child. You'll do cleaning and washing, see to the poultry and calves, jobs I usually do myself, but our son and his welfare will be none of your business.' She gave a sidelong half-smile at that, and as I agreed to take her she announced coyly, 'Oh, and I'll need Sundays off, missus, to go to Mass, and if you don't mind, Thursday evenings too for Benediction.' Thomas was nodding across at me when she said she could start the next week. I was breathing deeply throughout all this, but my husband hadn't spoken a word, which didn't surprise me. It was when she'd gone that he'd tell me what he'd been thinking – such was his way.

When I'd shown her the door, I took a look at Thomas, who was now wiping his chin and smacking his lips. 'Yes, I think she'll work out well; all you'll have to do is to keep an eye on her.' He eased himself back from the table. 'And I can see straightaway she'll be good with the boy.' Then he stood looking long at something beyond in the garden before winking at me. 'It'll give you less to be at, good woman. Give you time for other things now, you know.' Then turning to James, 'Bid me goodnight, young man, and don't forget your prayers.'

Biting my lip, afraid of what angry words might fall out, I took James by the hand and we went up the stairs together. My husband's voice followed us up to the child's room: 'And don't let there be a sound out of you tonight.'

I closed the door smartly. 'It will be all right, my pet; I promise.'

The child settled and smiled up at me. 'We'll always be together, won't we?'

'We will, James. We will.'

Back down in the kitchen, I stood square on my feet, arms folded under my apron and fire on my tongue. 'Thomas, can you still not see that I don't need help with the child.' I was shouting, hammering out each word. 'He's doing very well the way he is.'

He looked surprised. 'Oh, but there's something else besides, Harriet.' He paused to pick at something stuck in his teeth. 'The boy is beginning to develop, grows wilful already.' He pulled his lips together. 'I can see it in him plain. And you're inclined to yield.' He rapped the table with his spoon then. 'You spoil him, and you know what a spoiled child deserves.' He got up, brushed crumbs off his overalls. 'And we don't want that, do we!'

I bridled in a way most unusual for me, 'Surely, Thomas, I should know what's good for my own son.'

'Our son.'

His reprimand caught me like the lash of a whip.

'And only yesterday, for example, when he refused to do what you told him, he needed a scud and a clip on the ear, which is what he'll get in the future.'

This was beginning to be another row, and I thought to placate him somehow, but he kept on talking, his voice sounding like a saw grating, dully persistent: 'And you may say what you like, my dear woman, but she shall most certainly mind the boy from time to time. It would give her a break from the hens, and so on, for if she was overworked in the yard, she might leave us.'

He drew back his chair as though preparing to leave, but his words had fallen upon me heavy as sods and I sprang up like a wildcat, my response quick and immediate: 'No, Thomas! And a thousand times no! You promised it would never be so.'

But he still had the hard face on him and was looking at me in a strangely heated way now, his eyes lidded. 'I'm the one who needs you now, Harriet.' And I looked up as he stood there before me, darkly lowering; he seemed very worked up, and I drew away, afraid of his need, afraid to deny him. But he smiled at me all of a sudden, and his words, cold as clods, ran free as a line: 'I want you to come with me to the Long Acre next week when we'll have Anna May Reilly here; you could give me a hand with the sowing. And in the spring you and I will head out to work on the bog.'

I could hardly believe I was hearing him right. 'But what of the men?'

'I've told you again and again, if you'd listen, that we're short of men. The latest is Sammy Smith and a couple more gone to the States. Anyway, men are a costly item.'

He chewed at a straw in the corner of his mouth, waiting, impassive. But anger sliced through me as I thought of the bog and the bog holes and the dark brown watery depths that could suck a man in. It was a place I would never bring James, and my husband knew that right well.

The following Monday morning Anna May duly arrived and I headed off with her out to the byre, where Thomas had already started the milking. 'You'll see that the buckets are scalded,' I told her. 'No straws or specks in the milk, and keep it well stirred to distribute the cream.' With a nod, she started into the work at once: the scalding was done to perfection and our milk arrived in the kitchen white and clean. 'Now, go out to the stable,' I ordered, 'and bring the rest of the milk to the calves.' The morning passed, and I kept her busy like that, fairly heaped on the tasks. When she'd done in the yard, she washed the delft and scrubbed out the kitchen, and I watched as she kneaded the sheets in the sudsy tub, saw how, without being told, she knew to spread them over the hedge to dry in the sun.

She was stronger than she looked and very diligent, and Thomas grunted, wasn't he right after all?

Over the first few months I kept her occupied like that, followed her around as she worked, testing and checking, secretly wanting to find a fault. James, still very timorous, came following too, wouldn't go near her, but one day when she was up on a chair, washing a window, she blew down a bubble to him. He laughed, delighted at that, and when she got down he allowed her to take his hand. I felt myself tighten then for, diligent and all as she was, I must still be watchful. I couldn't forget the crucifix I had spotted on a cushion one day or the bits of brown cloth stamped with idolatrous images that peeped from under her blouse.

Afraid I would appear too mistrustful, I said nothing of these discoveries to Thomas, who would just call me away to wherever he chanced to be working. Aggrieved, I once asked him why he couldn't get Anna May to work with him in my stead, but he just curled his lip, looked down from his height. 'Now what, my good woman, would the neighbours make of an arrangement like that!'

He could be as smart as he liked, but from the start I was gravely troubled about the effect she might have on James.

Sometimes pure shrivelled with fear I was, and he wouldn't listen. But the old hymn always rang in my ears, nudging and guiding:

> Ask the Saviour to help you,
> Comfort, strengthen and keep you
> He is willing to aid you
> He will carry you through.

And so I would bring all my fears to the Lord.

CHAPTER 10

Ballymount's weekly prayer meeting was held in our own hay-loft, and the location suited Thomas well but more especially me. I always had James in his bed before we went and we'd only to cross the yard and be away from the house for an hour, leaving Anna May to sit by the fire and redden her shins.

The loft was cosy on winter nights with hoarded hay and bags of pollard and oats packed tight to the rafters, and we'd gather around, some of us on bits of chairs or milking stools, some limber young ones lying back on the sacks of meal. And here we'd offer our prayers and sing to the glory of God. We had so many joyous choruses with great rhythms, and often we'd find ourselves, the ones who were able, standing and swaying together in what amounted to rapture:

> Softly and tenderly Jesus is calling,
> Calling for you and for me;
> See, on the portals
> He's waiting and watching,
> Watching for you and for me.

It was to this humble loft that we brought all that troubled us, sometimes praying in silence, sometimes with hands raised up. Here I listened to the murmurings as each one offered up whatever was laid on their hearts: Minnie Tilson praying that Gertie Weir would be freed from doubt and Thomas praying for Jonah Forbes, who toiled on the African mission field. We made supplication too for our country divided now by a border where none was before, putting our neighbours the Stewarts in one country, ourselves in another: the Free State. Oh, what terrible, cruel and lonely times these were in our part of the world.

But when I tried to ask the Saviour for help with my own troubles, I could find no words – my mind buzzed with pieces of this and that, fluttered with the motes that hung in the shafts of lantern light, and I couldn't haul it in; a kind of dread grizzled in me even as we began to pray, as we always did, for our lost brethren in the Roman Church, singing:

> There were ninety and nine that safely lay
> In the shelter of the fold;
> But one was out on the hills away,
> Far off from the gates of gold
> Away on the mountains wild and bare,
> Away from the shepherd's tender care.

And as these words whined and rolled their sharp trebles around the loft, I had a fearful vision of my own son for a burning second, the merest flash: he was a grown man standing alone in a precipitous place devoid of pasture and soundless save for a whipping wind and the haunting cries of strange birds. I snapped the hymn book shut then. This was foolish and frightening. I looked around but found little comfort in the stolid singing faces and the prim felt hats. Suddenly I was compelled to gather myself up and, without as much as a nod to Thomas or anyone else, I hastily buttoned my coat and pushed through the people, who were still engorged with singing. I had to get down to the house, must get there at once, and so I went fumbling down the greasy outside steps of the loft, clinging in the dark to the pebble-dashed wall.

For almost an hour I'd forgotten that she was still in our house, but now I ran quickly, silently, across the dark yard and hurried into the kitchen, the words of the hymn still ringing in my ears. I pushed open the back door and, without stopping to light the scullery lamp, I strode into the house singing out as loud as I could, my voice striking the gloom, 'Lord, thou hast here thy ninety and nine; are they not enough for Thee . . .' I'd remind her that it was a Presbyterian house she worked in. But she wasn't in the kitchen to hear me.

I was panting a little now, anxiously listening, but there was neither wind nor rain that night and nothing stirred in the kitchen save the gentle shifting and settling of turf in the range and the murmur of the tilley. Where was she? Those beads of hers were lying on a chair even though I'd told her she must keep them at home, and I was tempted to throw them on the fire. Then over my head I heard the scurry of feet: James was out of his bed. I listened hard. There were sounds coming now, whispers and breathing. Without taking off my coat, I hurried up and met her halfway on the stairs. 'What is this?'

Bold as brass, she faced me. 'Ah, I was just putting the child to bed, missus.' She stood there, pert and brash, looking me in the eye.

'But I had him in bed before I left.'

My stomach went into a curdle and my mouth dried up. Oh, how well I knew it would come to this; she couldn't keep her hands to herself, couldn't stay in the kitchen, where she was bidden to be. I was seized by a rush of fury so red that I had to clench my hands into fists, afraid I'd be tempted. 'Go down now at once and remember your place. Your business with us is in the yard and the kitchen, not up the stairs. And it's time you were gone away home.'

She just gave a toss of her head at that and went off meekly enough, but I'd speak to Thomas, I would, as soon as he got in from the prayers. I'd tell him out straight about things I'd seen happening and the way she was crossing herself in front of the child.

Yet I didn't get round to speaking to Thomas for the longest time. He just wouldn't listen, would shoo me away if I wanted to talk: too busy for women's nonsense, he'd say; let the two of you sort it out yourselves, a bit of peace was wanted to get on with the work and the Long Meadow waiting the cut. And so it was bitter as gall when he made me go with him down to the Bottoms, where in angry silence I tore at the blue-bearded flax until my hands were raw. With each pull I'd think of James, the poor wean, in the charge of that woman. But I was helpless, for after the flax was done and laid out, I was summoned still further into the bigger fields, where the barley and oats were ready to harvest. And so with all this duty laid on my back, there was little time left to share with the child. Yet Thomas assured me, as I scalded my face with tears of vexation, that everything was going a humdinger in the new routine: James was well minded; his own stomach trouble had almost gone, and I must surely be happy the house was so clean.

Oh, I do believe he tried to be kind, my poor Thomas, yet kindness was quite beyond him, and when I'd protest I was losing touch with our child, he'd raise his eyebrows as though perplexed and then scold: 'You have to have sense, woman! You know right well that times are hard. Men cost, and money doesn't grow on a bush.' Then he'd shake his head at me as if I was simple. 'Can't you see it's the only way to manage? Or do you want us all to be out on the road.'

Oh, he was one hard, tight man, yet very religious, moral and just in all his dealings. Even so, when we went with James to our Sabbath worship, it pained me to see him praying and psalm-singing, innocent as a lamb before his Maker.

CHAPTER 11

At home it was a different story, where it began to seem as if Thomas and Anna May Reilly ruled the roost. She did, I could see, grow very fond of James, and day by day, in spite of the extra tasks I put on her, the bond strengthened between them. Coming in from the field, I'd often find her gabbling to him and I'd writhe to see him almost ignore me. Or I'd find them at play in the garden or up in the loft looking to see if the eggs had hatched, and I'd hear the silly half-chant of hers that went, 'James, whose good child are you?' and him responding with his innocent little-boy chuckle, 'I'm Anna May's own good child!' And they'd laugh together and I'd feel sick at heart with a small snake of fear crawling around in the pit of my stomach.

I pleaded often to have the Catholic hussy dismissed before she did serious damage. But Thomas just shrugged aside my worries and sensitivities, counted them women's silly nonsense, and grunted something about the protection ensured by the child's baptism and the benefits that would accrue in due course from the *Shorter Catechism* itself. Slowly, I began to agree with myself that my husband was kin to the yellow-eyed bitch we once had in the byre at home: a mangy animal that would lie for weeks in a stall, curled in a lump of hay, who never wanted any milk herself but didn't want us to get it either. He was busy, busy, busy, he said, and mustn't be troubled with any more nonsense about the boy and Anna May, his minder, for that's what she'd become: she was his minder, with me, his mother, looking on, seemingly acquiescent. And so I rose unspeaking in the dark, knuckle-blue mornings to the long grey hours of drudgery that were peppered with shards of fear; rose to work in bog and field among ragweed and rushes. And when night fell over the unspeaking white of the kitchen walls, I'd take up my needles and listen to the pendulum knock out the hours till Thomas took down the Bible and shuttered the day.

I grew increasingly anxious, and many's the night I couldn't sleep for thinking about it all. Once I dreamed that she had disappeared with him out the back door and hadn't come back. In the dream I followed her close: first through the blackcurrant bushes that grew near the kitchen door, watched her as she dodged past the outhouse and over the plank on the stream where the watercress grew, but I couldn't catch up. Awake at last and breathlessly tearful, I roused Thomas, who scolded and told me not to disturb him or had I forgotten the thresher was coming tomorrow. I tried to get back to sleep, but all night long I could see her running and weaving before me, a crucifix dangling from her neck and the child in her arms.

Next morning I rose with a headache and a smothering heaviness that clung to me like a wet coat and I went at once to the child's room. I breathed in relief to see him propped up in bed looking at his picture books, and I thought what a beautiful boy he was and what a handsome man he'd one day become. 'Come, my pet,' I crooned as I reached to cuddle him the way I always did, but casting his books aside he jumped up, remembering he was to go with Anna May to see the little sick heifer.

Another time I chanced to come early home from the Long

Acre and found the pair of them sitting together, silhouetted in the deep windowsill at the head of the stairs. He was chuckling away while she appeared to dangle some kind of bauble before his eyes, teasing him to catch it as she swung it in front of his face.

I ran up the stairs. 'What are you doing with my son?' I tried to be calm, afraid to tear the child away, afraid he might resist.

She swiftly replaced in her pocket the beads she was forever fiddling with, those winking brown beads. 'We're just playing, missus.'

'Oh no!' I cried. 'No one plays like that in this house!'

I drew myself up, severe and scalded, while the child looked on, sullen, his big eyes filling.

'Come, James,' and I pulled at him roughly, 'and you, would you kindly get down to the parlour, where the windows are in need of a wash.'

I myself would have sacked her there and then, but Thomas was on her side and she knew it. A lovely man, I once heard her say; would never see you short of a bob.

Helpless and angry, I sometimes looked at myself in the glass of an evening and thought, *Harriet Campbell, what are you made of at all that you can't stand up to this woman? Or indeed to your own husband?* But I'd been kept down too long by the warnings from scripture and was unable to vent my deep anger. Yet I would try to stand up, I would somehow tell him. But he was utterly without understanding, until at last my distress, unbounded, began to seep through me and impinge on himself: the potatoes were burned more often and the oatmeal ran out and a hen died. At length he rose up, not liking wheels to run other than smoothly. What was up? he wanted to know. Was it that Anna May was minding the child too much for my

liking or what was my problem? So I told him then what I'd
been holding back: it was the way she was teaching James about
Rome, the beads and the crucifixes. Silenced a bit by that, he
pledged he'd call her to heel, tell her out straight she'd have to
keep her religion to herself if she wanted to mind our son.
Somewhat appeased, I later heard her give him her word on
that. She said neither boo nor baa, and after this I saw nothing
more of those beads or crosses and life went on.

But one fair morning I was away from the fields and in the
town selling my eggs. I rested the baskets on the shafts of a cart
and was checking to see that none had been broken when Betty
Wallace came up to me, all eager and bustling. 'I see,' she says,
wiping her mouth with the back of her hand, 'I see your young
fellow's getting a taste for the Roman chapel.'

Shocked and angered by her impertinence, I turned away
from the baskets. 'What in the name of patience do you mean?'

She smirked and sniffed and sidled around me. 'You'd better
look to your son, Mrs Campbell.'

I lifted my chin and folded my arms. 'I don't know what you
are talking about.'

'I'm talking about Anna May Reilly, who sometimes takes
him out walking.' She paused here and took in air the way
people do when they're giving out news. 'Last Thursday,' and
she lowered her voice, 'I saw them heading into the RC chapel.
Yes, right inside the two of them went.'

Oh, I knew that chapel very well. We passed it every Sabbath
on our way to Meeting, a small blue-washed building which
like Ballymount had neither steeple nor bell. It was surrounded
by statues and crosses and sat brazen among the yellow-spitting
whins, smug and set apart, locked I was sure in some dark and
sinful design of its own. And I stood looking down at my feet

and the shoes that needed a polish, brown court shoes with spool heels, a present long ago from Thomas.

'Does your husband not know?'

Her voice penetrated the silence that seemed to have dropped on the town, and I seized the baskets, my knuckles white on the handles. I was certain Thomas knew nothing of such a terrible thing, or else he'd have reared up on us all, summoned the Bible, taken down the cane, slammed the door.

Betty went on standing. 'Anyway, I thought I should tell you before the Kirk Session got wind of it.' She pulled her coat around her and knotted her scarf. 'But I better be off. There's the band practice in the Lodge tonight, and it's my turn to make the tea.' She went, looking back only once. 'But don't worry your head about anything, Mrs Campbell. Just keep a close eye on that maid of yours.'

I stood there looking after her, a ringing in my ears, the street suddenly quiet and empty save for the cardboard figures that were coming and going from shops and carts, soundlessly clinching their bargains. So, in spite of all that she'd promised, Anna May Reilly was taking my son to the Roman chapel, into that dark and forbidden place with its terrible secrets. I'd have to be ever more vigilant. Stupefied, I could say nothing, just stole away sickened. But I'd tell Thomas, reveal it all – uncover it gently of course, for his temper was always unstable.

CHAPTER 12

As soon as we'd finished the dinner that very night and before Thomas could start on a job, I told him I wanted to talk. 'It's about James,' I ventured, and calm as I could I sat down and took up my knitting.

He yawned and stretched himself out on the sofa. 'More complaints to be sure.'

I cast on a few stitches, biding my time, preparing.

'Well, speak up, woman. I've a meeting later on in the Lodge.'

I put down my work and looked him in the eye. 'I need to let you know, Thomas, that Anna May Reilly isn't keeping the promise she made you.'

'Well?' And he raised his eyes to the ceiling as though wanting to hear no more.

I cleared my throat and reddened. 'She takes James into the RC chapel.'

He turned to me now, suddenly outraged and angry. 'Ah, hah! I should have known her ladyship couldn't be relied on to keep her word. Oh, I'll chastise her severely for this.' He glared at me as though it was all my fault. 'Now is there anything else I need to know before I rebuke her? We must have it all out in the open, know where we stand.'

But I'd said enough, was afraid to tell him the rest, like the time I'd caught James dipping his fingers into a jar, then dabbing at his face and chest. I'd seized the boy then and demanded to know what in the world he was at, but he'd just grinned and said he was blessing himself with 'holy water'.

Thomas was standing before me now, rubbing his hands together. 'This time I'll reprimand her with rigour, and then –' he pondered '– if she shows herself properly chastened we might give her another chance . . . like the fig tree in the Bible.'

Another chance? Utterly taken aback, I baulked at this proposition, didn't agree we should endure her presence another hour. But he paid me no heed.

He was frowning now, looking heated. 'Call the boy in.'

I heard the threat in his voice. 'But he's in bed, Thomas.'

'Well, get him out of it.' When James stood timid before him, his father was cold and stern. 'What's all this I've been hearing about you, son?' And without waiting for any reply, 'About the walks you take with Anna May, for example?'

The boy brightened. 'Oh yes, Father, and if she wants to pray, we go into her church. You can see Holy God there and Jesus all bleeding.'

I drew back in my chair and saw Thomas rise, take him by the shoulders and shake him. 'Listen to me, young man!' And his voice had a shudder like the reeds in the lake when a storm was on. 'First of all, you know very well we don't call our Maker "Holy God", and second, you must realize we never can see Him, never can entertain even an image of Him. The Bible forbids us.' Here he declaimed from the Book of Exodus: ' "Thou shalt not make unto thee any graven image, or any likeness of any thing that is in heaven above, or that is in the earth beneath, or that is in the water under the earth." Do you understand that?'

'But Father, Anna May—' James was daring to protest.

'No, my son!' Thomas shouted, interrupting. 'No! Anna May means well enough, but she is not one of us. Understand? Not one of us.' And he shook the wean again, more gently this time. 'Anna May dwells in darkness. She's a poor soul astray, lost in the night like that sheep from the flock.' He released the child, who was now looking frightened and ashamed. 'And let me hear no more of your ventures into that place or any more talk about Confessions or "Holy Marys",' and he looked to the wall where the cane hung. 'From now on, you'll just attend to what your mother and I have to say about God.' He held the boy away from him. 'Give me the second commandment now. Or can you be forgetting your scripture already?'

As I listened to James reciting the text my heart went out to him, but he had to be disciplined.

CHAPTER 13

Thomas did speak to Anna May of course, and I spotted her, all red in the face, hurrying out of his presence. After that I could see she was fairly subdued in herself, had much less to say. Yet I wasn't mollified; I'd been truly enraged to hear of that 'second chance'. But I'd a plan of my own to deal with that, and the very next night when Thomas had his boots off and was settled down on the sofa, I decided to broach the subject again.

I quietly finished up my own jobs: raked out the fire and wound the clock, then I took off my overall, hung it on the nail by the door and, sitting down, drew my old house-shoes out from under the table. They were in need of a patch but I'd wait till I got paid for the eggs. Thomas was looking through the *Celt* and, after some time, gave an unexpected chortle. 'Would you listen to this! It says you can buy stuff that puts living chicks into hatching eggs.' He threw the paper down then and turned on me with a grin. 'That bit of magic would save you some bother! It'd save a bit of money on the Indja Buck too.'

I thought of the handfuls of yellow meal Anna May scattered daily to the hens in the yard. It had been a wet summer so far: the hay had mildew and the yield of oats and barley would be down. Biting my lips, I got up and went to the range to start the porridge for his supper and then, cool as a chip of ice, I told him: 'Yes, Thomas, you're right. Perhaps we do need to make economies. Prices go up, and the money you give me doesn't go as far as it used to.'

When I'd called him over to the table and was pouring the stirabout into his bowl, I watched his face, but there was no darkness in it that night in spite of the poor weather and the turf soaking in the bog.

'So you're turned bookkeeper now, are you?' And he started to ladle up the porridge. 'Since when did your pretty woman's head get interested in figures?' He grinned at me. 'Now tell me what you'd suggest, pray.'

I knew he was despising me, but I went on boldly, knowing his passion for thrift: 'We could cut our cloth to suit our measure.'

'Ha!' And he put down his spoon with a bang. 'Now I know what you're after. Anna May again, of course. A thorn in your side if ever there was one.'

He snorted and pushed his dish away. 'But maybe you're right. The boy is growing up and needs no more of her coddling or anyone else's coddling either. He's turned five, after all, and we'll put him to school in September.' He looked at me through half-shut eyes. 'All right, tell her she can go. She's another expense we can now do well without.'

I smiled to myself and rolled up my knitting. Money was king after all.

When the breakfast was over the following morning and Thomas and James had gone to the yard, I found her out in the scullery polishing the globe of a lamp, the wick nicely trimmed; and behind her the vessels she'd dried lay in neat piles. She'd been with us nearly two years and would be here even longer, I knew, if she'd kept her word about her religion, but maybe it was as well she hadn't. And now I had to harden my heart, brace myself to spit out the necessary words.

'Put down your cloth, Anna May. I have something to say to you.'

Cocking her head, she slapped the duster over her shoulder. 'I'm ahead of myself, missus, doing the lamps so early, but I need to be speedy today. It's Benediction tonight and I want to be gone by seven.'

'We're letting you go, Anna May.' I was very cool. 'We need you no longer.'

But there was no gasp of shock or surprise; she just tossed her head. 'Right you be, missus, if that's what you want. I'll go for my bag this minute.' She still wore the impertinent face that I'd always mistrusted. 'You were always a hard one to work for anyway, and I'm not a bit sorry to leave you . . . except for the wee fellow.' She looked down at the floor, strangely forlorn of a sudden, but I didn't soften my heart.

'No doubt you'll find another place soon. Here's what we owe you in wages.'

In silence she took the ten-shilling note but continued to stand. 'Ah, the wee fellow, missus? I know he'll miss me, the cratur.'

I relented then and brought her round to the stable, where I knew he'd be petting the newborn calf. He was leaning over the pen and scarcely looked up at our entry.

'James, your mother tells me I'm wanted no longer.'

'Righto,' he chuckled without raising his head.

She raised her voice: 'I'm leaving today; won't be back any more.'

But he went on bending down to the calf. 'Look here, Anna May. Look at this fine wee bull.' He picked up a handful of straw for the calf to nuzzle. 'He has a star on his forehead and I'm going to call him Whitey.'

'Jamesey boy, have you not a word more for your old Anna May?' It was almost a whimper, but he didn't seem to be listening.

When she'd gone, I stayed talking to my son in the sweet-smelling stable. Tired of the calf, he asked about her, wanting to know, but I steered him away quick with talk about school and the book and the bag he'd be getting. As I joined him in stroking the calf, I felt his hand warm and secure in my own and I was well content. Clearly the Bible guided and warned, and now Thomas and I would wipe away all the papist smearing that had begun to smudge the young soul of our son and soon he'd be off to begin his book learning.

CHAPTER 14

Sunnyside, 1982

There was always so much to be done at The Cairn and no time to be doing it: calves to be fed and cattle rounded up, that child to be minded, minded in the face of much hardship and barring of ways, and I was made of stuff too soft and pliable, slack and bending, which only maturing years would harden. My curtains, bright yellow, stir now in a gentle breeze, and Bernadette comes to draw them, not close, just open enough for a bit of the sky to be seen, its dark canopy pierced by stars all a-twinkle, as James used to say. What a good boy he was growing up, always good. But, like the apple and the worm, there was something got into him.

Bernadette wants to close the window now, and I object to that since, far away in the darkness, away from the beds where the gardener snips, I listen always for something out there in the dark, something that might come on the bark of a fox or even on the mewl of a kitten, and it would call me by name; and if ever a star should fall, drop down through the deepening velvet of night, I would strain to hear, to catch that voice, but of course there'd be nothing at all, only an old woman breathing, breathing, and waiting to die. So, with a grudge, Bernadette leaves the window open and with a caution about draughts and chills goes on to tidy and straighten.

It's hard to get used to taking orders again, even here in this place, for it was only after Thomas's passing that I got my first taste of pure freedom and wondered I'd never missed it before in all the warp and weave of my life. It was such a racing feeling, like when you watch a couple of colts tearing round in a meadow: how they stop at the fence and throw back their necks and whinny as if to say they'd do it all over again. And I, would I live my life all over again? I think about this as Bernadette gives me a wave and leaves for the person next door. When I came here first, she asked if I wanted the 'sacrament' after Mass, but I told her no thanks, that Reverend Boyd would attend to my spiritual wants. If only I understood what those wants were. I know there's something needy inside me that worries, something darkly loitering, but I'm not going to work on that now or try to tease it out to make sense for I'd only upset myself and raise my blood pressure. I am dog-tired, truly tired of living, but I'm glad the window is open and the curtains not drawn.

It's ten o'clock now. All the trays are collected and the night hush sets in. I welcome the glow from the pink-shaded light that's left on in the passage and I listen to the creaks from the wooden floors. I don't like the nights: they're too long and there's not a sound to be heard, not even the bark of a dog. My pains are bad these times, and as they bite into my bones I lie and think, comb over the past. What if I'd married Johnny Williamson instead of Thomas? What if I'd run away from The Cairn like Eliza in Uncle Tom's Cabin? Well, given another go at my life I'd have a little more wisdom than what my mother and Church instilled in me. For one thing I'd have minded my boy myself through the early years, and I'd have stood up to Thomas, shown him the door whenever I needed, maybe even the boot! I chuckle at that in the dark.

And as for James, he would have joined the Lifeboys along with the Church of Ireland clergyman's son and learned to tie knots and rig up a tent for camping out on the beaches. Instead of which, at the age of nine, he was put out to hoke in the sheuchs with a spade and taught to clean drains. For ever since the day Thomas came on him curled in the boughs of the apple tree, a book in his hand (Treasure Island, *I think), he felt a need to toughen the boy. Yet when the father was away to a meeting, myself and James would go strolling and playing on the paths the other side of the meadow. And I smile to remember: he'd hold a buttercup under my chin and tell me how much I liked butter and we'd laugh together at that or we'd take up dandelion clocks and blow them away to tell time, all foolish games that his father would spurn. It was on one of these strolls that he shyly told me he'd got 'saved', himself and Molly McKinley: below in the Gospel Hall with the galvanized iron roof they'd given their hearts to the Lord, were redeemed by the Precious Blood. And oh! What joy filled my soul at his words. He was eleven years old at the time and we stood there close a moment, mother and son, our shoes all yellow with buttercup dust and the dandelions forgotten. Now that was all to the good in those days, yet looking back, I think that maybe we shouldn't have filled him so full of religion, stuffed him so tight with salvation and sin, that he baulked in the end as if sick, grew wilful and stubborn like an unbroken colt that refuses to take the bit.*

CHAPTER 15

As each of James's birthdays passed, my thoughts would fly back to the bedroom over my head where I'd laboured and waited, glad I needed to wait no more. For now, as he grew, everything seemed to happen at once, turn on a moment. Anna May Reilly still called on occasion, it's true, called for a drop of paraffin or to see if I'd any cast-offs, but I found I could suffer her easily now she was at a remove; I'd even make her a mug of tea on occasion, but if James was around I'd send him off smart on some errand or other. And she'd stay for a bit, give out the news if she had any, ask about Thomas and James, then away she'd go.

At that time I enjoyed the pleasant enough drudging sameness of days: the icicles dripped from the eaves, the snow melted, the river flowed on, and James was growing in grace and knowledge. He was turning out to be a helpful young fellow around the farm, and laying aside his own playthings, mostly marbles and hoops, he'd hurry off to make laps of hay alongside the hands his father had lately given in to employ – with a grudge, I might add.

And so the years went on. Childhood passed into boyhood, and with that passing there came, of course, the times of temptation, like when we found him playing conkers down in the lanes with the idle boys from the town and wanting to fish with them for minnows in the dirty stream that fed into the town lake. Satan was always active. 'It's the thin end of the wedge,' Thomas would bellow, for sure enough these and their like were pastimes that could lead to falling away, so we had to be stern, and as I'd empty his pockets of shrivelled chestnuts, I'd sing to him:

> Yield not to temptation, for yielding is sin;
> Each vict'ry will help you some other to win;
> Fight manfully onward, dark passions subdue;
> Look ever to Jesus, He will carry you through.
>
> Shun evil companions, bad language disdain,
> God's name hold in rev'rence, nor take it in vain;
> Be thoughtful and earnest, kindhearted and true;
> Look ever to Jesus, He will carry you through.

And I'd praise the Lord then to see my young son hang his head and hear him make his promises.

Up to his thirteenth birthday James still attended Ballymount's Sabbath School, where I'd taken on the role of superintendent, and it always lifted my spirits to see, after worship, those twenty or so children with shining faces fold their hands in prayer and praise. Florrie McKinley's daughter Molly was always there with her mother, who happened to be my assistant. Molly was of an age with James, and if I'd been blessed with a second child I'd have wanted one just like her: she'd be such a dear companion and sister for James. She was a good sweet girl, her wide-eyed face always lit up with a smile, clever too, and when we sang the hymn of the day she was our young accompanist on the harmonium. Occasionally I'd steal a look at James. Usually he stood at Molly's elbow as if ready to turn a page for her, and when I'd hear his young voice, still unbroken, rise just above the others, my very heart would melt:

> Children of the Heavenly King,
> As you journey sweetly sing,
> Sing your Saviour's worthy praise,
> Glorious in his works and ways.
>
> We are travelling home to God
> In the way our fathers trod;
> They are happy now, and we
> Soon their happiness will see.

We brought James to Meeting every Sabbath from the time he could walk, and through Bible Study, Catechism and Sabbath School he came early to faith. When I knelt to pray, morning and night, my plea was ever that, eschewing the ways of the world, he would go on to witness, and perhaps in the fullness of time be charged with a call to this very congregation. And I'd look at him singing there beside the harmonium, his head thrown back, freckled face slightly flushed, and I'd know that he was hovering on the edge of a time when, minnows and idle boys forgotten, he'd be moved to testify to Jesus as his personal Saviour. He was a good and steadfast child, more feeling than his father, cheerful and kind; an obedient little soul newly set out on his earthly pilgrimage. He was pliable as a green sally, and it was only up to us to shape him aright as he matured, tightening the twist or allowing judicious slack.

We'd invited Mrs McKinley and Molly to tea for that

thirteenth birthday, and Molly, all smiles in her Sunday coat and shiny button boots, arrived with something under her arm. 'This is for you.' She thrust a parcel at James. 'It's my favourite book, and I'd be glad if you liked it too.'

James, unaccustomed to gifts, held back.

'Oh, you must keep it,' she pleaded. 'It's *The Pilgrim's Progress.*'

Mrs McKinley and I smiled at each other, and I went at once to give Molly a hug, thinking her the nicest child I'd ever met. James had already begun to leaf through the pages and she was guiding him to the illustrations. Remarking to Mrs McKinley that the nights fell so quickly these January days, I crossed to the window. It was almost dark out there, silent too. The wind had dropped and all I could see was the black glass wet with condensation and the dancing light of the lamps reflected, nothing more, and again a scripture rose up in my mind: 'For now we see through a glass, darkly; but then face to face: now I know in part; but then shall I know even as also I am known.'

I tightened the string on my overall and turned back into the kitchen. A peculiar harmony, a haze like spun cotton lay over us all, a contentment that I thought I could touch so like a cloud it was, wispy, ready to fold and fleet. I looked at the two of them reading their book at the table and at motherly Mrs McKinley laying out slices of cake and I longed to put a stay on that moment, draw the bolt, remain shuttered and cloistered for ever in this space, this kitchen with its red cement floor and whitewashed walls. I crossed to the dresser, pretended to tidy some plates and, closing my eyes, offered a silent birthday prayer: 'Please God, may there always be a long road stretching smooth ahead of him.'

Tiring now of the book, the young ones were eager to run outside, but they were stopped in the doorway by the sudden appearance of Thomas, who came bustling in, blue with the cold and shaking off clouds of frosty air. They faltered as he laid a firm hand on the boy's shoulder. 'So, you think you're a big fellow now, eh!'

James looked crestfallen. 'What is it, Father? I hope I've done nothing amiss.'

Thomas smiled. 'No, never on the day of your birthday, young man, but we have to keep it like that.'

I sensed that Thomas wanted to give him a talk in the presence of Mrs McKinley – tell him about growing up, about morals and duty – but my husband hadn't a word for that kind of converse so instead, when James and Molly had gone, he just pulled out a chair and sat down to the table. Chafing his hands, he turned to Mrs McKinley. 'Isn't it good to see our young people close from the start? Keeps them from straying beyond the bounds.'

Mrs McKinley nodded. 'Aye, and when they've grown a bit we keep them dancing together in the Lodges!' And we all laughed together at that; it was such a long time away.

CHAPTER 16

It was only a couple of weeks after that same birthday when Reverend McGoldrick paid us another visit. Of course we expected he'd call around this time for he knew all about his people: the ins and outs of our births, deaths and marriages and far more besides, more than could have been good for him, I sometimes thought.

It was a cold sleety night with a dusting of snow on the hills when he came knocking at the front door. Thomas was lying back in his chair, undoing the stud on his collar, and as usual he looked to me. But that night I looked back at him, my face tight, thinking could he not stretch out those long legs of his, shift himself for once, or did he think I was his servant? Anyway, I left what I was at and went to lend my weight to the door, which was always stuck, swollen with damp and varnish, seldom used, and there was the minister, his coat glistening, shuffling his feet on the icy step. I drew him quickly to the warmth of the kitchen, where Thomas was hurriedly rousing himself and calling on James to come in at once from the scullery, where the boy was patching a bicycle tyre.

The minister stood for a while with his back to the range, his coat steaming. He was a tidy, stout little man with a wattle under his chin and a drip to his nose, and I always thought it a pity he hadn't a wife. He stood now among us and, after some chat about our health and the beasts and the weather, he offered a few scripture salutations and prayers, as was his custom. Then when the amens were pronounced, he turned directly to James. 'Well, my dear boy, I see thirteen years are just gone by, eh?' The minister was well warmed now and settled on the sofa. 'And what a big fellow you've become!'

'Thank you, sir.'

I could see James redden and twist in his body the way he did whenever Thomas chastised him, but the minister, unperturbed, was opening his arms to include the three of us. 'This is a time for family rejoicing, don't you think, a time of thanksgiving for the goodly span of years given this lad.'

I set down a cup and a slice of curny cake, as the minister turned again to James. 'You now leave your childhood behind, dear boy, slough it off, you know, become like a butterfly, and take up the burden of youth.' He coughed wheezily. 'But of course I expect you realize all this?'

'Yes, sir.'

I frowned as I poured out tea and watched the steam rise, drift for a while and disappear. That was the way of things, but surely there was no need for this heaviness, no need to cast clouds across the boy's life, and I longed to intervene. I wanted instead to go on talking (chirruping Thomas would say) about the weather or Ballymount. But Mr McGoldrick continued to stir his tea, slowly, gravely. 'You're a young lad arrived now on the threshold of manhood, and I consider it timely, you know, that you prepare to take your place at the Lord's Table.' He heaved himself into a new position, making the springs in the sofa creak. 'To partake of the Lord's Supper is a privilege proffered to you by the Saviour, an invitation and a wonderful duty required.' He went on stirring his tea, round and round and round. James stood before him and I couldn't but notice how clumsy and awkward my son had become, his poor wrists sticking out of his sleeves, short trousers too short, socks fallen about his ankles.

'Up till now you've been "speaking as a child",' the minister went on gently, 'you've been "understanding as a child", but now the time has come to "put away childish things".' He smiled up at James, who stood pale and silent, the bicycle tyre forgotten. I sighed and pulled my cardigan closer around me for the fire had gone low and the familiar words from the Bible did nothing to cheer me. I thought of all the old childish playthings still scattered about the place, simple home-made bits: the painted tin he used to pretend to drum on below in the field at the Twelfth, the little red cart with a wheel missing, the ball-on-the-rope and the kite made once by a friendly neighbour. But now Thomas was lowering himself on to the sofa beside the minister and giving James a prod with his finger. 'Do you understand what His Reverence is saying, son?'

James gave a nod as Mr McGoldrick chortled, 'There's a bit of study ahead of you, feller-me-lad, but it'll give you a break from thinning the turnips!'

Thomas was looking so upright now that I thought he'd burst. 'I'll miss him true enough in the fields, but he'll have to get down to the books and maybe you'd be good enough, your Reverence, to tease out a bit of what lies ahead of him?'

I thought my husband sounded very full of himself, cocked there beside the minister, forgetting it wasn't so long since he himself sat labouring night after night at the *Shorter Catechism* and the *Westminster Confession*, me at his elbow. He wasn't so eager then for the books, only badly wanting to be an elder.

'Pray be patient, Tom. Of course he understands me. The

boy knows much already, and I'll explain everything in due course.'

Mr McGoldrick was swollen with enthusiasm, his face creased into a smile. 'Tell me now, James, something of what you have learned; for example, you might tell me what the Catechism has to say of the Lord's Supper, eh?'

James looked anxiously at his father, saw the stern nod, and then breathlessly, rapidly, without giving pause, he began, ' "The Lord's Supper is a sacrament," sir, "wherein, by giving and receiving bread and wine according to Christ's appointment, his death is showed forth; and the worthy receivers are, not after a corporal and carnal manner but by faith, made partakers of his body and blood, with all his benefits, to their spiritual nourishment and growth in grace." ' And there wasn't as much as a gulping for air. Even Thomas himself had nothing to say after that; only the minister, softly nasal, murmured, 'You're a good scholar, James, quick to learn, and I'll always be glad to teach you.' He held the boy in his gaze. 'I'll teach you the meaning of "corporal and carnal" in due course and about transubstantiation, and I'll lay out for you the whole history of our Church so that you'll understand how we Presbyterians had to fight with might and main to preserve our godly inheritance and must go on fighting to preserve it.'

Pity flooded up in me for my child as he sat down now, twisting his legs through the rungs of his chair. I thought the minister would never stop, and the hour of his visitation wore on in a wedge of talk, thick as wet grass, big words sliding and slipping over the room like eels in the bed of a river: 'sanctification', 'justification', 'adoption' floating over the table and dresser, winding like gossamer through the filaments of the tilley. I was sure Thomas was only pretending to listen, and my own head ached as I struggled to be attentive while the sonorous voice dragged on, turgid and thick. It was too much for this time of the day, too much for a boy of thirteen. But at last the peroration was over and the minister was standing up, preparing to go. Stretching himself out, he gave us his blessing and pulled on his big woollen gloves. I saw him out to the door, but on the cold step with the night sky hanging black and starless behind him, he stopped and turned to grasp James's hand. 'And you won't feel a couple more years go by, young man, till you're eligible to join us in the Orange Order.'

CHAPTER 17

During all those years and in spite of much wholesome nurture in Ballymount, Thomas and I were forever worked up about the Roman Church. Now, whatever about my husband and the religious baggage on the Campbell side, I myself had good reason to fret for I'd had fear embedded in me like the roots of a bush, planted there by my own parents. Of the two, it was my mother who'd had the long thoughts, thoughts that dipped back into times before she was born, back to the 1859 Revival, which began, I was told, in Antrim and had spread like a fire through Ulster. I recall how affected my mother had been by her parents' recounting of that marvellous outpouring of spirit, which had enflamed the hearts of the poorest, both men and women, as they razed their whins and dug out furrows in thin rushy soil; had sent unlettered men to shed Gospel light on all, even on the Romans who languished in darkness. My mother told me these things while blacking my father's boots or mending his socks. And I'd listened eagerly, intently, wanting to know, wanting myself to drink from those waters that had once flowed over our land, filling drumlin and valley with sanctification. This fountain, my mother assured me, stayed open for all who'd partake of its health-giving draught, and so I was roused myself to seek out that spirit of 1859, to follow the clues she'd let fall whenever she spoke of those times.

In our seldom-used parlour back then was a press with a deep musty drawer that was hard to pull out. And as a girl of no more than thirteen or so (the same age as James when Mr McGoldrick came on that visit) I tugged and pulled at that drawer one day, delved into its depths looking for stories of 1859. Rummaging in the smells of old wool and mice and scraps of newspaper, I came at last on the inside part of a book that lay loose with staples rusting in the centrefold. I pulled it out and, hunkering alone in the parlour, I opened it up on my knee. I was wearing a long plaid skirt that day and as best I could, I smoothed out the badly creased paper looking for a title and soon came on words that drew me up: 'The Awful Disclosures of Maria Monk. Published 1836.' What could this be? I caught my breath and, kneeling down, began to read further. The paper was yellow and very crumpled, and sometimes the letters seemed to crawl in behind each other, but I persevered and slowly it dawned on me that it wasn't the Revival I was reading about; it was plainly the Roman Church.

Fearful now, I hurriedly folded the pages into my pinny and headed over to the haggart. Here, in the dim quiet, I furtively opened up the rest of that book, and to this day I can see the dark little speckles of mildew on the paper, crinkled and faded from lying wedged so long in that drawer at the back of the button box. And I recall how, with trembling fingers, I turned the limp leaves, almost fluffy with neglect. I read hesitantly at first but then faster, felt a tremor run through my growing-up body as I trawled through the tiny black print that yielded up stories, hideous and yet more hideous about nuns and priests and Confession boxes. Crouching there in the sweet-smelling hay on that Saturday afternoon in October, I felt soiled and ran to restore those pages to the drawer making sure they were well jammed in.

A few nights later Mother and Father solemnly sat me down in the kitchen. The work was done that evening and the lamp lit, and I sat meekly at the end of the table, already embarrassed, deeply affected by the defiling contents of what I'd read. Mother, still wearing her apron, was seated on a low chair by the range, looking put out to say the least, and Father, still in his overalls, was lying back in the old wooden armchair, his hands folded over his stomach. He started in at once about the book, and I knew immediately they had discovered I'd read it. I cringed as he tapped the toe of his boot on the floor and sucked in his lips. 'Through prying and deceit your eyes have been opened –' he looked at me hard '– and now you're ripe for guidance.'

It was as if they'd decided it was time for me to grow up. My face grew hot and I looked down at the floor, where a spider was walking across the bare boards. I shivered as Father took up his stick and pointed to the large framed text that hung on the whitewashed wall between the door and the window, 'What does that say, my girl?' His voice was sharp as an axe.

I looked at him. He knew very well what it said and so did I. It was Mother's copy of the Ulster Covenant signed in her own hand; his own 'men's copy' was above in the parlour. Didn't we all know everything about that covenant, for nothing much else was talked about at home or abroad, in church or in the town?

'Read it out.' His command was strident.

And so I went over to where the text hung by the cuckoo clock and I looked up again at the sprawling hedge of thickly black letters such as you'd see in the Bible. Then I looked at Mother, saw her nodding and complicit, and I began to read very slowly, a word at a time, while my heart hammered beneath my thin frock: ' "We, whose names are underwritten, women of Ulster, loyal subjects of our gracious king, being firmly persuaded that Home Rule would be disastrous to our Country –" ' and here my voice came out all ravelled like a bit of rope so that I had to struggle to go on ' "– desire to associate ourselves with the men of Ulster in their uncompromising opposition to the Home Rule Bill now before Parliament, whereby it is proposed . . ." ' And now the words began to peter out, ending in a tearful whimper as I sought to finish.

'And why was all that now?' Father demanded, ignoring my discomfiture.

I stood silent, twisting in my shoes. I had a good idea why it was. I knew that, for some reason, we had to protect ourselves, but he gave me no chance to speak; instead he was striking the arms of his chair with the flat of his hands.

'Why did over half a million of us sign that pledge on Ulster Day, the twenty-eighth day of September, in the nineteen hundred and twelfth year of our Lord?' He was shouting now. 'Why did we go in our groups of five hundred like the army sent out against Saul? Sir Edward Carson first! Why was all that, my girl?'

But neither he nor Mother wanted an answer from me; they knew it all. The cuckoo sent out a cheep from the clock, marking the half hour, and rain beat against the windowpane and still the two of them sat.

He leaned forward then, his face hunched between his shoulders, and I could see the fillings in his teeth as he glowered towards me. 'Well now, Miss Harriet, I'll tell you again why we signed, some of us even in blood: we signed to save us from Romanism, from Home Rule that would put us under the thumb of the pope. That's why we signed!' He stood up out of his chair and thumped the wall with his fist so hard that I thought he'd damage himself. 'Know this, young woman: Romanism has bred poverty, superstition and priestcraft throughout this land, and we must save ourselves with God's help.'

Mother, who had not spoken a word, looked at me now in something like sorrow. 'Harriet,' she murmured, 'remember always that we're Ulster people as well as Irish, and that, unlike most in this land, you've been brought up to believe in freedom of conscience as discerned through Holy Scripture.' I bowed my head submissively as she rose to pat my shoulder. 'Rome brings chains, my dear, but we Presbyterians know the freedom of the Gospel.' And she started to sing the familiar psalm, while Father, placated and spent, nodded along with her.

> O God our help in ages past,
> Our hope for years to come,
> Our shelter from the stormy blast
> And our eternal home.

And I went on standing under the framed text, shamed and humiliated.

CHAPTER 18

Sunnyside, 1982

That must have been almost seventy years ago, I do believe.

Bernadette comes in again now, and maybe her appearance is timely for it's often a painful struggle to recall those dark times. She brings me back to the present with a jolt. 'Sit up for me, petal; it's time for your tablets.' I obey and smile at her for, in spite of the strictures in this place, I enjoy the afternoons well enough: everything slows down, grows quiet as the residents nod off and the staff take their break. My heart isn't racing and jumping too badly today so I'll sit for a little while longer in my chair by the window. I keep looking and looking out there as if I'm afraid that the grasses and flowers might suddenly fade and vanish for ever, the way I soon will myself. Oh, I'm not afraid of facing my Maker, not troubled at all even though I'll bear the shreds of something that sullies. This is what niggles in me. But resolute, I turn away from dark thoughts and stiffen my back. I can still discipline myself, which I suppose is one of the blessings I got out of my life with Thomas.

When she has finished dishing the tablets out, Bernadette stands for a while and remarks, 'It's great you've such an attentive son coming so often to see you.' And I say nothing at all to that.

When she leaves, I go on sitting. It's September again and the sun is shining. Down along the avenue, a liquid light is flooding the spindly trees, turning their leaves to silver and gold and why I was thinking of Maria Monk and her 'awful disclosures' just now, I do not know. Memories can be so hard on a person. Their roots are entwined through a million wants and betrayals, and great strength is needed to pull some of them up and write them down.

It was from those long-ago times that the Roman Church began knitting long shadows into my life, causing me ever after to tighten my grip on the commonest things and leaving in me a bitterness like meadow sorrel. I recall how Rome had truly haunted our lives: given a special place by the new State, it had paraded in triumph with its canopies and statues through town and city, stamping us down as we hid behind curtained windows. There was also a thing called the 'Eucharistic Congress', a spectacle that occurred around the very time that Reverend McGoldrick was sitting with Thomas and me discussing James's future. We Protestants shrank into ourselves then, for the entire Catholic Free State was alight with a jubilant fervour, burned with an intensity that matched the fires of the 1859 Revival of my grandparents' days.

My own poor parents had signed the Ulster Covenant to safeguard their faith, but I wonder what they might do today, for the Irish state is kinder now: there's no longer a judge to say the law of the Church is higher than that of the land or a Roman bishop to make a pact with the government. Even so, the Catholic Church still rules with an iron hand today: many books are forbidden and until a few years ago contraception was very hard to come by. There happened, of course, what's called the Second Vatican Council, but this, while merciful to Protestants, was far too late for us Campbells.

My fingers still cramp, so I idle some more and look over to where my Bible lies on the table beside my bed. The embossed leather cover has stood the times well, and its golden-edged pages are caught, as I look, in a glint of sun, but aside from an occasional glance at the Gospel of John, I don't open that book any more. Yet there was once a time when I scanned those insubstantial pages closely and found in them transparent assurance that we, the people of Ulster, were in covenant with God just like the Children of Israel. But I don't know what I think any more. It grows dark as I sit; the days are drawing in, and I notice the leaves on the bigger trees are losing their suppleness, growing brittle, preparing themselves for a new season. The sun is low in the sky and soon Bernadette will be back to close my curtains once more.

CHAPTER 19

For so many years the pattern of our lives at The Cairn stayed even and unchanged. Thomas managed the farm, and I looked after the house and the dairy end of things: poultry, milking, calves and so on. James was a pupil in Ballymount's National School just a mile the other side of the church, and the master had told us from the start that the boy was good at his books. So it came as no surprise when he said there was nothing more he could teach our son, no point in holding him back for the Seventh Book; it was time for him to move on.

That day in July was his last day, and he came running in, threw his bag down on the sofa and pulled off his shoes. I had a cool drink of buttermilk ready for him but he'd hardly time. 'Where's my boots, Mother? I must hurry to get out and give a hand with the hay.'

But I quietened him down: 'Surely, my dear, the hay can wait till you have a bite. Book learning isn't the easiest job in the world.' I set down a plate. 'Was the master sorry to say goodbye?'

'No, but I was sorry to leave.'

He sat down at the table and began to butter a slice of bread.

'You were just going on five the day you went, couldn't wait to get your first book and then had it learned before you got home.'

I loved these quiet minutes I had with him when he came in from school; they were pieces of gold scattered over the greyest day and I'd surely miss them. We drew close then, spoke in little snatches of this and that, him about the master and the boys, and what he'd do when he was grown, things he mightn't speak of any other time. I looked at him as he ate and saw the shape of a well-grown sturdy young man, fully formed almost, like the sapling I'd planted the year before last at the end of the lane. Anna May Reilly and all her carry-on was a thing of the past.

He wiped the crumbs off his mouth. 'You know, Mother, it's hard to believe I'm finished there, but I told the master I'd go back to see him in September.'

'And what did he say to that?'

In reply he put on an old man's face and, mimicking, scratched his head and did the master's spluttery cough. 'Well, fellow-my-lad, if you were to come back in September, it's you might be teaching me.'

We were still laughing at the very idea when the door opened and Thomas roared in with a face on him. 'Does neither of you know that the hay's still out there to be cocked! Sitting here like the gentry, wasting the Lord's own time with talk about school and the master.'

We grew sober at once.

'But Thomas, it's his last day,' I protested. 'And we were just having a little celebration.'

'Last day nothing! I'll be blowed if it's his last day. There's all the days in the world waiting for him here in The Cairn if he's not got above the muck and the gutter that provides his daily bread.' And turning to James, 'Come on out of that. Get your boots on you. You're needed to twist the hay ropes.'

Although the master had dropped a word once in my ear about James's future education, I said nothing now. There was no point. I'd bide my time. Thomas was the master of words as well as of everything else so I often had recourse to imaginary conversations when he would listen and I would talk and maybe we'd sort things out. In my mind's eye he'd be tired and resting, his feet on the sofa with his eyes half closed, perhaps listening to 'Danny Boy' on the gramophone. And then I'd begin: 'Thomas, our boy is very clever, you know, and the master has said we might send him to board at the Protestant Chartered School.' But I could already hear Thomas retort, 'What are you talking about, woman? Maybe Sir James could learn how to screw back the wheel on the barrow that's lying out in the yard this month.' And I could see him stretch himself out the length of the sofa and reach for the Bible. I would protest a bit then but knew he'd be bound to add, 'Besides he's just learning to lead the prayers.' And that would be that. But Thomas wouldn't have taken Mr McGoldrick into account.

On the day of our minister's July visitation I gave the parlour the usual going-over and baked a sweet cake and a soda scone. When Thomas came in from the field, he was in better form than usual: the hay was drying well and he good-humouredly saw to it that James was tidy, all the seed combed out of his hair and his hands clean. Mind you, I thought our son would look well no matter what with his slow sweet smile and the cow's lick falling over his high Campbell forehead. I finished up what I'd been doing myself in the yard and hung my sacking apron on a nail in the scullery. Upstairs I took off my juice-stained flowery frock and drew out the sober grey cotton I'd made myself. It had grown a bit shabby – the cuffs and collar needed a wee bit of lace – but there was so little time. Lingering for a moment in front of the mottled mirror, I smiled at the strong intelligent face and, discarding a bit of red ribbon, I drew my hair to lie in a tidy knot across the nape of my neck.

When the time came, we sat quietly in a little row facing the minister, who peeled the silence away in gentle curls. He asked about our well-being: Thomas's pains, my own little cough, Sabbath-School work. Finally he turned to James: 'Now you, young man? I am fully satisfied that, under my wing, you underwent the most diligent and careful preparation for Communion, but what I'd like to know now is: do you also keep up with your school work?'

'I've finished with Ballymount School, sir.'

'Well done!' The minister beamed at me and Thomas. 'And what, my good people, are your plans for the boy now?'

Well, of course Thomas couldn't wait, had to jump in at once. 'That's all worked out, your Reverence. James is done with school. There's only the one book he'll need now, and that's the land here at The Cairn.' And he lay back and laughed so loudly that he began to splutter a bit. 'That's the studying he'll do. This place will belong to him in due course, and he must start learning to be a good steward. Still,' and he idly swung the fob of his watch, 'I'd be happy enough to send him as far as the tech in the town, where he'd learn a bit of woodwork, etc. and, more important, given the price of milk right now, that wouldn't cost me a penny.' My husband didn't as much as look my way while he spoke. 'Maybe he could go to the tech for a year or two and work with me here on the land at the same time. And we'd keep a close eye on his behaviour and morals.'

'Aye indeed,' the minister agreed in a friendly way, 'and I'm sure the boy would be willing to do all that, although a little fairy tells me,' and he looked coyly at James, 'that the Chartered School was looking forward to receiving him as a boarder for his entire secondary education.' Then, as if appealing to Thomas, 'It's a nice old building in its own grounds on the County Meath side of the Boyne and convenient to the train in Dundalk.'

'But what could he learn there now that he couldn't learn at the tech, tell me that?' Thomas sounded querulous and uppity. 'Greek and Latin and women's poetry, I'm sure.' And he snorted. 'What good would all that be to him if there'd be a cow calving or a belt in the thresher broken!'

'Hm. You have a fair point.' The minister, unruffled, let me replenish his cup. 'There are so many things to be learned as we pass through this life.'

I looked at my son, who seemed to be studying the pattern on the rug, and I glanced at my husband, who was now calmly biting into the cake, looking right pleased with himself.

Then the minister turned again to James, who almost seemed not present. 'You've learned so much already, my boy: the Sixth Book in school, the Bible and, more importantly still, I know you've accepted Jesus as your personal Saviour and testified to that. These are the things that count when we talk of learning.'

James fell to studying the rug again.

'Never be shy about your faith, lad; hold on to it like a precious jewel for you won't learn much of it at the tech.'

I set down the teapot then and stood up, emboldened by the minister's words. 'Pay heed, Thomas.' I almost stopped there, completely abashed at my daring, but I clenched my hands into fists and, looking to the minister for support, I prattled on: 'His

Reverence is right, Thomas. James would learn no Bible or Christian discipleship at the tech; he might even be a prey to the teaching of Rome.' I paused here, suddenly sure. 'I've heard it said that the boys are called to say what's called the "angelus prayer" right in their classroom.'

At once I could see the muscles in Thomas's jaws working and tighten, and I knew he hadn't known any of that, smart as he was.

'All right then!' he huffed in a minute. 'We'll give the place you mention a try.' He took up his knife again. 'There was no boarding school in my day, and if I find I can't do without him, he'll be back here, where he belongs.' And he slapped down his cup on the saucer.

For a minute there was silence. Not even a clock or a breath, until the minister's voice, soft as velvet, crept in: 'Well then, Mrs Campbell and Tom, would you like me to contact this school on your behalf and say the boy will attend this coming September?'

'You may do as you wish, sir, but don't say I didn't warn you.' And Thomas swept the cake crumbs on to the floor. Then standing up, he adjusted his braces. 'Now if you'll excuse us, your Reverence, we must get back to the work.' And together he and James reached for their boots.

I saw the minister off and sat down myself at the table, rested my head on my chin. I could see James already in blazer and cap, head of the school, receiving awards and everyone clapping, or else he was striding towards me in a clerical gown with a Bible under his arm.

CHAPTER 20

So, in early September 1934, I packed a trunk in James's bedroom and was only a little lonesome as I put in the clothes I'd carefully labelled: the woollen vests, the pullovers I'd knitted myself and the good twill shirts neatly mended; then on top of all, before closing the lid, I laid his Bible and hymn book, his Psalter and Catechism. My heart felt heavy. I'd miss him sorely, yet I couldn't but smile as he came whooping, excited, into the room to fasten the clasps on the trunk himself and give me a hug.

Downstairs his father was waiting, and soon James would be off to Dundalk and the train that would take him away to his school down the country, away from me and The Cairn for the very first time. Of course he was leaving his father too, but Thomas showed little feeling. Turning to James, he just scolded, 'And if you don't live up to the mark, you'll be home out of that as fast as a fox. We want no swanky ways around here or any fancy recitals.' He punched the air. ' "In all labour there is profit but the talk of the lips tendeth only to penury." So bear in mind that I'll have no dainty Johnny-jump-up about this place. There has never been the like on The Cairn and never will be.'

I was very annoyed that he should speak in this manner, but he cooled down as quickly as he'd risen and, maybe feeling a little of regret, called to the boy, who was standing silent by the door as if afraid to enter: 'Oh, come on in out of that, gason! Don't stand there like a daisy! The pony's already harnessed so just put your baggage into the trap and I'll let you take the reins as far as the road.'

I was still very angry but I stood there meekly, saying nothing, afraid that Thomas might change his mind even yet and keep James at home. Instead, I looked at my son as he picked up his little attaché case, felt myself wanting to adjust his tie once more, to straighten his collar, give him another hug, when there came a rattle and a tap on the window.

Now I always disliked people knocking on windows – why couldn't they use the door for that was its purpose? – and of course I knew rightly who it would be. I knew she'd be bound to come; knew she'd never stop dipping in and out of our lives in spite of my coldness. I knew too that, on his way home from school, their paths sometimes crossed near the Bottle Lane, which ran past the road to her own place. Several times too I'd had to intercept her on Fair Days when she was buying him Peggy's Leg or some other rubbish to ruin his teeth.

That was the worst of living in a small townland: you could never get away from the ones that annoyed you. And now she was here again, Anna May Reilly, her screwed-up headscarved face stuck with a grin in the windowpane. I tightened myself in displeasure, bit on my lip, but her sudden appearance shut Thomas up in a hurry for he never liked what he called his 'righteous wrath' to be seen in public and he went to open the door.

'Oh, come round, Anna May, come on round to the door. You just got us in time. We're about to set out.'

Holding the door for her, he turned and pointed at James. 'This fellow's away to be turned into a gentleman. To get a polish on the work you did when he was only a babby.' Chort-ling to himself, he took down his old brown coat from the peg and headed out to the yard, and in that moment I longed to strike him, slap his red face, make him wince.

Now the years had taught Anna May no manners for, taking no notice whatever of Thomas's departure or indeed of me, I saw her go straight to James, whose face was suddenly alight. Putting a hand on his arm, she prattled, 'Ah sure weren't you born a gentleman!' And I saw how she stroked the sleeve of his jacket and how he didn't draw away.

'I'll miss you, young fella, when I want a message done in the town. And I'll miss the bit of aul' crack we had.' She pressed a paper bag into his hand. 'Now here's a few sweets for the jour-ney, the bullseyes you like. You couldn't get enough of them whenever you came out to my place.' She winked at us both. 'And many's the time I was left short, I have to tell you!' I watched in silence as he took the sweets and gave her his hand, heard him thank her and tell her he wouldn't forget her when he was away at school. He looked so nice in his uniform, was so suddenly manly, and a lump was swelling at the back of my throat, severely paining, making me want to cry. Then she shook his hand, told him she'd say a prayer for him and with that she left.

He stuffed the bag in his trouser pocket and looked at me sheepishly. 'She only means well.'

But I wasn't for thinking along those lines, and all I could do was to tell him sharply that we mustn't keep Father waiting.

When he left for his school, it was all so quiet around The Cairn, but I got used to it after a bit. Thomas and I continued to go to Meeting, of course, as well as to the prayers in the loft, and we always remembered James in our intercessions. Sam Hanna called less often now, claiming a bad chest, but Anna May Reilly went on dropping in although she found it a struggle, she said, to make her way up the lane, for she'd put on so much weight, she was a burden to herself.

In the post every Tuesday there was a letter from James with news of his lessons and rugby or cricket, and he came home three times a year for his holidays, each time a bit taller and maybe a wee bit more distant but still the joy of my heart. Strangely, around this time Thomas seemed to lose interest in the boy's maturing, stopped asking to see his reports and wasn't nearly as stern, but that was likely because Thomas's own stomach trouble was getting worse: he wasn't feeling the best any more and had taken to seeing the doctor. That was the first real glimmer of illness, the first crack in my strong man's armour and a foreshadowing of times up ahead when I alone would be the one to do the admonishing and the advising, the guiding of our son on to pastures green.

CHAPTER 21

Oh, our daily happenings can have such a rough crustiness! Sometimes these events are so small that they run together like the stitches in a dressmaker's seam, smooth and barely noticed; but sometimes they cut into the soles of our feet and lame us. And while it's always our lot to suffer, to 'change and decay' as the hymn says, change can come uninvited. Thus it was that on 7 January 1938, with James already gone back to school, that Thomas himself suddenly commenced his dying. It started with just a slight fading as on a shirt collar hung out too long in the sun – so slight that I almost didn't notice it for he was often contrary in himself in the mornings and lately wasn't as eager to get down the stairs to pull on his boots. So I put it all down to a bout of indigestion due to the recent rich fare of pudding and cake.

I was the first down in the kitchen that morning and raking out the range to have his porridge ready when I heard him calling from the bedroom; not his loud accustomed shouting but more like a groan, like a grey scarf trailing, floating down through the banisters. And it dawned on me he was calling for help. So I left the pot down on the range and stood taken aback a minute, looking this way and that, the spoon still in my hand. Then I went out to the hall and waited calmly at the foot of the stairs, reluctant to know, shocked that such a terrible sound might have come from my husband. It was still almost dark, and through the little hall window I could see snow falling, swirling and spinning in great loops and hanks, swivelling over the laurels, over the roots of the flowers, over the stubborn scutch. Then I heard it again – 'Help!' – and the word was an irritant, combing through knots in my head. But still I stood at the end of the stairs. Unmoving, I noted the cracks in the old black tiles and the sheen on the red ones and thought how I needed to buy some more polish. Orrs in the town kept a good brand.

I was suddenly all of a shiver, and I tried to move but was as if stuck in a bog, squirming and twisting. What did he need my help for now, this great big man I'd obeyed all the years of my married life, the one we could never keep waiting? Was it my duty still to attend to his need when so often he hadn't been present in mine? I thought of the turf and the flax and of Anna May Reilly, and I went on standing, tracing my fingers, slow as slow, through the grey damp on the yellow wainscoting. He called again, kind of piteous this time, no longer demanding. *But let him call*, I said to myself. Many's the time it was me that called and he didn't come except with a roar and a shout: 'You're spoiling the boy'; 'You'll be late for the creamery'; 'Where's my dinner?'; and often 'Listen here, my good woman.' (How I hated to be called that.) But it was 'Harriet' now I heard. And it was such a long time since I'd heard my name on his lips that I softened and moved up a step on the stairs.

'Harriet! Help me, Harriet!'

And so I went up to the room. As I expected, he was lying on the bed, his face not the usual colour but greyish all over and old, so suddenly old. I put my cold hands to my heart, which was thumping badly. 'What's wrong with you, Thomas?'

'The doctor, the doctor.'

I noticed his breathing was harsh, the rasping in his chest like the gurgle from broken taps, and still I looked. He could fool me like this, I knew. It was a passing paroxysm. A dose of Epsom salts and he'd be back in the kitchen with his orders and me jumping around like a flea.

'Harriet, get Sam Hanna to go for the doctor.'

And I said, 'Yes, Thomas, I'll do that at once.'

Then I drew the coverlet up to his chin to keep him cosy and warm. I knew in my heart he'd soon be out in the fields again, his big body heaving, the muscles I often admired straining as he laboured to keep food on the table, us in our decent clothing and James at school. And so a feeling of kindliness swelled up in me like a flower. I'd go down to the scullery too and draw him a cup of cool water out of the earthen vat. But just as I was filling the cup, I heard a shuffling outside near the door: it was almost full daylight now and here was Sam Hanna himself (surely sent by God this morning) preparing to make an early start on the drains.

I set the cup down on the floor and went out to him, very composed: 'Leave what you're at, Sam Hanna, and go for the doctor: it's Thomas.' He stood for a second, shovel still in his hand. 'Just go!' I repeated, at which he gave a quick knowing nod and pedalled back into the town.

But something seemed to have come over me then for, completely forgetting the water, I found myself out barefoot in the orchard and James, still seeming a baby, snug in my arms. I was showing him the moon and the stars and telling him his father would always look after him. I took him then to Bally-mount and we played around the Campbell graves, encrusted with frothy ice, and found it a cheerful place with the velvety lichens caressing the gravestones that leaned around in a companionable way. Then on we went to the Lodge where the lads were polishing flutes and drums for the Walk in July, their knuckles all chilblained and blue. It was very cold in the night so I wrapped the child in the lining of my coat and lay down to rest for a while on the ferns that were crusted with frost, and the moss edged with rime. It was very still.

Then out of the dark, Sam Hanna comes suddenly rushing, all in a panic, his arms waving around him like bunches of twigs. He is calling and calling, his voice rising up through the black of the heavens. 'Where? Oh, where?' he appeals. 'Oh, where have you been? Come home out of this at once, come home. The doctor came when I roused him and His Reverence is here.' But I don't understand what Hanna is saying.

Now I think I must have been gone for a very long time, so long that when I got back they wrapped me in rugs. Cissie brought me upstairs to the room, where I saw my poor man stretched out like a bolster, flat on the bed where I'd so often tossed and turned, his jaw held shut by means of a Bible tied under his chin with a fair linen cloth, and Mr McGoldrick saying a prayer. My first thought then was that he'd shout no more. And the next, what would I do when I sought advice about calving or fixing the coppice fence or about our son?

Already I was wording a telegram to James's school.

CHAPTER 22

A neighbour met him at the bus and drove him out home. He was weeping inconsolably, his freckles showing in a face that was paler than ever I'd seen it. A sad sight in his fawn trousers and the little school cap he was still obliged to wear.

'Why didn't you send for me before?'

'It was very sudden; I sent word as soon as I cou—'

He cut me short: 'I'll go up now.'

He'd grown brusque, even churlish, but together we went up to the bedroom, dim now, the green curtains drawn on the close and empty air.

He opened the window, then sank to his knees by the bed. I put my arm around him as he wept, but lost and bewildered he shrugged me away from a place in him where I couldn't come. And I saw he was such a lonesome, poor thing, so lonely and lost, yet so sure to need me again for comfort and strength. I looked down on the fair head, hair already thinning. He was tall for his age, manly, and when he filled out, he'd be like his father, big and muscular, even handsome with his grand-father's high forehead and my own grey eyes. What age was he now? Almost seventeen? And with only a mother to guide and to care; no longer the father who, severe and cruel enough at times, had whipped him with words on the narrow road to sal-vation. The husband who'd scourged and chastised me too over the smallest of things: no pin in the hen-house door, no clean straw for the new calf.

But what terrible things I was thinking here beside the body of my dead man. I was surely committing a sin and must ask forgiveness. We should never speak ill of the dead, or even think ill of them. I must ask pardon of the Lord, pardon and strength: 'Ask the Saviour to help you, comfort, strengthen and keep you.' I looked around the big room that had never befriended me: nothing had changed, the curtains were still limp and green and the roses still swirled, only my man was gone. Was I going mad that such unholy thoughts were buzzing like bees in my mind? If I wasn't careful they'd put me away. Should I ask the doctor to give me a sleeping powder? But I have no pain. It's very strange to have no pain, not to be weeping the way a wife should; strange to have nothing at all warming my heart.

But James was weeping. He rose from his knees, adrift at last from the father he'd known as guide, as anchor, as judge too, whether about selling the cob or joining the Lodge, and I saw that his eyes were full of a plea: 'Won't you say a prayer, Mother?'

I was taken aback. 'Oh, I couldn't. Not here.' For I knew no words. Couldn't put any feelings into words, for in truth I had no feelings. It was as if the floor I'd been standing on had swivelled and spun, disappeared, leaving me hanging suspended in a great empty darkness. Where was Harriet? I panicked. Where was my old familiar self? That solid obedient little person who went about her tasks with never a complaint, said her prayers by night and day at the side of the big bed with the patchwork quilt. I groped for her, this woman, in the shadows, my hands swimming into the empty place. Then somewhere, not too far away, I thought I heard a small cry, the cry of a child restrained too long. And my son held me close while I spewed up bile in the bucket that stood by the washstand, held me until the passion had passed.

'It will be all right, Mother.'

He wiped my face with a cold wet cloth, and I looked up at him. He was crying still.

'Yes, it will be all right, son.'

And it would, for I'd 'take him like a chick under the shadow of my wings'. And, rubbing away the smudge of guilt that had clung to me fast and slick, I folded him close in my arms. From now on, it was only by showing care and compassion that I could best revere the memory of Thomas, who'd tried his best to raise a good son. But my husband's best had been always a boulder, hard and cold as Jacob's pillow.

So I roused myself, 'Come on, James, you must eat. You'll need your strength for tomorrow.' And I drew him away out of that room where he'd been born, where the red-rosy wallpaper continued to pile and swim, the petals floating and spinning, lightening my head.

CHAPTER 23

In the early light of the funeral morning I shivered as I donned my mourning clothes. I fingered the beetle-blackness of them, so black they were almost green, and the jet bead necklace he'd have scolded about, saying it cost a fortune. Cupping my face in my hands, I peered out into the half-light. It was guttery around the yard, the puddles shiny with rain, and away beyond the haggart I could see the last of a narrow moon and the lumpy hills speckled with snow. A hardy morning it was, with a bitter wind shaking the bare-boned tree in the garden, making it rattle and creak. Even the kitchen was cold that hour, for the range wasn't long lit and I felt stiff and uncomforted in the corrugated crepe of my dress that was as rough to my fingers as the sods I threw on the fire. James's suit hung ready at the back of the door, waiting for him, poor boy, the black cloth diamond already stitched by Cissie on to the left sleeve. But neither of us would eat. Even to eat seemed a betrayal; I knew that Thomas would have approved of our fast as a mark of respect, a salute to faithful elder and Orangeman, scrupulous husband and father.

So we sat there waiting together. I read aloud the requisite portion of scripture, and at my nod James took up the hymn the way he'd been taught: very softly at first, tremulous, then louder, and it warmed my heart to hear the young voice climb bravely over his tears, shearing the darkness, measuring out the familiar words so beloved of his father:

> Home at last, thy labour done,
> Safe and blest the victory won;
> Jordan passed, from sin set free,
> Angels now have welcomed thee.

I held him close as the black bandage of loss, draping and shrouding, thickened his tongue so that he had to struggle to finish.

When the time came, I didn't go to Ballymount Church. Attendance at funerals wasn't permitted to women, so James went without me. From the hall window I watched calmly as the black-plumed horses dragged the hearse slowly away from the house, the neighbours pushing their bicycles after and Anna May Reilly streeling behind. I saw the horses turn at the haggart: they'd pass the Big Field and then the meadow, where Thomas had laboured over the years, and then they'd be gone from my view.

Back in the kitchen I found the fire was almost out, so I lit the larger lamp and stoked up the range intending to make things right against their return, but a kind of lethargy came over me and I just dully sat. It was very still. Someone had stopped the clocks and silenced the cuckoo, and, very cold, I held out my hands to an emptiness thick as a fleece. I looked at his chair where it still proclaimed itself at the head of the table, and his cap, the Donegal tweed, that hung from a nail by the door. Once or twice I stiffened in something like fear, listening, but all I could hear was the wind and the rain and the bushes scraping, the way his boots always scraped on the floor when he'd come from the digging of drains. Once or twice I waited to hear his voice be it loud or soft, in command or question, but nothing stirred, nothing at all. So I rose to tidy his things away: the overalls worn at the knees and needing a wash, the bits of wire and spigot beside the pot he'd been mending, planning to fix it tomorrow, so quick he'd been taken, and I felt again the convulsion of sudden death, the cold grey slap and the barren space. Yet I couldn't weep though tears did well somewhere inside me, fresh and green as new-peeled rods, but oh, unsalted grief is a hollow place.

That afternoon, when all was over and the remains of the funeral meats were laid away in the scullery safe, I betook myself again to the comfort of the kitchen. It was peaceful there: the turf settling itself in the grate, throwing out a few sparks, and a streak of late sunlight falling over the table. Most of the neighbours had gone home; only James was left and he was still above in the parlour being consoled, no doubt by Molly, so I was surprised to hear a knock on the kitchen door and still more surprised to see Sam Hanna. About to leave, he stood there like a bent rush in the doorway, his tweed cap folded in his hands, his trousers already in their bicycle clips.

'Mrs Campbell, I'm sure there's nothing I can do to help you now, but—'

'There's nothing, thank you, Sam.' My voice was like ice.

'This is a sorrowful time indeed, but if ever you want for anything in the future, I'd be beholden to you if you'd inform me of your need.' And he went on standing there with the shiny boots on his turned-out feet and his long nose seeming to sniff out something. 'Often it can be hard for a woman to guide a youth on her own with the father gone.' He sniffed into the air again. 'I've raised a few of my own, so for advice et cetera – that is if you ever needed advice, for I know you're a brave quick woman – then just ask me. I well understand the trials and temptations of youth.'

I stared into the fire, my back like a ramrod, my lips bitten together.

'There's awful temptations around us. And boys need a father just as they need a Saviour.'

I stood up at that, angrily beating the air.

'Maybe this isn't the right time to discuss these issues.' He was muttering now. 'We could maybe go over them on my next pastoral visit.'

Dusk was beginning to fall as Hanna left, and the yard was swathed in a grey mist. From the hall window, I saw him stand and fiddle with his bicycle lamp and dry off the saddle just as Molly and James were emerging together from the front door. Hanna tipped his cap and, when Molly had gone on her way, I saw him approach James. The rain had stopped and the moon shone bright, and I could plainly see the two as they stood side by side on the step of the front door. They spoke together for maybe five minutes, heads nodding, feet shifting. When Hanna was gone and my son had come back to the kitchen, I could see how eaten up with grief he was, and I wasn't surprised that he'd nothing to say or any remark to make about the laying to rest of his father. And he made no mention of Hanna. But much later on, looking back, I knew they'd spoken that night about James's joining the Orange Order.

CHAPTER 24

Sunnyside, 1982

I have plenty of solitude here, and this is a state that has always eased and delighted me. I like to be alone and in tune with my thoughts, listening to their music, be it soft or shrill, and I recall the times in The Cairn when I so often retreated alone to the peace of the haggart with hurt and anger held under my arm like two injured birds.

Even so, in the few months after Thomas's death it was hard to get used to being alone, although I knew some relief in the knowledge that James would never be cruelly taunted or jeered at again in his own home, and I'd make up to him for all the hardness he'd so far endured.

But it's a law of life that a person gets used to anything no matter how bad it may be, and so I came round in my grieving, helped by the spring and by Cissie and, I suppose, by the occasional visit from Hanna and other Ballymount folk. Anna May Reilly came too – no show, of course, without Punch, but I'd never deter her for she was as good as the Celt for news – and I never rebuked her for leaving gates open or soiling the floor with the mud she brought in on her feet. She sometimes wanted to talk about James, referring to him always as 'the cratur', but I'd cut her off; couldn't bear to think she might ever know more than myself.

There's a knock on my door now, and it's Reverend Boyd, who's always smiling as though in a pact with his Maker. He sits down by my bed, fits himself into the visitor's chair and folds his hands over a Bible. First he talks about the usual things that float idly on top of everyone's mind like so many feathers: the Church, the weather and the government; later he slides us gently into religious fields, enquires about my prayers and if I'm at ease in my spirit. I know, of course, he's referring to what they call your 'inner being', a condition always of interest to Churches, and I'd love to tell him out straight that my inner being is a place he wouldn't want to discern because it's as full as a pit with you know what. I know right well that he's hinting at 'family discord', but I just let him hint, for what will be, will be. So, even as he talks, I close my eyes and sink down into my own familiar darkness and lock both him and the world out. It'd make you laugh, if you felt like a laugh. Cissie chides me for being like this, says I've grown crabbed, sour as bilberries. But I'm tired again; no fight left to fend off this weighted, pushed-down feeling that fills me. And I'm so aware of my heart and its fidgets, its tremulous workings. How it has lasted this long, I'll never know, with all it has suffered right back to that cruel day long ago when my mother took me from school as soon as I'd sense.

Now a bell comes sounding down the corridor; it's the little handbell they ring when they're bringing Communion to the Catholic residents, and along with the tinkle, a white-clad priest comes swaying and swishing past my door, his shoes ticking lightly on the soft uncarpeted wood while Reverend Boyd sits calm in his chair beside me, sturdily praying, 'Forgive us our debts, as we forgive our debtors . . .'

I make a pause now for my hands cramp with all this writing. My poor fingers that were once long and pretty, are gnarled and swollen at the joints as Bernadette has reminded me again. Yet, old age brings its own blessings, and I sometimes count these out just as the old hymn tells us to: 'Count your blessings, name them one by one, / And it will surprise you what the Lord hath done.'

How I used to love it long ago when we sang those words in Ballymount, and I count it a blessing that I still have a clear mind even if my body isn't that good any more, but I think my count stops at that for old age has its encumbrances, and along with stiff fingers I notice my sight is fading. But I don't think my past can ever fade although I would give anything at all to wipe much of it away. Still, memory is kind enough for it knows where to patch and when to blot out so that old pain from years ago can never engulf. I know grief too but I also know moments of joy, unexpected and fleeting, which balance the ugly heaviness of the forgiveness I go on withholding. I have no heart in me for pity any more; instead I dwell in my sunnier memories, and these are many: long summer evenings back at The Cairn, for example. Those hours were little snippets of heaven, and it is wonderful that they come to console me here in this shadowy backwater, bleak and loveless.

I look up now at the nurse who is giving me this new injection they've decided I must have. 'No, I didn't feel a thing, love.' She smiles and tidies up her bag of tricks, prepares to leave. 'You're a great soldier, Mrs Campbell.' And I know by the way she looks at me that she pities me. But I'm far beyond the reach of pity; what I need instead is valour, that old-fashioned thing we used to know as 'mettle'. And if I only had this valour, I'd reach out to my son, my once-beautiful child. But I haven't the strength and I haven't the will. I close my eyes against the nightlight that dimly burns, and I can see his young face, close as my own, and he looks as young as he did the day he left for the Chartered School. But here's

Bernadette and her tablets again, interrupting my thoughts. In this place it's hard to find the time or the space to think things through; there's always somebody annoying, intruding with pills and potions and, lately, sharp needles, and I hear her again even before she speaks: 'Sit up for me, petal. It's time . . .'

CHAPTER 25

In June 1939, the year after his father's death, James left school and two weeks later joined the Orange Order. That summer was quiet and uneventful, but, armed with a scholarship, he was preparing to go to Derry in September. I was delighted about this of course, as Magee College was a good place to prepare for ministry should he ever feel he was called. It had a fine reputation, the minister said: great biblical scholars had studied there. It was all in Mr McGoldrick's plan that James would keep on his Greek in Magee and take up Hebrew. He would stay in Derry for two and a half years, finishing eighteen months later in Trinity College, Dublin with his BA. After that it would be off to Union Theological College in Edinburgh.

But before he left for Derry, I knew I must sit him down as there was something important I badly needed to air. So one evening when the work was done and the pleasant hour of rest had fallen over the house and farm, I decided that this was the time for a talk. I took up the piece of embroidery I'd been working on and waited for him to come to the fire. It had been his habit since he left school to sit with me when he was finished for the day, and I was glad of this for we had only each other now, but that particular night he was late. I continued stitching for a while, musing on how life went on even without Thomas and how we were all dispensable in the end; this very scrap of embroidery would be here, for example, long after I was gone. *Would James keep mementos of me*, I wondered, *and what might they be?* As I bit off the thread, I heard water being poured into the basin in the scullery and his familiar soft whistling, a habit he'd had since a child. He wouldn't be long now and I moved to stir up the fire, for the summer night had turned a bit cool and I called, 'Are you coming in soon to sit down, son?'

The whistling stopped and then, from the scullery: 'Oh, I'll be going out tonight, Mother.'

Tensing, I drew myself up.

'Thought I'd go down to the Lodge for a bit. There's a few lads meeting there to practise flutes and accordions. The Twelfth's nearly upon us.'

Well of course I knew I should be glad he was taking himself off for he'd become a bit too quiet of late and, aside from the prayers and the taking of tea in the McKinleys' or Williamsons', he didn't go out much.

'James, before you go, would you come in here a minute? I want to talk to you.'

He came in wiping his hands on a towel. 'What's up, Mother?'

I looked at him as he stopped at the mirror to slick back his hair; what a real young man he was getting to be. I cleared my throat. 'Well, James, it's just that with Father gone, I thought it time we ironed out a few things.'

He replaced the comb in his pocket and, taking a look at his watch, he sat down. 'OK, Mother, let's hear it.'

I let my embroidery fall idle in my lap, the threads in a bit of a tangle. I would have to come to the point, be firm and open, the way Thomas would have wanted.

'I won't be here in The Cairn for ever, James.' I felt choked a bit but went on: 'And we need to talk about that.'

He got up, crossed to the window, and I went over to join him. Out there lay the acres Thomas had farmed, the fields where my son and I had grown close together and the twisty lanes that ran down to the river.

'You know this will all be yours.'

He turned to me, frowning. 'But Mother, what would I want with all this? Sure you know I'm not cut out for a farmer.'

He paced the floor just as his father had done. I'd known how unwelcome a talk like this would be, a shadow falling across a young mind where as yet there was nothing but Greek and Hebrew and wisdom sprung from the Bible.

'James, my son,' I hastened to add, 'don't I know very well it won't be the lands around The Cairn you'll work: you'll most likely be tilling the fields of God –'

He nodded a smiling assent.

'– so I have given all this some thought, you know, have discussed it in detail already with Harry McWhirter, that good man out of the congregation.'

'The auctioneer?'

'Yes, and as he farms a bit on the side, he knows what he's talking about. Well, I've taken his advice . . . which is to sell most of this land. Someone in the congregation has already expressed interest in buying.'

James looked up quickly now. 'Do you mean to say the Big Meadow and the paddocks would no longer be ours?' There was a wistful note in his voice.

'No, nor the Little Pasture that runs down to the river. But James,' and I beamed, 'there'll be something at last to put in the bank.' I was counting it out on my fingers now. 'There'll be a chequebook, and I'll have ready money for the balance on your fees, money for all the books you'll be needing in college.'

I looked at his patched boots and the shine on the knees of his trousers. What a lot of scraping together and stitching I was having to do to kit him out for Derry, and my eyes were red from darning socks, already twice darned, turning shirt collars and patching elbows. The money was tight.

'But what of this house? What of the rest of the land? What of the lanes?' He sounded anxious, for The Cairn, after all, was 'the rock from which he'd been hewn'.

'Ah,' and I smiled at him broadly, 'here now's the plan. If you were blessed with a call you wouldn't be needing The Cairn, would you? You'd live in a manse provided by the Church but with such a poor income you couldn't put by for retirement.'

I was surprising myself at how businesslike I sounded, and I think even James was impressed.

'Well, what Harry suggested was that after I *go*, you could let the house and the remaining two fields and get them back as soon as you'd retired from ministry.'

He gave me a hearty hug. 'Ah, Mother, I see what you mean, and it's a wonderful plan altogether, but that's all away down the road.'

He went back to the mirror and peered once more at his face, once more at his watch, and I felt a need to rein him in a bit. 'But James, supposing you were to stray off the path on which you've been set, supposing you were to be called in another direction entirely . . .' And I wagged a finger at him. 'It wouldn't be the first time I'd seen a young man set out with the best of godly leanings, change tack and go on instead to join the guards or something.'

He laughed. 'Well, if that were ever to happen, I'd still have the house and the wee bit of land, wouldn't I! But one thing's certain, Mother: I will not be a farmer!'

I was standing beside him now and noticed how handsome he was, and what a fine figure he'd cut at the Lodge dance, which was coming up very soon. He'd never be short of girls, my James. I let myself think of the ones in the church: pretty Mabel Delap with her beautiful curls, Priscilla Johnson out of the choir and Marjorie Ingram who took care of the minister's robes, all good solid Presbyterian girls; he could take his pick, but Molly McKinley, pedalling the little harmonium Sabbath by Sabbath, had to be the cream of the crop.

He kissed me briefly. 'Now that we've that all sorted, Mother, you can relax and I'll get down to meet the lads.' I wondered who else he'd be meeting. He flattened the quiff in his hair with a spit and, then taking up his cap, he whooped. 'Did you hear that Silver Buttons is to play again at the Twelfth dance? He's a dab hand with the accordion.' I chuckled to myself. No, I hadn't heard that.

He went off whistling across the yard, and I thanked God that all was well with us, the future now planned, gave thanks too for the stable, secure place we enjoyed in Ballymount, where faith, fellowship and fun abounded in our own church family.

CHAPTER 26

A week or so later came the Twelfth and the dance, and with it all the excitement. I'd never joined the Order myself and felt it beyond me now to attend the 'walks' in the North, but of course James had gone and now they were all returned, Orangemen and Orangewomen, their drumming and marching over. Hot and flushed, with their sleeves rolled up and fife cases under their arms, they'd be off no doubt to get ready now for the Lodge's 'Grand Dance'. I too was readying myself to go down to the Lodge that evening, not of course to dance, for those days were done, but to help with the supper we always provided for the hungry marchers. I was just going down to squeeze into the wee kitchen with Sarah Williamson and Betty Wallace, to spread butter on thick slabs of white bread and curny bread and pile it on big tin trays ready for serving. That's how I'd spend the night of the Twelfth, but the fun and fellowship was always great for we were all Protestants together, mostly Presbyterians, and mostly members of our own congregation into the bargain.

Before going down that night, I went up to wash myself in the bedroom. Just as I was pouring the water from the big jug into the bowl with the roses on it, I heard James come in through the back door below. I called down to him, glad to hear him home, but he made no reply. I thought he was a bit more reserved since our talk, a little remote perhaps, but I put this reticence down to part of his newly gained manhood, and while I knew I mustn't be meddlesome, I admit I pined a bit for the times when he used to tell me everything. We'd been like twins, you could say, closer even than twins. That closeness was hard to describe: it was a bit like living inside yourself, and I shuddered to think that this could ever change. But I'd just go on dreaming my dreams for him and trust he'd depend on his own good sense and avoid temptation when he went out in the world.

With these thoughts flitting through my head, I put on my flowery dress with the tie-back belt, and as I plaited my hair, I heard him move around in the kitchen below, then water being poured from the butt into a tin basin. So I hurried downstairs. He had his shirt off, and as he bent over the basin I noticed that his poor neck was badly burned, and at once I thought of Nivea and him a small boy crying after too much sun.

'Well, James, was the "walk" a good one?'

'Aye. Good enough, but it rained till we got to Enniskillen.'

'Will you be heading down now to the dance?'

'Aye.'

So I left him then to carry on with his young embarrassed ablutions. I had to learn to stand back.

Later on, at the dance, I couldn't help looking out for him, but it was hard to see who was who. The smoky atmosphere was terrible, and there was a strong smell of porter as the crowd heaved and swayed to the music. The big red-faced men in their serge suits held their partners tight in great muscling arms making them look like squashed flowers, and I listened with pleasure as all the old dances were called: foxtrots and flings and finally the ladies' choice, when the woman got a chance to pick her own partner. And there was Molly McKinley, standing and waiting with the other girls by the wall. She was now a buxom young woman as nice and fresh-faced as ever, her dark hair smoothed to a tidy bun, her long neck graceful, dress modest and plain. She was full of music too and at the church's Harvest Festival the congregation listened enchanted whenever she took the solo, her sweet voice soaring to the very gates of heaven. But above all these charms was her virtuous nature, the perfect example for our Sunday School children. All told, she was like good wheaten bread, and might one day, dare I think it, make the perfect wife for my son.

She was looking around her now. I saw her step out, neat as a pin and, crossing the floor, she stood facing him. I smiled to see this, although my poor boy stayed nailed to the wall, his hands in his pockets. He could be so annoyingly slow at times, and I longed to give him a nudge. But then I could see she was laughing and, pulling his hands away from his pockets herself, she took him off smart by the elbow. When they got going, they danced so well as a couple, and I sat down for a bit just to watch, looked at them long as they changed from the waltz to a quickstep with the good old Orange tune, 'Dolly's Brae'. As they passed me in the dance, she waved and smiled, looked so happy, but then who wouldn't be happy in the arms of James Campbell?

As I sat dreaming, the women were getting busy in the little kitchen behind me. I could hear them laughing as they worked so, with one last glance at my son and his partner, I went in to give them a hand. The kitchen was full of steam, and there was hardly room for the three of us, but feeling happy in myself, I hummed a tune as I laid thin wafers of brawn and Spam on the slices of bread, and I smiled to myself as I held the white enamel buckets for Sarah to fill with sugary tea. When supper was called, I lost sight of the pair in the ensuing turmoil, and although I searched everywhere I didn't spot them again that night. I smiled to myself as I belted up my coat and prepared to go home. *Oh, would they?* I dared to wonder. And how happy James would be with her. Still, I knew I must leave everything with the Lord for he would work his purpose out no matter what: 'Commit to the Lord whatever you do, and he will establish your plans.'

CHAPTER 27

James went up to Magee in early September, and I was left on my own once again but I began to believe he was gradually sensing a call. It delighted me to hear all that he was learning in Derry. He was keeping on his Greek and had taken up Theology – something I didn't know about at all except that, as he explained, it concerned the study of God, the very idea of which filled me with awe. He was doing Hebrew as well, and he even copied out for me a few strange-looking letters of the alphabet, naming them aleph, beth, gimmel, daleth and so on. How I'd have loved to be alongside him, studying with him, but even so I was learning, through him, what a wide and various world we lived in and what God-given freedoms were ours to explore it with.

It was lonesome enough at home, I suppose, with both him and Thomas gone and me rattling around by myself in that big empty house: no farm hands to feed any more, only the hens and the garden to be attended to. Cissie called now and again, along with a few of the neighbours, and Anna May Reilly dropped in on occasion too. Although she had slowed down a bit, she was still really the same old 'two and six', trotting round the townland, taking in all she heard and telling it out again to the world and his wife. She'd improved quite a bit with the passage of years, and while I didn't know exactly why she went on coming to the house, especially with James gone, I never in charity turned her away. But I was still suspicious of her and still fiercely resented the bond that had cunningly formed while my son was a child. She knew too much about him, knew things that maybe I, his mother, didn't know. I prayed long and hard about this, prayed that their crooked attachment would yield to the abrasions of time. Yet my prayer was weak and half-hearted for I'd been told (by someone who'd know) that if you worked on the mind of a child until he was seven, worked as if kneading and pressing the softest of dough, you were already shaping the man. And she'd known him for a good two years, and maybe that was enough. Still I'd loved him myself with the burning fervour that only a mother can know, had loved him beyond human telling and must surely have loved him out of her reach. But you never could tell.

Badly in need of ordinary chat with other women – Thomas would have called it gossip – I took to visiting Florrie McKinley, herself now a widow, and I sometimes dropped in to see Sarah. Every so often Sam Hanna called on his pastoral rounds, and sometimes a couple of folk from the prayers, for Ballymount continued to be the centre of my life. I was forever grateful for the assurance and promise I found in its very walls, and it was there that I worshipped, renewing my soul week by week. I was proud too, I have to admit, always proud of our Presbyterian heritage, for which, I believed, I would die: 'Be strong and courageous, do not be in dread of them, for it is the Lord your God who goes with you.' So I kept up my attendance along with my Church work. The midweek prayers were ever inspirational, and what a privilege it was to be able to bring before the Lord all the sorrows and worries that lay on my heart, for I missed Thomas and very often fretted for James especially if the day was too wet to *plouther* around in the yard.

Now I took out the latest letter from James again for another read and sat down with it on the sofa. I settled myself to peruse the creased pages for maybe the tenth time. It was the next best thing to having him here with me.

Strand Road, Derry
20 November, 1939

Dear Mother,
Thank you for your last letter and all the news. I am glad to hear that you are well and keeping up with your prayers and church attendance now you're on your own. We can never go too far wrong if we live in the light of the Gospel. And yes, I agree that Mr McGoldrick is a jewel in the crown of the Church for he gives his entire life to it.

I must say I feel truly blessed to be studying here in Magee and the sense of my being called grows stronger by the day. Magee gives a great grounding, I think, to future ministers, and I am kept pretty busy just finding my feet and getting to know the other men in my year. There were fourteen of us to begin with, but two have already left for England, to do their bit in the war, which seems very close now: we have blackouts here, the city is full of sailors, and from my window I can see the escort vessels waiting in the Foyle, ready to assist on the Atlantic. But me? I'll bide my time, wait for the Lord's command and will join up if He, my Captain, summons.

Meanwhile term has begun, and we have lectures on Old Testament and New Testament as well as Systematic

Theology (I think I explained about that in my last letter). Then there's Church History, which I find very interesting; it's answering a lot of the questions I have about our Church, and I begin to see for myself why it is that the Presbyterians south of the Border keep so much to themselves. As for the study of Hebrew, I must say I get really immersed in it and also Greek, which I was already well up on, thanks to Mr McGoldrick. It is quite breathtaking to read the Bible in the original languages. Terrible to think that Roman Catholics are discouraged from reading God's Word: 'Pray ye therefore the Lord of the harvest that he will send forth labourers into his harvest.'

But it's not all study here! In the evenings we students lead prayer meetings in local churches. First Derry is my favourite. Churches here are all very big compared with Ballymount and at first I found them quite awesome. In First Derry for example, just before the service starts the sexton strides majestically in, carrying, on a cushion, the big church edition of the Bible. Just imagine! And then, in a most dignified way, he climbs into the pulpit and lays the Book down on the minister's lectern.

Services here are a bit different from at home: there are marvellous choirs with organs worked by electricity. Not like Ballymount's and old George sitting behind a curtain with a bellows. On weekdays we have the usual teas, and so on, to attend, and ladies' circles where garments are knitted for sailors' children. I haven't preached yet, but when I do it will be on Judges 7 and 8; you know those chapters well: 'A sword for the Lord and for Gideon'. And didn't the Reverend Duncan give us a great stirring message at last year's Orange service?

My name is down for giving my testimony, the Lord be praised! And I will do this fairly soon and with a full heart. When we give our testimony, we can choose a hymn to go with it, and I know already what I'll pick: it will be 'Sound the Battle Cry! See the Foe is Nigh' with its magnificent chorus:

> *Rouse then Soldiers, rally round the banner,*
> *Ready, steady, pass the word along;*
> *Onward, forward, shout aloud Hosanna!*
> *Christ is captain of the mighty throng.*

It's a great rousing hymn, isn't it, and of course a great Orange favourite. Do you remember how we used to sing it in the kitchen at home and how poor Father was nearly always out of tune?

And now a little about the social side of life, which you like all women are ever most interested in. To begin, Presbyterians up here in the North don't go to dances the way we do back home but instead they have soirées and socials where games are played. These games can sometimes appear childish but I join in, knowing that their excellent purpose is to keep us from sinning.

And, finally, Mother, Molly writes that she'll be up here for a weekend soon if she can get a lift to the train in Dundalk. I will be very glad to see her and have already arranged for her to stay in Macintoshs', members of First Derry congregation. I know she'll be comfortable with them. Best of all, she tells me she'd like to give her testimony the night I give mine. Won't it be wonderful if we can represent our little Ballymount together as we proclaim our faith in the saving blood of Christ Jesus?

I folded one sheet behind the other. What a good boy he was and what a life he had ahead of him. Ballymount too would be greatly pleased as it followed the life and progress of this wandering son. I read on, skimping over the last few lines: 'Mother dear, I hope to hear from you soon again. Greet our people in Ballymount for me.' And then came the PS, which had me smiling: 'You will see Molly in church this Sunday so please tell her I'll be able to meet her at the train in Derry, and remind her to bring her umbrella.'

Well, of course I'd remind Molly for I was frequenting her home a fair bit now since James's departure. Amazing to think how in a few short weeks Florrie and I had grown so close, each of us eager to see the bond strengthen between these, our young people. Sometimes I would go over to Florrie's place or she would call to The Cairn, but whether here or there, we'd sit knitting and chatting, and after we'd combed the news of the day and the news of the Church, we'd get round to the talk about 'our two' as we put it. So, putting the letter into my pocket, I pulled on my coat and headed to Florrie's once more, full of the latest news from Derry.

When I arrived, Molly was still at work, for which I was glad as it gave her mother and me the chance to discuss the more sensitive things should this be our wish. So I read out bits of the letter and we settled into our chat. As Florrie poured out the tea, she chuckled. 'Aye, they're moving along very nicely, those two, and isn't it a terror she's going to Derry to see him.' Then she tapped at the table with her fingers. 'Molly'll be eighteen next birthday, too early to marry I think, but she has a mind of her own and doesn't take kindly to having the topic as much as mentioned.' And Florrie rolled her eyes.

'Och, it's as well that she's somewhat demure like that,' I remarked. 'One day she'll make a fine wife for a minister.' And we smiled at each other, agreed how nice it would be if they married and ended up some day in Ballymount Manse, though they'd be poor as the mice.

When the dog started to bark in the yard, we hushed, knew it was Molly come home, and at once her mother was up on her feet, clucking about her daughter's wet coat and the rain: 'You're drowned, my girl, and look famished. Another long day stuck behind that old till, slaving away for Wilson, and him I suppose as contrary as ever.' She hung the coat on a chair in front of the fire. 'I'm thinking you'd be happy to leave him for something else.'

Molly greeted me sweetly, then turning to Florrie, 'Remember, Mother, that poor Mr Wilson is badly bothered with pains. He doesn't intend to be vexed.' Florrie just sniffed at that before adding that Owenie Brady would be available to give her a lift to the train the following weekend. With a quiet nod, Molly folded away her scarf and her gloves and then, as though the thought of going to Derry had just occurred to her, 'Oh, I'll be needing two frocks for my visit, I think? Maybe the grey one? And the pink for special occasions?' She was blushing a little and, sensing her excitement, I couldn't help saying as I rose to leave, 'James tells me you're hoping to testify together?'

She paused for a moment then, her eyes raised to the light, said, 'Yes, Mrs Campbell. I suggested to him we might do that in Derry, and what a privilege it will be.'

I left them soon after, dear daughter and mother, and on my way home I couldn't but think what a treasure she was and how well got the two of them were, James and herself, and how, God willing before very long, they might become husband and wife in the very place where Thomas and I had ourselves tied the knot. I was bold to think that far ahead, but I hoped and prayed, knowing that Molly would patiently wait until he'd finished his studies, good girl that she was.

CHAPTER 28

The war rumbled on, and another young man of James's year left and joined up. James himself stayed on and continued to do well at his studies; indeed he brought home quite a few prizes to add to the ones in the parlour bookcase: in his very first year he came first in Church History and first in Ethics; a lot to be proud of. But in the long holidays, scholar's gown laid aside, he happily worked the few fields along with a man I hired for a couple of months in the year. Things were difficult enough without Thomas, but with the money brought in from the sale of the land we were able to manage much better, and during his holidays James and I could enjoy time together if there was no work to be done and if Molly was busy in Wilson's.

Often we'd go down to the river, him to fish and me to sit idly by on the banks and watch. It was always so pleasant to sit there: I'd bring a rug and a bit of embroidery, and we'd keep each other company under the dripping trees on soft after-noons. It was a lovely scene no matter the season: grey sky with the clouds bundled up and the water rucked like green velvet, best for the fish, he said. And I'd watch him, the lean frame of him, casting his line high behind him into the arc of the sky and then following it up with a swift forward movement so that it sang whistling into the river, dropping its bait with the slight-est *flop*. Then he'd sit silent for hours, an eye on his line.

Our talk was always desultory, for our lives ran in the same courses and we knew each other's thoughts much of the time. It occurred to me too that we must look a strange pair sitting there, me with my greying hair bent over needlework, him strong and young and handsome, and I'd wonder sometimes what energies were flowing through him, what his secret desires were. Sometimes I'd be tempted to ask, but just as I'd be about to speak, the line would go taut or he'd stand to manoeuvre his bait and the opportunity would pass.

These little outings that he and I took were like perfect pearls, but one damp afternoon in February, just a week before he returned to Derry, something happened to dull them. It was really far too cold for sewing, but I had just finished off my daisy stitches that day and was about to snip off the thread when I heard voices in the distance. This was unusual for our quiet was seldom disturbed. They were musical voices, and then, in a moment, two young women emerged from the trees behind us, a remarkably pretty girl with dark auburn hair, the other nondescript, and together they laughed and chattered along.

The pretty one stepped forward when she saw us and then hesitated. 'Oh, we are so sorry to disturb you.' She sounded cheerful and friendly and I noticed her lovely smile. 'We'll find another place.'

But James, ever the gentleman, told her, 'No, you needn't do that. You're welcome to join us.' And he rose to his feet. 'We'd likely be the better of a bit of outside company in any case.' He looked over at me and I really did wonder why he had to be so inviting, but that was my son for you, always welcoming of people even when it wasn't in any way necessary.

'This is my mother and I'm James, James Campbell.'

'This is my sister Marie and I'm Dolores, both Dohertys, of course!' And she laughed. 'But are you sure we won't disturb the fish? There's plenty of room further up.'

This made me wonder irritably why they hadn't gone 'further up' as she put it, in the first place. But James was drawn: 'Och no! Stay where you are.'

I noticed he was blushing as they sat down near us. The one called 'Dolores' was wearing a nice woollen coat, blue with a sprinkle of snowflakes, and a full skirt which she drew in under her legs before seating herself. She didn't seem to mind that the grass on the bank might be damp or leave a stain and, tucking her ankles under her, she smiled at me in a warm, friendly way. 'Delighted to meet you, Mrs Campbell.'

I must say I was impressed by her nice manners and educated-sounding voice.

'What a pleasant way to spend an afternoon,' she remarked then. 'It's a little bit chilly, but I suppose with this overcast sky, the fish must be jumping, as they say.'

'Indeed!' said I. 'And do you do some fishing yourself?'

'Oh yes,' she replied with enthusiasm. 'I do indeed, but I'm afraid I'm only an amateur. I'm still at the hook-and-worm stage.'

She smiled at James, and he smiled back, one of his long, wide-mouthed smiles reserved for so few, and again he flung his line over the river. 'It's very easy to get on to fly-fishing, you know. I could teach you if you liked.'

She raised an eyebrow.

'I could bring you over to Lough Sheelin next time I go.' He was all in a fluster. 'You and Marie. I go over every year, you know, when the mayfly is rising.'

But she just laughed at that. She was a winsome young

woman, and I was proud to see that she admired my son but I was anxious too. She sounded like a local girl, but although I racked my brains, I couldn't come up with any Dohertys; maybe they were new to the town or maybe they were from the next townland. They certainly weren't Presbyterians with such names, although they could be Church of Ireland, for you never could tell with them. She could be Methodist of course, but surely to goodness she'd never be RC!

As soon as they'd left, I looked at James, searching his face for any sign of what he might be thinking. But there was nothing I could read in the untroubled eyes that looked back into mine. 'Worried are you, Mother, that you might have some competition?' He laughed, but I had such a bad feeling and knew the helplessness of not being able to name what I feared. As he reeled in his line, he read my thoughts. 'You needn't worry about me, Mother, for you must know I belong to Molly.'

I could see he was trying to lighten my darkened mood so I responded quickly in a more cheerful tone, 'Oh, don't I know, James! From the time you were children, it was plain you and Molly were cut out for each other.' I gave myself a shake and gathered my threads. I could be really so silly at times for James after all was up in Magee, likely heading to ordination, and with the great Reverend Dr Samuel Stewart as his mentor there, he'd hardly slide off the course set before him. I scolded myself: he and Molly were devoted to each other, just as they'd always been and over so many years. As we picked ourselves up that day, we were a little quieter than usual. He had caught nothing, and the Doherty girl preyed on my mind.

The remaining days of that spring-term holiday were uneventful: he studied a bit and went down to the Lodge once or twice, and almost every evening Molly came up to the house to sit with us around the wireless and listen as Churchill addressed the nation. Some nights James went down to her place and together they went to the midweek prayers, but more often they took long walks and would be gone till well after dusk had set in. I was pleased and touched by their charming courtship, and I bit my lip when recalling that long-ago evening when I was fifteen: Thomas's bike and the ditch and the can of buttermilk. Still I was worried, and sometimes anxiety stained my days, but I'd give myself another good talking-to. Wasn't my lovely son engrossed after all in his books in Derry, and hadn't I heard him speak of the essays he had to write on things like 'The Law and the Prophets'? And besides, there wasn't much time in Magee for fishing with all the work to be done round the churches. Moreover, I prayed that one of these days he'd sense a call for, like Christian in *The Pilgrim's Progress*, he was making his way to the 'Celestial City', as all of us were. But I didn't know how long that way would turn out to be, or how stony and hard on the feet, or how many awkward twists I'd encounter.

CHAPTER 29

In a flash his years in Derry were over, all the exams passed with flying colours, and in the spring he began the first of four terms in Trinity College, Dublin. But whatever it was about Dublin, he wasn't himself from the very first time he started there, and now here he was, in his final year, grown all moody, morose and irritable. He continued to write to me of course, but these Dublin letters had none of the Derry verve.

It was the last of those long university holidays, April 1943, and to cheer him up I concocted his favourite dinners and asked Molly over for tea, but he just went on being up and down in himself, very moody. If he'd been a girl, I'd have put it all down to the time of the month. So I puzzled my head: perhaps it was a little difficulty with his studies or maybe he and Molly were in disagreement over some trifle. I couldn't be sure, but on one occasion when I invited her over, he told me sharply that I shouldn't have done so without asking him first as he'd already planned to go out. I was really shocked by this, and when Molly arrived I was very embarrassed. She had little to say when I told her, but it was clear she was very put out and didn't sit long.

And it dawned on me as that holiday passed that he seemed to be going out more often, never saying where. Sometimes he came in looking pleased with himself, sometimes whistling, but on the day he let Molly down he'd come in very late in the evening with a puss on him. When I tried to ask him what was wrong and where on earth he'd got to, he just brushed me aside. 'I was out, Mother' was all he would say.

I looked at him crossly. 'Well, Molly was here as you know, and she wasn't well pleased, I can tell you.'

He stuck his thumbs in his waistcoat pockets and angled his feet. 'I'll be seeing Molly tomorrow night, but she must know I can't always be here when she calls. I've a life to live.'

'You'd need to explain all that to her then if you don't want to lose her.' Annoyed, I swiped at the table. 'There are lads in Ballymount would be queuing up to get her.'

He was angry now. 'What I'll explain is this: I don't need people expecting me to be here and there, do this, do that, wanting to know where I am every minute.'

I was quite astonished at that, silenced indeed, for here was my son telling me plain to mind my own business. Well, this to be sure took the wind from my sails, but it had been as well to let him know he was truly out of favour. But the very next day, when he gave me a hug and said he was sorry to have addressed me so rudely, I forgave him at once, and when he added that Molly was coming for supper, I was quite elated, his tantrum forgotten.

That evening was pleasant enough – I made a nice tart and reddened the fire – but they were both far more silent than usual, which led me to think there were things they wanted to say to each other. So I took myself off up the stairs to give them some private time, though they'd get plenty of that, I thought, if they'd just step outside and look at the stars. But somehow I didn't think Molly would be greatly taken by stars.

I knew I'd be very relieved when James went back to Trinity at the end of the month. His studies might settle him down a bit.

CHAPTER 30

Just before his final exams, he came home for a weekend and on the Saturday morning he took himself off on a walk to the river. While he was gone, I busied myself rootling around upstairs, tidying up and so on. When I got to his bedroom, I saw, sticking out of a drawer, the corner of his Orange sash, so I went at once to replace it in the cardboard box where I knew he kept all his regalia. Now, the dear only knows, I hadn't been looking for his diary, hadn't even known he kept such a thing, but here, in that drawer, it was suddenly before me, just a little black book, and I couldn't contain myself. 'Page 1', it said in his own neat hand, and I allowed my eyes to run over the rest of the words.

8 April 1943
It's almost midnight. I have locked the back door and drawn the bolts, and now before I say my prayers and read my scripture portion I'll gather up my thoughts in the privacy of this book, my nearest friend. I feel tired and grumpy tonight but I'm so often like that these days.

Had a bit of a quarrel with Mother the other night. I was very hasty and this I regret, but when I'm at home I do need to come and go as I please, to the places I want. I also tend to quarrel with Molly. Some nights I go into the town on my own or else just go roaming abroad, feeling so wistful

and lonesome and longing, for what I don't have. My
comings and goings don't please my mother, I know, and I
do get home rather late, but I'd so love to meet that
beautiful someone again. I dream of her often, and always
she's wearing the same blue coat. I have looked and searched
in the town but think she may have departed the district,
and when I'm back at college and walk in the Green, I often
wonder if one day I'll see her face among others and if she'll
recognize me.

I gave a hand in the yard this morning and then, after the
dinner, I went across to the prayers. Molly was there and she
gave witness again so that a few were stirred to faith. She's
really a very good girl, a little too stout maybe but a hard
worker, and gratifying that she shuns idle shows, spurning
make-up and all extravagance in her dress. She's a good
daughter too, just herself and her mother. I walked her home
after the meeting tonight and was relieved she never
mentioned me not being there the other day when she called.
It was a lovely night for a walk: the moon just on the wane,
the sky star-filled, and we held hands. Passing through the
grove at the foot of her lane, I was almost overcome by an urge
to embrace her fully, but she drew quickly away and I
respected her modesty, knowing that I too must exercise
self-control as scripture adjures. Oh, I'm feeling very jittery
and on edge tonight, so irritable. Perhaps I need a tonic for
my nerves . . . or something else . . .

As I continued to read, the big clock in the hall boomed
eleven; the morning was wearing on and he might soon be in,
but I proceeded, couldn't stop myself – it was like being sucked
into a bog.

10 April 1943

*Went over to the Lodge for an hour in the evening and heard
the lads practise their flutes; we won't feel the Twelfth coming
round yet again. After that I went over to Molly's place,
although I was feeling fatigued and would have much
preferred to go home. But we had some fine hymn singing
there with a few from the church, and Mrs McKinley,
accompanying us on the harmonium, insisted that Molly and
I sing our duet one more time. To tell the truth I'm utterly
tired of that duet, but together we dutifully rendered, 'I've
Found a Friend'. And at least our effort was well received.
Later on in the evening, Molly asked if we might picnic alone
before I go back to Trinity, but I said neither nay nor yea,
wouldn't commit. Had a little argument with her about the
need to discipline children, but I conceded her point for I
couldn't be bothered disputing. She has a fairly good brain
and should be in a college instead of minding the till in a shop.
It occurs to me though that I've rarely heard her laughing:
hers is a much more earnest nature, and I have to admit to
myself she's sometimes a little wearing. I've never thought of
her like this before and maybe it's just the mood I'm in, but I
really was very bored tonight and she had on such a dowdy
old frock. Now that's a mean thought and I shouldn't be
thinking it. Oh, I expect I'll get over feeling like this. Maybe I
should try to liven her up a little: religion isn't supposed to be
glum after all. Yet I'm unbearably restless these days and
sometimes don't know what end of myself is up. Of course
Mother notices I'm frequently out of humour, but thankfully
Molly never does, or else I'd be quizzed till the cows came
home. She's not the most sensitive person, and I do wish she
wouldn't keep nagging at me, insisting I don't really love her*

*at all. Well, maybe I don't and maybe I do, or maybe I just
don't get the hang of girls.*

*Back home by 10 p.m. Worked on some Greek verses for a
while, Sappho's love poems. I translated one for Molly the
other day but she was disapproving, dismayed to think I
should be reading the like in Trinity College. I had to smile at
that. Maybe I could teach her a little for she's right quick but
lacks breadth.*

Retired early.

Here followed a few pages of scribbles and sketchings before
I was driven on again.

14 April 1943, Sunday

*I went to church with Mother today. She's getting on a bit and
can be lonely when I'm away but she derives great solace from
her faith. After the dinner she lay down to rest, and Molly was
visiting her ailing grandmother, which pleased me greatly for I
wanted to walk on my own for a change.*

*It was great to be free and I felt so light-hearted after
morning worship and all the glorious hymn singing. I hadn't
walked alone for the longest time and I struck out gaily, crossed
the Long Acre and entered the woods that lie just beyond the
Little Pasture. It was a great spring day, the fields ringed
around by daffodils and the woods alive with forget-me-nots
and primroses, while high in the Scotch pines the crows
clattered around their nests. I just needed to be alone then,
wanting to savour beauty's own sweet melancholy. I wandered
on for an hour or more and came to the paths that run parallel
to the river, narrow dry trails rutted by the roots of trees. I sat
down here and leaned against the trunk of a chestnut tree and*

thought again of the girl who, with her sister, happened upon me and Mother the day I was fishing – it's over a year ago now – and how flustered I'd got that day, blathering away as I did about Sheelin. But she'd said nothing to that, only laughed some more, and I blushed in my body now, foolishly wondering if she too had remembered.

But all that slipped speedily out of my mind for I was drowsy with the hush and the freshness of the air and, lying back, I closed my eyes, yielding to nature's balm. It was perfectly quiet there that hour save for the crows and the wind riffling the bushes, and I think I must have dozed off for a bit for I was suddenly roused as if shaken by someone. There was a pattering of leaves, a shuffling that drew nearer, and then, almost beside me, the parting of light branches revealed a girl. Well, and I smile to recall it, I was ready to jump up at once and stalk off in annoyance at having my peace disturbed, when she turned and in sheer disbelief I saw who it was: it was the one I had thought of over and over. She was very close to me now and just as I remembered her. I sat rigid, tight as a mouse's ear, behind that sheltering tree, sure of not being seen, and I watched her strolling along, traipsing the nearby path and swinging a sally rod loose in her hand. She was wearing a pretty blue frock with a pattern of daisies, her hair falling loose, dark and curling, revealing bare shoulders. I hardly dared to breathe as I watched her draw closer: she was singing softly to herself, red lips parted, and her face turned up to the sun's glint so that I could see the curve of her cheeks and the tender line of her brow. My breaths came fast. In a minute I knew she would pass me by, in a minute she'd be gone like a faerie woman, and I panicked. So I stood up as quick as I could for my limbs were

trembling, 'all my bones were out of joint; my heart like wax',
as the psalmist says.

My sudden appearance startled her greatly and she drew
back frowning, but then she smiled, shone her face on me, and
I felt a spasm in my stomach. She held out her hand. 'Oh, I
remember you,' she said, 'that day long ago by the river,
yourself and your mother?' Like tiny bells, her words came
trilling and rippling along chords, and she took my hand and
there was the fragrance of lily of the valley. Then she asked if I
still went fishing, and when I told her I did but hadn't been
lucky of late, she laughed again at that, and I saw the laughter
ripple along her entire lissom body. She appeared to wish to
move on at that, but I knew I mustn't let her for I needed to
say more, needed to let loose from me all that I couldn't
release either at home or with Molly. And I was wanting to
tell her things, oh, wanted much more than that, so I heard
myself say something foolish about her enjoying these woods
as much as I did, and of a sudden a wild temerity rose up in
me, born of longing, I suppose, to ask if we might meet here
again before I returned to my studies in Dublin. She looked at
me somewhat warily out of the side of her eye and gave me a
long sweet smile the like of which I'd never before received
from a woman. With that she was gone almost as suddenly as
she'd come, sauntering away through the sun-spattered
woodland paths, stopping just once to turn and laugh back to
where I went on standing under the tree.

When I got home, I slipped quickly through the back door
and into the scullery; splashed my face with plenty of cold
water and had a good careful look at myself in the mirror
fearing I'd be different, but it was the same old face I saw,
with only a trace of acne remaining.

In the kitchen I was relieved that no one seemed to notice me coming in, and the chat went on without a break. Sam Hanna was having a mug of tea with Mother and Cissie, and later on Molly came by with some of the special cake she'd made for Sunday. I walked her home as usual tonight, although I was just choking with guilt. I kept going when we got to the grove at the foot of her lane, didn't stop, and I prayed Molly wouldn't notice, but I don't think she detected a thing for, as we walked, she just chattered away about Mr McGoldrick and the hymns for the following Sunday.

Now here at last I can stretch myself out in the quiet of my own room and savour my thoughts to the fullest. I'm very worked up. I write her name, slowly, like this, spelling it out: 'D-o-l-o-r-e-s'. There! I've set it down: 'Dolores,' I repeat aloud. Beautiful name though connected somehow with sorrow, and it's Dolores who fills my thoughts this night, colours them in, and at the close of this wonderful day I know that something has come alive in me.

I'll snuff out the light soon. Too tired to pray or read my Bible. Have promised to help Sam clean out the sheuchs tomorrow. Don't think I'll get much sleep tonight.

After this I couldn't turn one other page. I snapped the book shut and shoved it to the back of the drawer, under his things where I'd found it. Turning round to the mirror on his dressing table, I saw my face: it was washed and pale like eggshells. I would have to do something about this: I would write to Reverend McGoldrick.

I planned to take up my pen there and then. I'd be blunt, wouldn't put a tooth in it; I'd tell His Reverence there were untoward things going on with my son, and if we weren't careful, though I wasn't yet sure about this, we could lose him to Rome. The boy was losing his senses, letting down a good girl from the Church and seeming in thrall to another woman. Let there be no mistake about that, for I had my proofs. I hoped the minister would give him a talking-to. Or was there no one in the college who would take him to task before it was all too late, and who was the Presbyterian chaplain in Trinity anyway?

But planning was as far as I got.

CHAPTER 31

It came as no surprise to me then to learn on the day after James's graduation from Trinity College that, instead of going on to Edinburgh in September as planned, he'd take a year off to help out at home. This made me very suspicious: there must have been goings-on during his last term in Dublin, some unsuitable activities, for there was something afoot, some doings that seemed to have come to a head just as soon as his degree was conferred. I was also very annoyed about his plan as we needed no help – Sam Hanna and his son were now doing the little that needed to be done – but James was adamant. Moreover, I was worried about him: something in him seemed to have turned; his mind wasn't right, and I feared a break-down, thought of the place in Monaghan, where people went for their nerves, but that was a thought too far.

As the autumn came in, however, he worked well with the men at the thresher, and our pattern of life went on unchanged for a while, though he went less often to the Lodge and on occasion was absent from Meeting. After the little harvest was reaped and the crops brought home, winter set in, and as the land lay resting, he assured me he'd be busy keeping up with his books. But I couldn't fool myself into thinking that there was nothing else going on in his head. To my dismay, he'd broken it off with Molly, told her he didn't love her the way a man should, and the poor girl came to me sobbing her heart out, and Florrie too in distress. But I didn't dare mention the irregular hours he kept when I never knew if he was in bed or gone away out or that once I got a strange scent on the jacket that hung on the back of his bedroom door. I was so afraid to confront him; afraid it would incense him, make everything worse.

In January we happened to have a pig to kill and, standing at the gable end of the house one morning, I couldn't believe I was seeing my gentle son take up the weapon and wield it; saw him, who loved to be singing Psalms and reciting Greek, huddle with a couple of men in a corner, heard the volley of animal screams, saw blood pouring, and my stomach curdled. He still had much in him I didn't know of, and yet, an hour later when he came into the kitchen, where the window was open to sunshine, and the muslin curtain billowed gently, you'd never have known a thing: he just wiped his hands and gave me a hug, grateful for the buttered bread and summery raspberry jam. Nor did he mention the scraping and salting that would need to be done before the pork could be stored in the dairy. He'd always been considerate like that, sensitive. Yet until this morning I hadn't known what was in him, and I grew uneasy, realized there was much concealed.

As the weeks went on, he managed to keep himself busy enough about the place, indeed he was always helpful and willing, but there came one dark morning when he left with Sam Hanna to bring two bullocks to the fair in Drumbeg. They were gone from the house about five o'clock, and when I'd shut the gate behind them, I found myself creeping into his room. I always had to be looking, searching and probing, and nothing would do me but I'd discover what sullied him.

At six o'clock it was still very dark so I took a lamp. His room was filled with shadows that bowed and swung, lighting up King Billy, who hung over the bed, and it was very cold, a deep biting cold as, summer and winter, we slept with our windows wide open. In the flickering light I could make out pyjamas in a twist on the sheets and beside the bed a candle stump, matches, a few collar studs and his Bible lying open.

But it was all so quiet at that dark empty hour, and the house of a sudden seemed full of noises, floors creaking and squeaking, and I held my breath, the lamp trembling in my hand, but all I could hear was the whine of the wind in the keyhole. My skin was prickling and I wished I was anywhere else, but I had to find out, had to understand what was happening to him. I looked to the drawer in his dressing table. It was firmly closed, but I steadied myself to approach it again. *What harm would it do?* I sought only for hope after all, for reassurance about his nervous condition, yet craved more than that if I was honest. I stood a minute to think and imagined much that caused me to tighten my jaws. But I needed to hurry.

Dawn was beginning to break, and on the wall outside the black and white cat was leisurely strolling, picking her way through the weeds; she'd been with us a long time, maybe twelve years. We'd got her out of a litter, and when Thomas put the kittens in a sack and drowned all but one of them, I remember how James had loudly complained, protested with such anguished cries that his father said he'd give him a clatter if he didn't stop his noising. What a long time ago that was, and as the cat yawned in the pale morning air, she alone, of all round The Cairn, seemed unchanged; faithful old Sailor was long gone.

Resolute now, I drew the book out again from under his

socks and handkerchiefs. Why did he never hide it? For it was making me do things I'd never have done in this sneaky under-hand way – me who had always condemned deceit in whatever form – but I knew very well that to confront a man, be it husband or grown-up son, was not in my nature, and I have to thank my upbringing for that: it was bred in my bones.

Setting the lamp down on a table, I carefully lowered the wick, saw the tails of smoke curl black through the globe. Then I closed the window and sat down on the bed. There were so many pages, all closely written, but I flicked back through them until I found the place I was looking for: the time of his graduation and sure enough it was there.

25 June 1943, Trinity Term, my digs in Rathmines
Today I was conferred with my BA in Trinity. Molly refused
the invitation to attend the ceremony. Mother came on her
own, and I was quite distracted thinking of how, when she'd
be gone for her bus, I'd be meeting D.

I laid the book down on my knee and looked to the window, saw the pink and grey dawn in a spare, unpromising sky. Oh, the deceit of him and the cunning. The blood was now filling my face in a heated surge, but I was still determined to know for sure what I feared most of all. I would brace myself to see it set out in the hand I had once so admired.

She is visiting her aunt in Dublin and I met her, as we'd
arranged, by the linden tree in Stillorgan. We walked the
length of the pier in Dún Laoghaire and I listened again to
those sweetest of syllables running and rippling like the notes of
a scale. My dear mother tells me sometimes that I need a good

*rest but if only she knew what it is I really need. Anyway I'm
filled with a loathing of home and hot-water jars. Poor Molly
is milk warmed up, the other champagne. I have no idea at
all what Mother is thinking these days for she's such an astute
little person and wise beyond the ways of women.*

Well, wasn't that grand of him! I slapped the book down on
the bedstead. If I was as wise as he thought, I'd go to him at
once; I'd lay this diary before him and all that was on my mind.
But I was afraid, afraid of my own son. Frantically, I flicked on
a few pages.

30 August 1943
*Home again now and so glad I've altered my Edinburgh
plans. I need time to sort myself out for I don't understand
what's occurring in me. D fills my thoughts, and I search for
words to describe her: she is Aphrodite, beautiful, virtuous
beyond reproach; she makes the world spin, makes it cast its
colours like petals. I would take the cherry tree as a symbol
of love but it is short-lived, so instead I'll choose the
amaranthus, the mythical flower that never dies. I burn;
I can't be away from her. So no, I won't be leaving The
Cairn just yet.*

This was not the boy I'd reared. I held the book tight, a finger keeping the place, and looked down to the yard, where the
rooster strutted and crowed and the cat lay asleep on the wall.
Away beyond the byre the chickens scratched, and overhead the
clouds were beginning to gather in little yellowish-grey whorls.
What was a mother to do when her son was so threatened, so
tempted, with the snare lying low and the devil roaring? I took

up the Bible from his bedside. His father had presented him with this the day of his First Communion in Ballymount. Turning to Ephesians 6:12, I read aloud the familiar words, ' "We wrestle not against flesh and blood, but against principalities, against powers, against the rulers of the darkness of this world, against spiritual wickedness in high places." '

I could do nothing now but pray: I'd ask the Saviour to carry me through whatever else must be disclosed and so I opened the book again:

14 September 1943
I am living in such a strange place now. The Cairn with its
pious industry is dry as a fallen faggot, no longer a refuge,
and yet only to be near her, I'd bide here for ever. Ballymount,
my church, is a black block on which I stumble as I move ever
deeper down through a valley that's scented with violets and
lilies, open to the sun. Oh my beloved, what have you done to
me? 'You came, and I was mad for you – you cooled my mind
that burned with longing . . .' Sappho again.

Cooled his mind! I'd cool his mind for him when he got home, but I couldn't move a step, not one. I felt very warm now, and of a sudden the room had started to tilt, so I made to stretch out on his bed. The ceiling was turning in on itself, meeting the yellow walls with their sprays of ivy, waltzing and weaving, and sweat oozed cold on my forehead. Then just as abruptly the room stopped spinning, was still again and I was sitting up, smoothing my hands over and over. Something would have to be done, and soon, but I didn't know what. Thomas used to say there was a hole in every bag of troubles, and I knew he'd have found the hole in this one already: for a start, he'd have taken the horsewhip down from its hook in the stable, and I honestly wished he was here again now. I don't know how long I stayed in that room, but I was still upstairs when I heard the boyo himself come home. It must have been nearly three o'clock in the afternoon, and I winced when I heard him call up to me from the scullery. I greeted him curtly, so brimful of anger and sorrow, I just couldn't say more; 'a soft answer turneth away wrath' and I had no softness in me at all. I wanted to tell him how full of deceit he was, how full of lies, hypocrisy, stealth, but I was afraid to; instead I just told him there was a bit of cold meat in the safe and that I was going to lie down for a bit. But I stood for a while out on the landing at the head of the stairs, listening. He'd be washing his hands, drying his face, changing his coat, and in a minute he'd go to the kitchen and eat his dinner. And that would be that. I stole off to my room then, where it was quiet, and on my bed, overlooked by the rose-covered wallpaper he'd scribbled on once as a child, I lay down and I cried. All the rest of that day tears leaked like lakes from my eyes, but towards night I recovered myself: I would 'gird my loins' and somehow find the hole in this bag of troubles.

CHAPTER 32

I held off for a couple of months, planning and plotting, then decided I'd seek out Anna May and not wait for her to drop in at The Cairn; her visits were very sporadic and the dear knows when she'd be back again. So one day when I needed to buy more wool for the jumper I was knitting, I got out my bicycle and decided to pay her a visit before heading to the shop.

I left home early while James was still in his bed. It was a particularly dank morning, a bar of fog lying over the nearby fields and the air webbed with grey. Rain threatened but there was a scent of spring all around: primroses abounding and gentians; the growth had already begun. I'd need to remind Hanna to cut the grass in the graveyard, but he was getting a bit stiff in himself, and of course James wasn't at all as I'd expected during his year away from the books. He was spending too much time away from the house, out at night, gallivanting here and there, was grown secretive. And when I asked, he'd just chat away, his closed face not betraying a thing. I squirmed to hear, for I knew about the unhealthy stirring, the ugly arousal that made him come singing in through the door of an evening or not come at all till it was nearly time to get up, and sleepless I'd lie listening for the creak on the stair. I did want to challenge him but something forbade me now, something other than my own upbringing: it was the fear of knowing, fear of hearing the truth from his lips.

But I'd push on out to Anna May's. Here at the end of the lane it was very muddy and I had trouble shoving the bicycle out to the road. Ours was always a wet and guttery place with a kind of wintry hauntingness hanging over the hills like muslin, and the fields full of thistles and ragweed and rushes. As I pedalled along, a sharp little breeze tugged at my headscarf, and I fought to draw it tighter. It was very quiet that morning, only the drips off the hedges and the lonesome call of a curlew in from the coast. The town was almost deserted, and I was glad of that: no cars, no shopkeepers at their doors, only a horse and cart on the way to the creamery, only myself like a ghost, sliding through the streets, slipping around corners not wanting to be seen.

It was gone eleven o'clock when I got to her place. What would I say? How would I phrase the questions that lay on my heart? A streak of red shame burned in my breast as I propped the bicycle against the stone at her door. What would Thomas think of me now? Or the elders? Or James? As I glanced at the two little prying windows, a lean wall-eyed dog came bristling and growling and then her 'Oh, it's yourself, Mrs Campbell,' and not a bit flustered. 'Down, Bran! Don't mind him, missus. No harm in him at all, he'll only nip you.' I let her draw me inside with a wave of her hand. 'Isn't it a treat to see you out here, missus. And how are you keeping these days?'

She took up some holy water from a vessel near the door, blessed herself and pointed me to a chair, where sullen and fearful I sat shrouded in disbelief, staring at the earthen floor, the rough-whited walls, the candles and the holy pictures. Everywhere I looked there were saints and popes and strings of beads, and then that peculiar sweetish Catholic smell, something like smoky cabbage. Spreading her hands palm down on her apron, she looked at me hard and bold, a servant no longer but full as a bucket of something she wanted to say.

It was only mid-morning but it was dark enough in her cottage. Rain dripped from the thatch and bounced off the window, and then, as we sat in the gloom, I felt her sidle up to me in a way that I found disagreeable. 'Oh, and your James now? How is he doing? How is he handling all the excitement?'

I looked away. How indeed was my son?

She poked at the smouldering turf. 'Ah, didn't I dandle him on my knee when he was no more than a babby!' She bent to stroke the dog and rambled on: 'And didn't I teach him things any time he came out to me here!' She laughed to herself. 'He didn't know an ace from a jack at the first.' She wagged a finger at me. 'But that was before he went up to the North and got to be too good for his old Anna May, couldn't bid his old pal the time of day for a while. Got snooty a bit and far too busy.' She wagged a finger and looked at me slyly. 'But, you know, missus, he's back to himself now, back one hundred per cent, wouldn't you say?'

My ears were filled with a ringing sound and I felt dizzy. 'What are you talking about?'

She leaned over then and put her face close to mine so that I could smell her dried-up body smell. I drew back but she moved nearer. 'Sure isn't that what comes of having a mot!' She looked into my face, and I remembered the squint in her left eye and how I'd often mistaken it for a wink. She shoved the dog away from her. 'Not Miss McKinley any more of course, good and all as she was.'

'So?' I parried, searching her face.

'Well, isn't she a Doherty girl. Dolores. Very nice too; she works in a bank in Shantra, and the talk is they're going to marry.' She looked sideways at me, questioning. 'Sure the whole town knows it.' She folded her arms calmly over a hole in her jumper. 'And he's receiving instruction from a priest.'

Well, I was silent at that: 'poured out like water, my heart like wax'. A coldness as of a wet cloth fell over my face, and the words rattled around me like hailstones, biting and sting-ing. I must have paled, blenched and looked a poor crooked wraith.

'Ah now, don't be telling me you didn't know?'

Turf shifted in the hearth and smoke blew back down the chimney. The wind had got up and I felt a sickening chill twist-ing through me, but still I sat tight.

'Ah ha, so he keeps his doings to himself, does he?'

She gave the dog a swipe away from a loaf on the table. 'Always a deep one, even as a child, but I thought he'd have told his own mother.' She shook her head. 'I surely thought he'd have done that.'

I was unsettled now, convulsed by a fear that shook me the way a storm takes the roots of a bush in winter. 'What else?'

She stood proud and important, comfortable, arms folded while her words sank down in me, slow and wavering, heavy. 'Receiving instruction' meant grilles and black robes, leather belts and whippings; it meant enforced obeisance. 'Receiving instruction' was Rome's coercion and control; it was abandon-ment of family and friends and values.

'And I think a wedding's to be soon. But sure, you'll be get-ting an invite yourself –' she shook herself out '– or I'll be having a word in his ear!'

I jumped up and left her at that, could hear no more.

Stunned, I took up my bicycle. I wouldn't go for the wool now; blinded by tears, I'd head back to the safety of home, try to understand what I'd heard, lay it all out, piece by piece, make sense of it. But when I got to The Cairn, all I could do was lie down on the kitchen sofa and bury my face in the cross-stitched cushion where he and I used to play. He'd live to regret it, he would. Rome would have her way with him, make him swear to all kinds of unbiblical things. I sat up in a while, dizzy with anger, ground my teeth and cursed my own son, reviled him for a coward, for casting away the Reformed Faith we'd so carefully planted and nurtured in him over the years.

Hours later I could hear him whistling as he took the pony out of the shafts, the full musical whistle that used to make me sing. He'd likely been away at a fair and would be here in a minute looking for his dinner, but I'd pass no remarks, would ask no questions. I pulled myself together and with steel in my soul got up off the sofa and went clattering out to the yard to shut in the hens.

In the fading light I could just make him out on the far side of the haggart: he had his coat off and was heaving the harness on to a nail in the wall. And I stood and watched him, a sapling bent in spite of all that we'd taught him. The moon was rising in the early night, and as he turned and began to walk towards the house I could see he was smiling, his head thrown back to the air, his neck exposed, and I thought how all of him was exposed now like a peeled sally, and I saw him then as he was. He came near where I was standing, striding, easily loping, strong as a tree although warped. The misty air hung over all, enshrouding, clinging with cold wet hands. I looked up at him, saw his face framed in the door of the haggart and I went out to meet him, detached and pitiless. 'What are you going to do now, son?'

It was such an ordinary night, and he looked at me full in the face and replied, calm as calm, 'Oh, I think I'll just go to the prayers, Mother, when I've eaten my dinner.'

Then I watched as the colour of shame crept over his bared neck, heard my voice come smooth and deliberate: 'James, you must know, "God is not mocked, for whatever one sows, that will he also reap."' And the words fluttered like rags on a barbed-wire fence, cutting and catching. Neither of us spoke after that, and I turned away from him, for 'A fool gives full vent to his spirit, but a wise man quietly holds it back.' But as I moved over the cobbles, I felt a great hollowness, brassy and hard, scud over the yard. It went curving over the byre and, clear as day, away beyond the cart house, I saw the 'scarlet coloured beast full of blasphemy', just as the Bible said. And I was filled with a terror I didn't know how to express.

CHAPTER 33

The following morning, when I'd a little more strength and had somewhat cooled down, I collared him in the kitchen, stood out in front of him, barred his way just as he was making for the door. My voice shook with passion: 'I know very well what you're up to, my son. Your lies and deceit, your vile cunning!' A glaze was veiling his eyes, but twisting my apron into a knot, I carried on: 'I'm not a simpleton, James.' He made no response other than to shove past me and hurl himself out the back door. I waited, hoping he'd return that we might talk again, but by midnight he hadn't come back.

The most I could do after that was to go and buttonhole Molly, who hadn't darkened our door for many a while. So the very next day I set out for McKinleys'. The cow parsley was growing well in the hedges, milky, on the thick hollow stalks we used to break off, James and I, for pea-shooters. Poor Florrie was away in Monaghan for a couple of weeks with a nervous condition brought on by worrying about her daughter and it was Molly who had the running of the McKinley house now.

I found her out in the garden pruning some roses, her head bent under a hat trimmed with snippets of heather and concocted no doubt by herself. Maybe she should have been a milliner instead of going from school to work in a shop, but when her father died, her mother had to be supported, and

Molly, ever obedient and self-negating, had taken up her position at that till where she'd sat ever since. Sometimes I wondered if this wasn't behind the drop of acidity in an otherwise sweet nature, and as I beheld her now, bent over the flower bed, the narrow tight-belted body leaning and snipping, leaning and snipping, I was chilled. She looked up as soon as she heard my step on the gravel path, her face longer and thinner. I ventured over the well-kept lawn until I stood beside her. 'You keep yourself busy, Molly.'

She went on snipping.

'I need to talk to you, ask you some things.'

She was wearing white peep-toe shoes that day, and she stood up straight, one hand on her hip, newly impertinent. 'Do you indeed?'

I was taken aback by this incivility, even though I already knew she had a fairly tough streak, and what I wanted to ask was hard to thin out into words. We stood there by the rose bed, silently waiting, for hours it seemed: her looking at her shoes, me at the hedge over which tiny spiders were spinning their webs. Then at last, when I could contain myself no longer, I asked what was happening between her and James.

'What is happening?' she echoed as if confounded. 'I wouldn't know since I haven't seen James in many a while.'

'Have you heard the rumours?'

She bent her head and I couldn't read her face.

'You must tell me what you think.'

'I don't know what I think, Mrs Campbell.' She laid the secateurs aside and carefully removed her garden gloves and the hat, which she twirled in her fingers, causing bits of the heather to drop.

'I expect you know why I wanted to meet you?'

She shrugged, brushed down her frock, pursed her lips till I longed to shake her.

'You must tell me what you know about James.'

She didn't reply at once but, slowly gathering herself up, bristled and dabbed at her nose with one of the hankies she always had in her sleeve. 'Every Tom, Dick and Harry knows more about him than I do. It's the people in town you should ask. He's your son after all, Mrs Campbell!' She looked away now, colour spilling into her cheeks, and I couldn't help feeling sorry.

'And what about you?'

She threw back her head. 'Oh nothing about me. I'll be all right.'

'But Molly . . .' I faltered. 'But Molly, what about James?'

She shrugged and went on twirling the hat in her fingers almost as though she didn't care.

'You know of course what this will mean for him? That she's not one of us?'

'I know all of that, Mrs Campbell, but,' and her voice took on the tone she used when she gave her testimony, 'this is a time when faith in the providence of God is called for.'

I looked past her to where a cart was going by in the lane and a man was calling up his donkey. Far away a rooster crowed, and in the distance I could just make out the tip of Ballymount's gable.

'We have all erred in our ways.' She looked at me very pointedly as if she thought me somehow to blame and gathered herself up, fluffed herself out, came over all virtuous: 'But James is choosing the broad way that leads to destruction, just as the Bible tells us it will, and so we must pray for him.' She looked to the sky and took a breath. 'Not that he will come back to me, for he won't do that, nor would I have him at any cost, but we must pray that he'll hear the Lord calling him back, and that he'll return to the fold even if he never resumes his studies.'

I breathed slowly and deeply. She had stopped at last. And I must say how coldly her words fell on me, chilling my soul with righteousness. So there was nothing she could do. And my son would yield up his heritage to Rome, along with that of future generations of Campbells. I left her self-satisfied there in her garden and took up my own unbridled sorrow, tucked it like a bird into my coat. Chastened, I hurried home needing to be by myself, for sometimes, if I'd no one around to distract me, I'd a knack of sorting things out in my mind, bringing again a bit of sense to myself.

CHAPTER 34

As I cycled back, my spirits lifted a little. I knew I could put that down to the sunshine and the little spring breezes that stirred in the grasses, to the flowers, the celandines and violets. And I'd put Molly behind me even if only for an hour.

It must have been about five o'clock when I reached The Cairn. Everything was quiet there save for the sound of my boots on the cobbles: the hens were asleep and there wasn't even a budge from the dog. No sign that James had returned. With an unlooked-for lightness of heart, I went into the house and took up my tasks and knitted some more of the stocking I had up on the needles. About ten o'clock I went up to bed, and a great peace further enfolded me, a peace so deep and so thick I could almost touch it. I believed that God had come back and that, as someone had said, 'All would be well. All manner of thing would be well.' Then I heard him come in.

Well, it was about eleven o'clock when he entered, charged into the house like a stallion, in no way at all like his usual coming, and he stayed below in the scullery, loud and noisy, scolding, berating himself, kicking things over. So, with my peace well broken, I got out of my bed and went down to the scullery door, my heart beating fast. I didn't know what I would find, but I saw enough to make me retreat. There he stood, his face contorted and red, fists clenched, his grey eyes staring so dead, that I quickly withdrew. From the kitchen I listened some more, shivered with new apprehension, but when it was quiet again out there, I braced myself and went out to him. 'James, my dear boy?' But he thrust my question aside and, sweeping past me, made for the stairs.

Shocked and anxious, I put this out of mind as best I could, knowing he wouldn't enlighten me until he was good and ready. I was determined to carry on no matter what life would cast up, and in the following weeks, if you didn't know what was going on you'd think all was normal: just a mother and son going silent about their business. Cissie knew plenty of course but seemed to think it wiser to keep her counsel, and the Protestant pride bred into me sealed my heart against asking her questions.

Then something happened that turned my world upside down. It was the first week in June in fact, and the Twelfth was on the horizon again. But you wouldn't have really known it was coming for I hadn't seen him head off in the evenings of late to attend a meeting or practise his flute in the Lodge. The Lodge was my final hope, and I prayed that his brethren would kindly but firmly take him in hand, whatever he was at, and he'd surely be obliged to listen to them. Whenever I queried his erratic attendance, he'd just shake his head and go off, rudely slamming doors behind him. And as for Hanna, the true blue, well, he just didn't want to know, so I assumed James must have told him where to get off, which would surely have come as quite a surprise to the elder.

Anyway, James and I chanced to be sitting together in the garden one day and I was glad of a sense of peace. He was read-ing the *Celt*, and I was trying to knit but the wool kept sticking to the needles. It was very sultry that afternoon: thunder rumbled in the distance and the sky was heavy with rain, and I found myself wondering why he wasn't in the next field, where they were struggling to dry out the new-mown hay before the next shower. It was proving a rainy summer so far and things would be late. Presently, he put down the paper. 'Mother, I have something to tell you.' And he looked so earnest, so solemn, so unusually confiding that I laid my work aside at once. Now was the time he would tell me all.

My breath came fast. 'You know you can tell me anything, James. It's not right to have secrets between us.' I actually found this quite hard to say, for it seemed a bit mean, underhand in a way, knowing as much as I did. But I was hoping against hope that he'd make a clean breast to me now, disclose his innermost thoughts, rebuke himself for all the unwholesome feelings I knew he was harbouring, the dubious doings; and I was wanting to hear that, after all his casting aside of Molly, he would go to her now again and with the past forgotten ask for her hand in marriage. All this I hoped he might say, and I'd throw my arms about him then and give thanks to the Lord. So, coyly I drew the wool from my basket and, starting to knit a new row, I waited – a very long time, it seemed. Knit one, slip one, pass the slip stitch over, and when he began to speak at last, it was as if he addressed the ground, sometimes clenching his hands, sometimes cracking his knuckles.

'This will be hard on you, Mother.'

I went on knitting, in and out, my fingers missing and catching, and a singing in my ears. I wished he would hurry, blurt it all out, get it over, for I was prepared to forgive and forget with the whole of my heart.

'You may not wish to know what I have to say.'

I jabbed the needles together into the ball of wool and looked at him, felt sorry for him. To come clean wouldn't be easy, but there was a steely look in his eyes, glassy and grey, that reminded me of how Thomas used to look when he was bent on doing something contrary.

'It's about the Lodge, Mother.'

The sky loosened itself now, and the air fell free, and shoals of disappointment came swimming around me. My hope was confounded. So it was only the Lodge he would talk about now after all.

'Well, son,' I encouraged, hiding my let-down feelings as best I could, 'you know I'm always happy to hear about the Lodge.' Anything to keep the talk going.

'I've left it.'

'You mean for a while?'

'No, Mother. I've resigned from the Order.'

I sat up with a jerk now, knitting put down.

'I have written to the worshipful master in Belfast as well as to the brethren here.'

His voice seemed to come from far off now, and I felt as if I was plodding a step at a time across the bed of the town lake. Then I caught myself on, sat up straight, shook out my wool and waited.

But he was taking my hands in his, warm and confiding, and saying, 'Listen, Mother. There was a time when I truly saw the Order as the seal on my Christian faith.'

I pulled away and took up my knitting again, plain and purl, over and under, and the air tightened round me once more as before a thunderstorm. What was he talking about?

'I knew,' he went on, 'as all of us continue to know, that the Order defends the Protestant religion and opposes what it sees as Rome's fatal errors.'

I nodded, eager now. 'Of course it does. That's exactly how your father would have put it.'

'But there's more to it than that.' He looked away from me now as if trying to unravel his thoughts. 'The point is: I have come to see that the roots of the Order lie in bitter sectarian conflict, not in the Gospel.'

Well, it's said that time can stand still, and it stood still right there, so unmoving it was that nothing could be heard but the *coo-coo* of the wood pigeons and, over the hedge, the low voices of men and the *grook-grook* of their hay rakes. Pictures of the king and the Covenant, of Thomas and Ballymount flicked through my mind one after another, and now, no longer timid and waiting but crested with anger, I rose to face him. 'How dare you!' My voice rang out red. 'How dare you speak like this about the Order, the very capstone of our faith.'

My words plunged like wild horses into the air, beating it out. I had never been angry with him before, and I drew back now, chastened, hoping, until at last I heard him say quietly, 'I dare all for the Gospel, Mother.' And he looked so pious that I had to hold on to my hands. 'You see, I've been led by the Holy Spirit to some people in Dublin.' He was murmuring now. 'And through fellowship with them, I've come to understand that while the Order is Christian, it has become polluted by irregular rituals.'

'Hah!' I snapped. 'I think it's the Roman Church you're talking about.'

He flushed at this but said nothing so I went on: 'You must surely know there are times when Satan can come in the guise of the Holy Spirit, be transformed into an angel of light.'

We were now standing facing each other. I felt violated, crushed, as if held in a dark fist; the world was going all skew-ways and I wished again that Thomas was here or even a couple of elders, someone to restore my disturbed boy to his senses for he wasn't himself: all these foolish words, this rant-ing about pagans and rituals.

'Why are you talking like this?' I demanded at last.

In answer he placed his hands on my shoulders, and I could feel his fingers gripping so tight that they hurt, and he looked into my face, his eyes hard. 'I have never before voiced this to anyone, Mother, but since you ask, I'll tell you what happened one night in the Lodge.'

I tried to free myself of his grip, draw away from him. He was heated and talking gibberish now, and I was afraid for him but he held me still.

'I was three or four years in the Order when some brethren came and asked me to join what they called the Royal Arch Purple.'

'James, that's enough.' I tried to free myself of his grip. 'You're quite overwrought.'

'No, I must tell you this. I agreed to join it, and so, when the time came, I was blindfolded by these good Christian men and made to go barefoot on what they called the Travels Through the Wilderness.'

'Hush, James, hush.' I was growing flustered. 'No more talk like this.'

But he ignored my agitation and went on: 'They assured me this was symbolic of the Children of Israel going to the Prom-ised Land.'

'Stop it! Stop it at once!'

He was breathing hard. 'It was such a humiliating experience—'

'Your father never spoke of such things, and—'

'No. Father was greatly deceived, as many of our good folk are.'

Sickened, I drew away from him and picking up my basket of knitting made as if to go, but he took my arm. 'You must hear all, now that I've begun.' He held on to me. 'There was a noxious smell of drink in the Lodge the night of that institution, and I was anxious. All I wanted to do was to get away home, but they detained me, and while I was still blindfolded, they put me in some kind of a blanket and kicked me around the Lodge Hall – they called this Riding the Goat.'

I recalled Leviticus 16:22: 'And the goat shall bear upon him all their iniquities unto a land not inhabited: and he shall let go the goat in the wilderness.' Stunned, I remembered seeing a live goat once being dragged into a Lodge dance one night, and I'd pitied the creature so mocked, but here now was my son telling me that he himself had undergone similar shame and derision. Yet I still couldn't take in what he was saying, didn't know how to respond. There was surely something amiss with him. Was all his perverted and secret carry-on with that woman undoing his head? Should I speak with Sam Hanna after all, seek advice, open my heart?

James released his grip on me then. 'That was the night,' he cried, 'the night you thought I'd gone totally mad in the scullery.' I opened my eyes, bewildered, but made no response as he shouted, his voice like a hammer, 'Well Mother, I tell you this now: I can stomach the Order no longer.'

I shrank into myself at that, was afraid he might somehow grow violent, but his voice quickly fell low again: 'Oh, I can do nothing but pray.'

'Pray for what?' I soothed, not grasping or guessing his meaning.

'Pray that those Christian people who choose to remain in the Order will restore its purity.'

'You are speaking sheer nonsense, my son.'

But he was standing tall, looking me in the face, and then, muttering something about integrity, he hurried off in the direction of the meadow, while I went on sitting, my head in a screw. The Order was next to Ballymount, Ballymount next to God, and oh, here was a chasm, a rift, as if a well-plotted chart without seam had suffered a rip in its fabric. Was this what came of him learning too much in the university? Or was it that wretched Doherty woman's influence? I wound up the wool, which was greasy with sweat, and closed the lid of my basket. Oh, if only Thomas was here. He'd soon have chastened the boy and restored him to his right mind.

In the next field the grass was steaming, and the flies had begun to swarm about my head. 'Please God, help my son,' I prayed hopelessly. 'I don't understand him any more; I can't follow where he's going.'

CHAPTER 35

But sorrow doesn't stay put away; it has spurs and outcroppings and, like a weed with tangled roots in grey-eyed rocks and crannied walls, it is often ineradicable. I was out a few days later painting the white picket fence that Thomas had put up shortly after we were married so that I could make a 'lady's garden'. I had neglected it often of late, but that particular day I decided I needed to be doing something active to occupy and ease my haunted mind. So I scrubbed the fence down and took the can of paint from the shed. It was a perfect morning for the job: bright and cool, and I leaned into the task trying to feel nothing but the weft of the brush in my hand and the *shush-shush* of the bristles sweeping the wooden rails. I'd think only of the brush and the paint. I'd chase darkness away. And so I was busy, but then, needing to stretch my back, I stood up and, chancing to raise my head, I saw them. Away over the fence, away past the scutch and the laurels, I saw them coming, small at first yet distinct. I was startled and fairly taken aback. I shielded my eyes with my hand the better to see, and there, plain as day, they were walking right up the lane with unhurried steps, herself in a yellow frock (I recognized her at once) and him in the good grey flannels I'd ironed yesterday; now they were opening the five-barred gate, now stopping to make it fast, fiddling and fumbling with the bolt, their heads together.

Quickly I thrust my brush into a jar of turpentine and shoved it under the hedge, then turned on my heel and hurried indoors. Inside, from the little hall window, I stood and watched. It was like a magic lantern show. Frame after frame, they came: strolling at ease past the pond and the raspberry patch, skirting the stream with the watercress and on then to the wicket gate that led to the garden path. Here, he opened the latch and guided her through, his hand on her arm. When they got as far as the water butt, they stopped and looked up together and I saw him point out some detail on the chimney or maybe the roof. It was almost as if, together, they owned the place.

I could watch no more but withdrew to the kitchen, where most of our lives had been lived and our soul-searching done. What did he mean by bringing her here to this house? Agitated, I stalked around from window to window, finally betaking myself to the parlour. I'd ask her to leave, so I would, this RC woman who'd weaselled her way into my son's affections and likely to ruin him; she wouldn't darken my door with her beads and her wily ways. But I needn't have worried for James came into the room on his own.

I turned to him smartly. 'Where is she?'

'Out in the garden.'

He took a step towards me but I drew back. 'You shouldn't have brought her here. You know how things are.'

'I want to make them better.'

I lowered myself into Thomas's chair, and he came over, dropped on to a stool beside me. I was as full as a cup with emotion. 'There's only one way you can do that.'

He looked up at me, pleading. 'I'm in torment, Mother.'

'It's nothing to the torment ahead of you if you carry on as you're doing.'

He was off the stool now and kneeling before me. 'Mother, you and Father gave me everything I have: educated me, reared me in the Presbyterian tradition, led me to Jesus as Saviour.'

I looked down at the floor, still the same old red cement, and sadly recalled the Bible Studies and the prayers in the loft, the *Shorter Catechism* and Mr McGoldrick's eloquent sermons. 'And have you forgotten all that already? Has your assurance all fallen so swift away that you now need a priest to "instruct" you? Teach you again about Jesus?'

I couldn't bring myself to look at him, looked instead at my grey worsted skirt almost worn through save for a tidy patch on the seam. So often he'd sat on my lap listening to my silly stories about the three red hens and the elephant who sprayed a tailor. We'd always laughed together at that, imagining the tailor to be Sam Hanna. But there was no jollity now.

He shook his head. 'No, Mother, it's not like that, not like that at all, for I haven't lost faith.' He looked to the floor. 'It's my faith keeps me strong, and if I marry Dolores, nothing will change that.' He dropped his voice. 'And should we ever be blessed with children, they'll be guided by the freedom of their own consciences to live as they will.'

I just had to laugh at that. 'You innocent simpleton! Freedom in Rome?'

He ignored that, and we sat lost in a fog of silence that was broken only by a cricket chirping behind the empty grate.

He spoke at last, cracking his knuckles: 'Mother, you must know it distresses me deeply to wound you like this, but,' and he reached for my hands, took them into his own like two injured creatures, 'I might as well drown myself as live without

Dolores.' He went on holding my hands in his as he spoke. 'Not for all that Rome can do to me, not for the Presbyterian Church, not even for you, Mother, could I give her up.'

I sucked in a breath. 'And what about Molly?'

'Ah, Molly!' His face assumed a blank expression. 'She's a very good person; she's been my friend and companion throughout the years, and her faith has always inspired me, but,' and he ran his fingers through his hair, 'she's not Dolores.'

I was smarting now. 'What will you do about your studies then and your vocation, if ever you had one?'

He flushed at that, looked down at the floor. 'I should have told you this before now: I'm going to Dublin at the end of next month to train as a teacher.'

When there seemed to be nothing more to say, we just sat on unspeaking in the fading light, until at last, withdrawing my hands from his, I rose and, going over to the press, took down the Bible as his father would have done. I knew where I'd find the passage: it was in the Book of Exodus, chapter thirty-four, twelfth verse. 'Listen to this.' And I read slowly, a word at a time: ' "Take heed to thyself, lest thou make a covenant with the inhabitants of the land whither thou goest, lest it be for a snare in the midst of thee." And that, my son, is the Word of Almighty God.'

He left me then, went out like Judas into the night, and I heard their voices urgently commingle in the garden, their steps hesitating, then receding. I went on sitting in the parlour till I was famished, clenching the dark in my fists, and I thought of Susan McAdam sighing and sobbing because she was childless and how I'd told her that what she wouldn't laugh over, she wouldn't cry over. And I thought of other women too and of Rachel who wept for her children 'and would not be comforted because they were not'. But I wouldn't sit here lamenting for ever; I had plenty of fight left in me and I'd make plans. '*Trust in the Lord with all your heart*,' I told myself, '*and do not lean on your own understanding.*' I would take counsel of Reverend McGoldrick face to face.

CHAPTER 36

So the very next Sunday as soon as worship was ended I told our minister the whole of my story though he probably knew plenty already. He received it coldly, as I'd expected he would, and ordered us both – me and James – to come to the manse the next morning. Such expediency put me into a bit of a flap to be sure, yet I was hopeful for Mr McGoldrick would surely trim the lad's sails and make him see reason.

Next day, all set and ready to go, I waited for James in the kitchen. I was nervous and anxious but he went on foothering about in the scullery, fumbling with his boots, not in a bit of a hurry. So I called out to him, my voice losing itself in the shadows, my mouth dry, 'We'll be late. Are you nearly ready?' But there was no reply, just some more shuffling and throat-clearing, and when at last he came into the kitchen, he was silent and morose, reminding me of his father.

He stooped to fix his bicycle clips. 'This is all a waste of time, and you must know that. And anyway you know right well what he's going to say.'

'I have no idea what he'll say,' I snapped. 'But maybe he'll throw some light on your situation.'

'I don't need any of his light, Mother. I know very well what I'm doing.' He shrugged on his coat.

'Know what you're doing! You're as innocent as the day you

were born.' I felt my face grow hot. 'Life isn't all about books and fishing, you know, or inordinate feelings.' And I choked with pity for myself. 'There's things like perdition and betrayal and falsehood.' I whipped my coat down off the peg and swung my arms into the sleeves. 'We'd better get going.'

But even as I spoke, my anger was draining away, for he stood there looking at me and I thought for a minute he was going to cry; yet he just went on standing until at last I took his elbow. 'Come on, son. We have to face up to this.' And, squirrelling away my thin shred of hope, I elbowed him out the door, where he gave his bike a bad-tempered heft.

We didn't speak as we cycled. No sound save for pedals creaking. I could smell the earthiness of hedges and ditches as we rode along in the shade of chestnut and sycamore. But I was nervous, caught between his angry confusion and my own eagerness to hear what the minister would have to say.

In the manse study we sat side by side in grim silence while the housekeeper set down a tea tray and filled the cups. The room was dark, full of books and papers, untidy too, but I supposed that was because Mr McGoldrick was a scholar. Somewhere in the house a clock struck ten, and then, as if barely noticing us, the minister was easing himself into the chair behind the desk, a squat little man with his side-whiskers and that perpetual drip from his nose. He took out a very large handkerchief, wiped his glasses and looked at us sitting before him.

'Now, my good people, what's this I am hearing?'

I let go of the handbag I'd been twisting in my lap. 'Your Reverence, it's what I was saying yesterday after worship . . .'

He reached out to play with a paperknife. 'I see.' Then casting his eyes down on the big green blotter, he spluttered, 'What a difficult situation you've got yourself into, young man.'

A hush fell over the room now. A fly buzzed behind the orange blind that was drawn against the morning sun and a pale gold light filled the room. Eventually I heard my son speak. I was quite taken aback by his voice, which had a strange confident edge to it all of a sudden, a challenge almost. 'What do you mean, your Reverence?'

I held my breath, not daring to look up, yet the minister sounded unruffled, even inviting. 'Well, this girl, you know.' And he folded his hands over the buttons on his waistcoat.

I glanced at my son again, pitying him now. He looked so vulnerable, the white-knuckled hands and those too-short sleeves. It was cruel to see him like this, almost hunted, and I was so afraid of everything.

'It has come to me, young man, that you are walking out with a girl.' And the minister looked at some papers before him. 'A girl by the name of Donata Doherty?' He coughed wheezily into his hankie. 'Is this so?'

'Her name is Dolores, your Reverence. Dolores Doherty.'

I kept my head down, not wanting to look.

The minister frowned. 'And she's not a Presbyterian, eh? Not a Protestant in short?'

'No, sir.'

I looked again at James, my poor son. His face was flushed, and I felt my heart thumping. The two of us sat there like a clumsy parcel waiting to be untied and so out of place in that decorous room where everything else was correct: the flocked wallpaper, the brass pen holder presented by the congregation, the picture of Jesus knocking at the door and the clock ticking away.

'Dolores is a practising member of the Roman Catholic Church, sir.'

I put out my hand then as if to prevent him from saying anything more, for he could be very forward sometimes, too quick to jump in. But the minister was sighing heavily now, his face red, jowls quivering. 'I am told that you plan to become engaged?' He leaned over the desk to us, his fingers brattling and beating on the blotter.

'Yes, sir, and to marry eventually.'

Reverend McGoldrick stood up then with a new fierce energy and, taking a step behind him to the tall bookcase with glass doors, he selected a volume and blew what might have been dust off it. Holding my breath, I watched as he flicked through the book until he found a particular page and then, glaring at us over his glasses, he addressed us urgently. 'Now listen carefully to this: "For a mixed marriage, the Church" – that is the RC Church of course – "requires three conditions." Attend well. It says, "That the Catholic party be allowed free exercise of religion, that all the offspring" – *all* the offspring, mind – "are to be brought up Catholics, and that the Catholic party promise to do all that is possible to convert the non-Catholic." Convert us, I ask you! Convert us to their false popish doctrines!' He was almost howling with indignation. Pausing to catch his breath and blow his nose, he glared fiercely at us. 'And here is the position that affects us even in this present day, so listen carefully: "The latest legislation affecting mixed marriages is that of the decree Ne Temere, which went into effect –" Now, where was I?' And he fumbled for his place on the page. 'Oh yes. "– went into effect on 18 April 1908. By this decree all marriages everywhere in the Latin Church between Catholics and non-Catholics are invalid unless they take place in the presence of an accredited priest and two witnesses."' He was swollen now with emotion, and his eyes bulged. 'Now there you have it.' He slapped the book shut. 'If you go down the road to matrimony with this girl, young man, you're finished, as plain as that – you and all you've ever dreamed of doing.'

I looked at James out of the side of my eye and saw him calmly adjust his tie. 'What do you mean, sir?'

The minister sighed. 'You must understand that the Roman Church is ruthless and powerful, and if she gets her claws into you she'll worry you like a cat with a mouse.' He looked at me then, and again at James, and he shook his head. 'No, I think you still fail to get my meaning.'

He sat down behind the desk again, and it occurred to me how old he looked and how wise and indeed how patient.

'But let me explain more fully,' he continued in a softer voice such as he used when addressing the children in Sunday School. 'Let me remind you that you'd be required to publicly renounce your Presbyterianism; that you'd have to kneel before a Roman priest and make confession of a faith foreign to you – you who've been raised in a tradition which, above all, prizes freedom of conscience grounded in the Bible.' He grew increasingly heated as if he was preaching a sermon, and spittle formed at the corners of his mouth. 'They'd even want to baptize you again, which is totally scurrilous and unbiblical.' He drew breath again. 'I tell you, young man, that the entire Presbyterian Church would cry out in abhorrence against such an alliance, not to mention your dear mother here or your poor father, who must turn in his grave were this grievous wrong to be committed.' And the minister, twisting in his chair, wrung his hands.

Throughout all this I tried not to look pleased for I felt grateful. With Thomas gone, there was no one to be strict with the boy or give him guidance, and it was such a relief that at last he was learning the bare truth. Yet, in a minute, I was hearing terrible words fall from my son's mouth, heavy, deliberate. 'Yes, sir,' he was saying, 'I understand you well. But my plan is to marry Dolores no matter about any Church.'

By now the tea in our cups had grown cold, and Reverend McGoldrick was shaking his head in a kind of bewildered sadness. He made another attempt to convince James: 'You have abandoned the Order, I know, but have you given thought to resuming your theological studies?' His little eyes bulged blue in their red sockets and he tugged at his side-whiskers. 'Surely, oh surely, you must see what a satanic nest of vipers you are stumbling towards.'

The housekeeper put her head in to collect the tray, but the minister waved her away and, as if knowing he'd done his duty, stood up suddenly, looked at his watch and concluded the meeting with a new briskness. 'I am sure I've given the two of you enough to think about for a while, but before we part let us offer up this dire situation in prayer.'

I meekly closed my eyes and clenched my hands into urgent fists for I felt a great need to escape the gravelly voice that, fruity and deep, was talking to God about me and my son as if we were china ornaments. I could see the toes of James's brown shoes twisting under his chair, and I stiffened, grieving again for my child even as I feared for him.

As we left the manse, the minister shook our hands. 'I'll ask your visiting elder, Samuel Hanna, to call on you again in a week or so. That should give you both ample time to think over what I've said, and perhaps we might look at things in a different light then, eh?' He was quite calm now. 'And may I suggest, James, that you attend the prayers next week along with your mother? It would be a good thing to bring this difficulty into the fellowship of the congregation.' He led us to the door. James went first, pale and tight-lipped, and me so flustered and uncertain that I nearly forgot my handbag.

Back at The Cairn, I threw my hat down on the kitchen table. James had come home along with me and I'd hoped that he'd taken the minister's words to heart, had begun to repent already and would soon confess his waywardness, see his folly, but neither of us had spoken on the way. Now he was gone to his room, and I knew in my heart that in a minute or two I'd hear the back door shut and he'd be gone again off down the lane meeting herself and doing the dear knows what, him telling her his misfortunes no doubt, what Mr McGoldrick had said and herself crooning back in pious tones. I could see it all: he'd be crying too for he was a soft one, and she'd be lulling over him, holding him, for she'd have him to herself, would marry him. I smacked at my lips. *Oh, he could just go and do what he liked.* I stood up at that and struck the range with a poker, struck so hard that the lid on the kettle jumped. *Let him be gone from me now and all that we taught him; let him splatter himself with holy water, dangle papist beads and go to Masses for all he is worth, for there'll be a hard outcome in the end when he finds himself coiled and toiled in the snares of Rome, imprisoned and not able to do a thing to help himself.*

CHAPTER 37

Sunnyside, 1982

What a long time ago all that is. Fretfully I turn away from this memory and scold myself for having ruminated too long. Ruminating is bad for me: it raises my blood pressure, makes me anxious, but it's not so easy to staunch this flow of thoughts about matters that distress me, and nothing has changed. So to blot thoughts out, I turn to counting the pale squares on the wallpaper and the curtains' spattered yellow shapes that remind me of fried eggs. What a terrible meeting that was with old McGoldrick. He laid down the law, not that it made any odds.

Now Bernadette, cheerful and brisk, comes with her tray. 'Snoozing again, are we? Take up your tea now, petal, there's a good woman.' Petal. Those big dog daisies. We did that when we were children, pulled off petals one at a time: 'He loves me, he loves me not.' A fickle little word is love, here today and gone tomorrow, handy to have up your sleeve. But I've learned plenty over the years, come to know that many RCs are just as upright and kind as my dear friend Cissie. Bernadette pulls a face now as I pick up the bread. 'You'll have to get more of that rub for your fingers, missus; they look all swoll. Maybe a neighbour could get you some?'

And I think at once of the congregation folk, especially Sarah and Molly McKinley. Most of the others are passed over: Betty Wallace, Isaiah Wilson, Willie Forbes, all gone to their Maker, Florrie and Sam Hanna too.

The young one stands silent now, making sure I take my tablets, but when she's gone, I continue thinking about how I wait here, paper-thin in the knotty gnarls of my body, growing a little more tired every day like a butterfly in the killing jar James used to have when he studied Biology. And sometimes I wonder about God. What or who is God? Is he there at all? Is anyone there in the miles of sky that's so big, so wide? Or is it only the moon and the stars I see as they spin through the dark, curving, disappearing into a place with no end? Oh, these are such faithless, fruitless thoughts, and I'll put them away. Yet I don't know where else to seek comfort.

I'm very tired today and am glad the Home has fallen quiet. It's time for the afternoon rest. I was never one for taking a nap myself, not even when the hours hung heavy during the last few months on my own in The Cairn, and it's no different here: I still like to be up and doing a bit if I'm able, even if it's only a walk around the room, moving this and that on my table, sometimes folding and unfolding the purple shawl.

But time is running away, and I begin to know a kind of urgency. I have to try to get everything done before I depart this life, have everything sorted and clean, no creases, no secrets remaining. And this writing, so often a struggle, helps to excise some of the poison that has narrowed my veins and even constrained my last will and testament.

CHAPTER 38

After that meeting with Mr McGoldrick, I gave up caring: it didn't matter that a button was missing off my coat or that my shoes needed to be heeled. My concentration just flew out the window. In the middle of counting the eggs I'd find myself falling into a kind of a doze, and once Sam Hanna came upon me asleep over a cup of tea that I'd poured and was still untouched on the table. 'What, my dear woman, has you like this?' he'd queried, and I'd roused myself quick, told him it was nothing at all whatsoever and that we should all attend to our own business. But it was hard to attend: everything was crowding in on top of me, and my sleep was disturbed by lurid nightmares in shocking colours.

On one occasion I dreamed I was in an outhouse throwing a heap of mangles into the chopper. Cissie Lynch was with me and, in a jumble of words, was gabbling about a new cathedral in Cavan town and about a Mass. In the dream my stomach lurched, and I felt a compulsion to learn more about this Mass. Yet, as I stood beside the crusher, a Bible verse spoke in my heart. 'Turn ye not unto idols,' it said, 'nor make to yourselves molten gods.' But sticky as honey was my desire to go, to lay my own eyes on the Mass, the great beast I believed we read about in Revelation 13. Yet I shrank into my skin, folded myself up, afraid. And so I dallied beside the chopper with my thoughts flying around like dandelion clocks. The sun was throwing long dusty ribbons that streamed through the cobwebby outhouse, and I smelled the mangles and the tied-up colt in the next stable where the pony harness hung, polished and shining, ready for Sabbath, and then in a breathless rush: 'I'll go with you, Cissie. I'll go!'

Then at once I seemed to be in the kitchen counting out hen money, a coin at a time on the table, and oh, here was Thomas, risen from the dead, watching me. And when I was taking my coat off the peg, he turned and asked, 'What would you be at, woman?' Big, inquisitive, barring my way, he pulled himself up. 'Now, tell me, where would you be off to?'

The hairs stood up on my neck, and my hands were clammy, but my voice stayed calm as I told him I was going to visit some Ballymount folk who'd strayed.

He stood there seeking my eyes. 'You mean "strayed" like that old one who never darkens the door of the church?'

'Yes, like her.'

'And you need your hen money for that?'

I said nothing.

'Well, if it's the Lord's work that you're about, go and do it.'

I pocketed the coins.

'Don't give her too much.'

And I knew in the dream, knew what a daring thing I was doing.

Next I was arrived with Cissie in Cavan town, and there, straight ahead of me, rose the new cathedral, gleaming white and reaching a pointed finger into the heavens. Suddenly I was on my own and, labouring greatly, my legs like water, I managed to climb up hundreds of steps. Great embossed doors lay open before me, and therefrom shone a brilliance which forced me to shield my eyes. From the cavernous interior there issued a strange sweet smell and a bluish smoke wreathing itself about vast grey pillars, and I heard the voice of the prophet Isaiah: 'The incense you bring me is a stench in my nostrils.' But I paid no heed, only went deeper into the smoke that hung in the multicoloured shafts of light, which came pouring in through stained-glass windows. The walls were painted in garish shades of purple and orange and gold and a violent green; statues were everywhere. Saints looked sad and forlorn in their haloes or else severe, and there was Mary, woebegone and pale, in a cast of brown plaster and gilded blue robe.

I moved on. Standing in front of a colossal crucifix, I shuddered to look on the burnished body of Jesus, a body the colour of walnut, stretched and nailed and bleeding, the poor sinewy legs twisted and nailed to a shape to fit the polished wood, and my stomach heaved. But I gazed some more, and before me I saw a white and dazzling mound like the Ark of the Covenant down off Mount Ararat, and before a great table of stone stood a priest with his back to the people. He was robed in red and was lifting platters and cups of gold and silver so high that the lights of a thousand candles danced in them. And as he stood he repeated strange words over and over in a high sing-song voice, while boys in lacy white frocks flitted around him, dipping and darting across polished red tiles, and little bells tinkled. Behind me I could hear much bustle and movement: people were kneeling and bowing, and over it all hung the sickly odour of Rome. This was the Mass. I turned to the people and asked what the priest was doing, and they said he was presenting Jesus as sacrifice. I cried out then, 'No! Oh no, no, no! He mustn't do that, for the Bible tells us that Christ was sacrificed only once for all.' But I shouldn't have spoken so loud, for on hearing my voice the priest swiftly turned and raised a great stick which he threw down before me. It was the rod of Aaron slithering over the green-marbled floor, a serpent that roiled and twisted, and the words of the prophet Ezekiel went rolling upward, echoing through the vaults: 'Thou hast been in Eden.'

Awake at last and still thrashing about from that terrible nightmare, it took me some time to recover.

CHAPTER 39

Not long after that I was out one day in the yard collecting a few bits and pieces of wood and turf for the fire when I heard Cissie call to me over the hedge. Just back from a pilgrimage to Lourdes and full of jollity, she carelessly threw her bicycle down in the laurels and, arms akimbo, came up to me. 'Well, look at yourself toiling away on your own.' And she laughed. 'Where's that big lazy son of yours?'

I started to protest for, in spite of all, I wouldn't have him disparaged like that, but without more ado she took a step to the house and, cupping her hands, called up to his window, 'Yoo-hoo, James Campbell! I know you're up there! Come on down out of that and give your mother a hand.' She shook her head and smiled at me. 'Too much dreaming; too much moonlight. That's what.'

I left off gathering my bits of sticks and wiped myself down. 'I've told you he's thinking of going to train as a teacher and is probably at his books.'

She gave me a funny look. 'So that's what you call it?'

I glanced towards the house and saw him come slowly out through the back door. He was yawning and rubbing his eyes as he crossed towards us.

'Hello, Cissie. And isn't this the grand fine day?'

'Well, is that all you have to say to me?'

'It's enough for now.' He reddened and bent to pick up a few bits of turf and pretended to throw one at her.

She winked at him. 'Nothing to say about that sweetheart of yours?'

He flashed her a smile, and of a sudden they seemed like old friends and I felt cold and tired, 'dark and cheerless' as the hymn said.

But she turned to me laughing. 'And Harriet, you'll have to head off to Dublin and get yourself a new outfit for the big day. They have lovely costumes in Switzers, I'm told.'

Angered and stricken, I bent again to the ground, where a few sticks remained. I'd pick all of these up, one at a time, one at a time, but I'd say not a word, for if I chose to speak I'd be like a slasher, cut through them both, say terrible things. I gathered up all that remained to be gathered, the two of them watching, then said I'd put on the kettle. But he had to be off, said he'd other things to do, and he bade Cissie a quick farewell. When he'd gone, she shook her head and remarked that the young ones had powerful red blood in their veins these days or something like that, something that scalded me anyway.

As I rattled out the mugs on the kitchen table, I stared at her crossly. 'Why must you encourage him?'

'For being in love?' She sounded perplexed. 'Maybe you don't remember how it was, Harriet?' I gaped as she took up her tea and lay back in the chair, a smile on her lips. 'The stars, Harriet? And the harvest moon in September bellying over the fields and the stubble bright yellow? And how you knew that if you started to sing you could go on forever.'

She looked at me hard, wanting a response, but I said nothing, just raked the ashes out of the firebox; this wasn't the time for poetry.

'Your fellow is young the way you and I were once.'

I smoothed the apron over my faded dimity frock and felt my too-thin knees. 'Cissie, you just don't understand.'

'Well you've told me often enough.' She sighed. 'And I know what it is to you that James will marry a Catholic.'

Again the words had a sting.

She shook herself down, ready to comfort. 'And Harriet, if I had a son – which of course I don't – I'd feel exactly the same if he hooked up with a Protestant.' She paused, frowning. 'But then maybe I'd get around to remembering that there's really only one God and that he'll be our judge when all is over.'

Easy for her to talk! So I just took up the brush and started to sweep and sweep. I would tell her the way things were, enlighten her somewhat about moonlight and stars and the judgment of God, make her see sense. But how could I possibly bring her to understand our fear of cardinals and popes and the secret rumbling of dark sexual things, and fear above all of Rome's searching power, its silky-gloved hand reaching with steel, its unchallengeable ruthlessness? And if I tried to explain, I'd only go on being seen as a narrow-minded bigot. I was very het up, but she just sat there like an ornament until at last I put the brush down and leaned on the handle. 'Now Cissie, listen to me, you just listen.' And I felt like a preacher spreading the Word. 'For us Presbyterians it's all very different.'

She nodded, waiting to hear what I had to say, and I thought how full to the brim this kitchen was with years and years of waiting: Thomas tinkering at the clock that would never keep time, Anna May late, the minister coming to call and our son not home from the fair. Now us here, but I couldn't wait any longer. 'There's more to it, Cissie, than just marrying someone who digs with the other foot.'

She set her mug firmly down on the table and folded her arms, and I saw the kindliness of welcome, the openness in her.

'Presbyterians are very few in this part of the world.'

I struggled to be patient, not hurtful, but I was like a hen picking at grain as I tried to sort out my words, sieve them for sense.

'The Catholic Church is so big, so powerful, so menacing . . .' I faltered. 'And sometimes we are very afraid that it will over-power us, hold us as naught, oppress and negate us.'

Cissie shook her head. 'Ah, there's no need at all to be ner-vous like that, Harriet. Just think of the priests and the holy nuns, and all the good work they do, and sure isn't it all the same in the end? Anyway, do you think it would matter to God where James said his prayers, now would it?'

Well, I just had to smile at that, for my friend could be somewhat simple at times, see-through simple like a washed windowpane.

'No, I am sure that wouldn't matter to our Heavenly Father.' I drew myself up then, stood straight as a pillar, fire in my face and sweeping my body. 'But what does matter –' I was almost shouting '– is when the road to God is blocked with thickets of dogmas and doctrines that Jesus never taught. That's what's of consequence, Cissie Lynch, that's what counts. The Lord Jesus never taught his disciples about Purgatory or that babies who died unbaptized would go to Limbo, or that we had to confess our sins to priests.'

I was well worked up now and had taken a duster, was furi-ously wiping and mopping. I looked over to the press where the Bible lay but knew I'd no need to take it down for I knew what the apostle said about salvation: we must work it out ourselves, he said, 'with fear and trembling'.

Cissie tried to butt in, to protest I was sure, but I hadn't finished: I would say what I had to say for the sake of Thomas and Ballymount. 'Do you really understand anything about freedom, Cissie?'

She frowned.

'Well, let me tell you something about it. Freedom is such a big word for us Presbyterians.' I paused and thought of the birds in their wayward flitterings through boundary-free heavens. 'Have you ever thought of what it's really like to be free, Cissie? To hear the voice of God come pure and unadulterated from scripture? To discern that Voice in prayer and in your own conscience?' I was almost breathless now. 'And do you know what it's like to have the freedom to govern your own woman's body?' Spent and folded down from those heights of emotion, I sagged into a chair.

Cissie came over to me, put her arm around me. 'Ah look, Harriet, leave all that old worrisome business to the Church. Just try to put things like that behind you, see reason in the light of day and come to your senses. The simple plain fact is only that your son is going with a girl from a decent family, and it's likely she'll marry your son.' I turned away, but she went on, arms folded in triumph, 'Now there's none of your "freedoms" lost in any of that, is there!'

I batted her words away: 'That girl can be as lovely and decent as she likes, but she brings a stain upon our people that will not readily be expunged.'

Cissie rose at that, had nothing more to say, my poor, sadly blinded friend. In silence we walked together as far as the head of the lane. I watched her turn in at her own gate and knew that in spite of all that she stood for, and in spite of me, we'd go on being friends.

CHAPTER 40

I was alone one evening when I saw Sam Hanna coming across the yard, sent no doubt by the minister. He was guiding his bicycle past the puddles, and the dog barking behind him. I wasn't a bit surprised to see him for I'd already begun to feel the steady stream of the church's rejection, seeping at first, then flooding cold and insinuate. Minnie Gilmore no longer left me her copy of the *Presbyterian Herald*, and Willie Johnson wouldn't do a message for me in the town last week; too busy with silage, he said.

I sat Hanna down with a cup of tea, which he stirred well for a while and then tapped the edge of the cup with his spoon before finally placing it in the saucer. No, he'd have nothing to eat, thank you kindly, and he didn't take sugar, he was sweet enough himself. When the tea was swallowed, he wiped his mouth and leaned back in the chair, and I saw there only a piteous little man charged to watch over the Campbells, to correct where correction was needed and report back to the Kirk Session. I knew it was his duty to admonish and rebuke as the Good Book exhorted: 'Brethren, if a man be overtaken in a fault, ye who are spiritual restore such an one in the spirit of meekness.'

But that night there was nothing meek about the tailor once he got going. He pushed the cup and saucer aside and turned to face me, and I looked back into his little piggy eyes, smaller without the glasses. His wrists were smudged with chalk and a few white threads still clung to his coat sleeve. When he spoke at last, his Adam's apple bobbed in his scrawny neck and the exhortation began: initially a trickle, then a deluge. He spoke heatedly at first, his words tumbling out, little spittle-covered barbs, but then, disconcertingly, he grew almost tender as if approaching a small wounded creature. Which in truth I was.

He asked where James was; could he not be with us? But I knew my son had gone out. The tailor had known James, he said, all his life in fact, and had high hopes for him, and would he not now see the error of his ways, come to his senses before it was too late. Molly McKinley was a lovely pure girl if ever there was one, and surely to goodness he'd never bow the knee to the Roman Church. On and on he went then, about the Border and the Covenant and the price paid by Presbyterians for their freedom. It was such a ramble that my head spun, and I wished only that he would leave me and pedal away out of my sight. But he wouldn't go yet. We Presbyterians had learned to be tough, he reminded me. Our hard-won heritage was greatly prized and a sure sign of God's covenant with his chosen people. That covenant was like the Ark of the Israelites itself, never to be violated. And he thumped the table. 'As it is written, "I will bring a sword upon you, that shall avenge the quarrel of my covenant and I will send the pestilence among you; and ye shall be delivered into the hand of the enemy."'

I got up to light the lamp, and as the soft glow slowly filled the room, anger and not a little fear was rising up in me. These were God's own words from Leviticus, he said, and here was James Campbell breaking that covenant and sure to be taken by the arch-enemy if he didn't repent of his ways. He asked if

I would like him to pray with me, but I declined for I had very little faith in my own prayers any more and none at all in the tailor's. I heard the outer gates clang after him, and then, feeling chilled and distraught, I made myself a cup of cocoa and headed up the stairs.

At first I couldn't find sleep. Echoes of his talking lashed around me, and I lay listening to the wind soughing in the trees and worried that I might have forgotten to turn the key in the back door. From across the fields a dog gave an occasional bark, but otherwise there wasn't a sound. Below in the hall the big clock chimed the quarter-hours, and it must have gone three before the candle guttered out and I slept.

CHAPTER 41

Sunnyside, 1982

It's not always easy to sleep in this place and last night I'd a very peculiar dream, so peculiar that I'll set it out now in full. I dreamt I was alone in the parlour at home, a strange place to be since that room was so seldom used. Thomas and I had sat here just once in a while to entertain the minister maybe or James to read his book. James was the only reader in the family, me and Thomas keeping to the Anglo Celt, *the* Presbyterian Herald *and the Bible.*

And it seemed that the fire was just lately lit for its flames were hardly flames at all, just little yellow ribbons licking the black grate, flickering over the marbled tiles with the scenes of Abraham and Isaac etched in them. I was sitting tall on the narrow black horsehair sofa that scratched the backs of my legs the way it had always done; the wallpaper had come loose, had pulled away from the plaster, and the prints, damp in their gilt frames, lay curled behind spotted glass. That parlour was such a desolate room for it knew only watery streaks of morning sun. The curtains hung faded and thin, their redness bleached to a sickly pink, and I said to myself we must get them replaced with bright yellow perhaps, for we needed to let more sun come through.

Then, in the dream, I got up off the sofa and went over to the low shelves in the corner where the books were kept, all of them belonging to James, and I drew out The Pilgrim's Progress, Martin Rattler *and* Settlers in Canada. *I turned over a few pages, spotted with mould and breathing out must, and I read again the labels inside, which said, 'For Sabbath School Attendance', 'For Diligence in Scripture Study', 'For '100% Answering in the Sabbath School Examinations'. What a diligent pupil he'd been. Calm now, I took hold of these books with their green and gold bindings and marbled covers ribbed in leather and I dashed them down to the floor as if they secreted poison out of their little black veins, and I listened to the hard thud of them as they hit the linoleum. There would be no more prizes like those.*

After that I floated, the way you do in a dream, silent, unfeeling, to the shelf above the books where we kept the few photos we owned. There was one of Reverend McGoldrick's predecessor and one of Ballymount, and in front of these a yellowing snapshot of Thomas with James on his knee, looking wistful. My husband appears grey and thin in himself in this, and he's looking down on the child in a kind of holy admonishment, with maybe on his lips that psalm of reproach that was forever plained in our house. But it was into the face of the child that I looked long, the innocent open face, and I told him how sorry I was about everything, how desperately sorry.

Then a kind of sadness dropped around me like the folds of a veil, and laying the picture of Thomas and James aside I turned to the final photo, which I held to the light of the window, gentle and steady. This was my favourite picture of James. He was about eighteen months old here, seated on a cushion and wearing the little coat I'd worked for him in moss stitch. In the dream, I stand and gaze at him for a long time. His fair hair has the beginnings of a curl, and he looks so healthy and sated, smiling a fat pink smile at the world. It was an age, I thought, since I'd studied that photo so keenly and now, taking it up in my hand, my lips bitten tight, I started to mangle it. The edges were sharp and cut into my palms, but using my nails I tore through the smiling pink face and, with a storm rushing through me, I twisted it all to a screw. After that and serene as if watching a sunset, I released the photo and saw the pieces uncurl and untwist in my hand like a butterfly crushed, and, looking down at my feet, the fragments were falling, scattered and cold, on the parlour floor – like ashes, I thought, or maybe the bruised wings of angels.

When I woke I felt quite ill for I found that the dream still lay beside me like a cold little corpse. I was fairly shaken and, sitting up, I rang my bell. Bernadette came running at once to ask what was wrong and did I want the doctor. But when I quieted down, I was able to tell her I was all right; it was just that you couldn't tuck in a corpse, couldn't make it comfortable in the folds of your own waking body, at which she said I was rambling and would bring some warm milk.

CHAPTER 42

Oh, it was a fine romance, I can tell you, and the talk of the whole townland. Of course neither James nor I went to the prayers that week not even at the behest of our minister. For one thing I couldn't abide the thought of sitting there with ones like Betty Wallace or Sam Hanna, his ears cocked, more interested in the content of the prayers than in the prayers themselves. And when I thought of the droning prayer voices: 'If only, Father, you would undertake to save your servant James, et cetera, et cetera,' I felt sick.

But I wouldn't let them best me or send me into a kind of exile from the church, so I went again to the Ladies' Sewing Circle in the church hall. That hall was a cold draughty place, even in summer, its sad yellow walls adorned only by the likeness of a long-dead minister and gravel-grey pictures of Calvin and Knox. My Sabbath School with its sweetly singing children was long gone.

I entered quietly, hesitantly, not letting the latch make a sound, and there were the women, sitting around as usual on the wooden forms, their heads nodding and tongues wagging as they knitted socks for our men in the ongoing war. I stood watching them spool out the greasy grey wool and I drew breath, felt I must leave at once, but Betty Wallace spotted me and, as with the flurry and flight of starlings, their chatter immediately stopped. They all started in at me, Sarah Williamson first, smiling that threatening kind of smile of hers, 'Well, surprise, surprise!' And her smile widened into a grin that reminded me somehow of our pony when he bucked at taking the bit, and they all turned to look at me as I stood by the door, work bag in my hand. Then one of them called out, 'Would you look at what the cat's brought in. Haven't seen you this long time, Harriet.' And they laughed as they resumed their chattering and stitching, heads bent, smiling chins visible under their hats. I sat down on the end of a form and spent a minute or two rummaging in my bag for threads to match the work I was doing. As I threaded a needle and jabbed it into my work piece, I was filled with something akin to hatred of those good women.

'Tell us then,' said another one after a while, 'how is your James?' She turned to me with a half-closed eye, her knitting stopped as she leaned and waited. I bent over the piece in my hoop, pulled a thread through the beige linen cloth and started to work on a daisy chain. I'd choose off-white for the petals and then pink for the tips. But there was a snag in the thread and I'd have to unpick.

They all started at me then, clucking hens. 'It's such a to-do, my dear.'

I went on struggling, unpicking, until finally the thread ran free.

'Does the minister know, can you tell us?'

'And the elders?'

'And what about your poor husband? I'm sure he must be turning in his grave.'

'It's said too that your James is out of the Order.'

As they picked and pecked at me, I silently stitched away

until I could stand it no longer. I lifted my head at last and looked at them where they sat, bundled together in their big tweed coats and felt hats, knitting laid aside on their laps, and I blurted, 'Well, if he's left it, so what! God's ways are not our ways.'

They appeared to bridle at that, show righteous displeasure. 'Oh, but we can be sure that this carry-on is none of God's ways,' said one.

I sat up quick, put down my work and looked at them banded together, comfortable as mice in a bag of flour, and I dared to rouse them: 'Could one of you now that are so full of what's right have the courage to stand up and spell out for us here the thoughts of Almighty God?' I stifled the catch in my breath and pointed to the grey blurry pictures that hung near the empty fireplace. 'Would one of you dare to stand here in front of our fathers and tell us what God has in mind?' I could feel my words hit home like the blows of a hammer, shocking even myself.

But the women just sniggered and took up their knitting again, needles clicking and clacking in renewed harmony as they provoked me still: 'Surely to goodness, Harriet Campbell, don't we know right well what God's will is! It's as plain as day in Holy Writ.'

'And not,' another smirked, 'in the antics of the Roman Catholic Church.'

But I could say no more. I was all dried up, my thinking astray. I silently stitched away for a while, but with every jab I made in the cloth, I thought of my son and my body turned to water. At last I rose, and without a word, went off on my own, stumbled across the knotty grey floorboards that had once welcomed myself and the children to Sabbath School.

Outside, the daisies, buttercups and red-berried hedges worked together to soothe me, but the women had stirred my fire. I would sit James down as soon as a chance arose, just as I did when he was a child, and I'd bid him attend, remind him again of what would be required of him: the outrageous recanting, the humiliation. I'd be very forceful this time, would fully express my wrath, which was righteous indeed, and I'd somehow cajole him into changing his ways before it was all too late.

CHAPTER 43

But I never did sit him down again, for he was gone before I knew it and embarked on teacher training. In a way I was relieved to see him go, for he'd be out of her way and engaged in the books again, but I regretted I'd lost yet another chance to reason with him. He wrote to me frequently from Dublin, little wretched letters full of words that never mentioned the books and barely concealed unease and confusion. Yet apart from sending him the *Presbyterian Herald* a couple of times, I didn't respond to a single one of those missives. He was heartbroken, he'd write in one letter, and in the next he'd say he was happy in spite of all; then he'd be angry and defiant or else confessing a little to sadness and guilt. And so the recitation ran on and on, letter by letter, lifting my hopes and then shattering them on the hard thing in my heart. He was in love, he pleaded, and could he have my forgiveness? But no – and I tore that letter up, threw it on the fire – he could not have my forgiveness, not ever. And yet I went on reading his letters as if by tormenting myself I could find ease, but there was no sign in any of them that he might give that girl up, not a sign. I sensed of course that he was deeply conflicted, but I had no pity for him; there was pity only for myself, and I'd sit for hours hugging myself to myself: poor Harriet, so this is the reward from your only child and this the reward from your congregation that, with all its preaching about faith and love, looks down on you now in rebuke.

Later on he wrote that everything required of him by the Catholic Church would be done only for her and for her alone. He emphasized this over and over again, almost like an apology, and it made me ill to read it. He and two others were undergoing a 'six-week period of instruction' with someone he referred to as Father Brady, and in due course he would be confirmed by Archbishop McQuaid himself, a man greatly feared by Protestants; yet he wrote he was beginning to understand that what was happening to him was God's holy will, even though he still had his times of doubt. Savagely, I tore up that letter too and burned it.

Yet I continued to read what he sent with an interest that grew in me like an obsession. He wrote that he had told his spiritual adviser about these doubts of his, and to help clear his mind he had been counselled to spend a week or two in Mary Queen of Apostles, a monastery in Kerry. I was fairly stunned by this. What was a 'monastery' about? And what was a 'spiritual adviser'? It quite sounded as if a foreign person was writing to me and not my own Presbyterian boy.

I sneered angrily as I read these epistles. He was truly leading a double life, for how could someone reared in Ballymount and in the simple precepts of the Presbyterian Church reconcile to himself all this nonsense? It had to be very hard for him, but let him at it if that was the way he wanted to go. I tore up the long handwritten pages of his most recent letter, threw these too on the flames. After this, and roused by anger, I went straight to the press in the corner of the kitchen and, rooting in the back, found the packet of postcards I'd bought in the last church sale. I peeled off one and sat down with it at the kitchen table. I unscrewed the lid of the ink bottle, dipped my nib and, leaning my head on my hand, wrote carefully, soberly, the way I had always approached God's Holy Writ, a word at a time: ' "I have somewhat against thee, because thou hast left thy first love. Remember therefore from whence thou art fallen, and repent, and do the first works; or else I will come unto thee quickly, and will remove thy candlestick out of his place, except thou repent." Revelation 2:4–6.'

Just that. But I couldn't bring myself to post it. A postcard like that seemed too final, and yet, when I sat down calm to consider it all, I was amazed that finality hadn't come long before now; in truth, I sometimes secretly wished for it.

CHAPTER 44

In due course yet another letter arrived that further roused my ire: this one was postmarked 'Ballybunion' and was written in his firm neat hand on the middle pages torn from a copybook.

May 1945

Dear Mother,

I trust you keep well. Since I have no news at all of you and since you won't reply to my letters, my only recourse is to keep writing until you return them unopened, and so that you won't be at a loss to know where to post, I'll always write my address on the back of the envelope. I have got my H.Dip.Ed., completed my training, and will now look for a teaching post. I am told there's a vacancy coming up in September at the Christian Brothers' school in Crockban, about ten miles the other side of Ballymount.

Daily I pray God that you and I can be reconciled. I know only too well how difficult all this must be for you but it is not easy for me either. I am gravely troubled at times, not only by anxiety about you but troubled also in my own spirit. Sometimes it feels as if I am setting out into an empty, dark wilderness that's full of lamentation from the past. I've no map and no guide. I do believe it's the Holy Spirit that keeps me going, but sometimes I feel truly lost and God-forsaken. I've come to rest awhile in this monastery and to pray about all that is happening in my life and in Dolores's and indeed in yours too. Brother Joseph has even suggested that Dolores and I ought not to marry. But it is our full intention to wed, and we have been making plans for some time now.

I think Mr McGoldrick must have retired as I have had some communication from a new Ballymount minister, Reverend Boyd, a very nice letter in which he expressed the hope that I would meet him. I have declined, however, since I believe that such a meeting would further muddle my thinking and moreover be pointless. I know he would plead with me not to convert to Catholicism, but the plain truth is that I must convert if I am to make Dolores happy and allow her to keep the solemn vows of obedience she made to her own Church. You and Father made solemn vows too at baptism on my behalf, but that was different and yet, truthfully, I don't really understand how it can be different.

After that I pledged never, ever to open another letter from him, for after hearing about that place in Kerry I could read no more. In any case, that turned out to be the last letter I'd receive from him.

CHAPTER 45

One warm sunny day not long afterwards, just before the Twelfth in fact, I had another visit from Anna May Reilly, who came struggling down the lane and over the yard as if she owned the place. Normally on that day I'd have been down in the Lodge helping the women: shaking out the flag with its purple star on the orange background and the St George's cross on the corner, polishing the cabinet where all the regalia was stored. But I wasn't brave enough to join them now. Instead I had only Anna May Reilly beside me. She lowered herself on to a chair without being asked, and I looked at her with suspicion. 'What in particular takes you here today, may I ask?'

Ignoring my question, she just shook herself out of the old astrakhan coat and adjusted her hat. 'Isn't it only like yesterday, missus, the time you were needing help, and I came here to see yourself and Mr Campbell, God rest him.'

Cringing at the memory, I moved quietly about the kitchen, pretending to be busy, poking at the fire, wiping down the table.

'So you wonder why I'm here today?' She rummaged in her bag. 'Well, I have this for you.'

She simpered and held out an envelope. 'That's yours, missus. Your invite.'

It was a little blue envelope, slightly soiled, with flowers

213

around the edge and my own name written small in neat letters. Ignoring it, I jumped up at once and started swiftly into dusting the top of the range with the goose wing, going into every little cranny: hither and thither over the hot black surface I went, before casting the sweepings into the firebox and slamming it shut. *Ah ha!* He'd known better than to give it to me himself, knew so well what I'd say. She moved as if to put her arm through mine but I drew quickly away.

'Oh, don't be put out, missus. This wee job is the least I could do for them. He's all in a heap, and I told him I'd give him a hand. There's not too many will get one of these, you know.'

I put down the goose wing then and stood for a minute looking out the window. The rose bush was scratching at the glass as it had done for years in spite of how Thomas had always said we should prune it better, and the gate to the paddock swung crooked and loose, its hinges broken. And her voice came at my back, hatefully burning: 'Poor missus, didn't the young rascal keep you well in the dark.' I watched as she put the envelope in behind a jug on the dresser and heard her mutter in a kind of amusement, 'Oh, the rapscallion! Wait till I get my hands on him, and I'll have something to say to him!' She went on talking like this, smiling and twisting her hands together and then, as if she could no longer contain it: 'Oh, and I'm his sponsor, you know, for getting him received.'

I let down the window with a bang then for a bit of fresh air and stayed looking out. There was hardly a sign of life in the whole of the yard that afternoon: just a couple of magpies clacking in the Scotch pine next to the potato plantation and a cock crowing.

'It's said by some that you're not too happy, missus, about James and Dolores?'

In reply, I showed her the door.

When she'd gone, I took a step to the jug, opened the envelope and read:

DOLORES ANNE DOHERTY AND

JAMES THOMAS CAMPBELL

REQUEST THE PLEASURE OF YOUR COMPANY

AT THEIR MARRIAGE CEREMONY

ON FRIDAY, 24TH AUGUST 1945 AT 10 A.M.

IN THE CHURCH OF ST JUDE, BOXTOWN, DUBLIN

It was only a little white card. No mention of mothers and fathers. No mention of any reception. And I knew where I'd put it!

When that date came around, I took myself off down the lane, didn't know where I was going or what I was doing, just any old place to be away from my thinking. I pulled at the grasses, picked bits of montbretia and the hours wore on until at last it was evening and dark and the day was over.

Cissie called to The Cairn a week after the wedding, and, in spite of myself, I wanted to hear what had happened that day in the Church of St Jude.

'You were at it, last Friday?'

She smoothed her skirt over her knees. 'Of course I was at it, and you could have been there too. There was no one to stop you.'

'Who all was there?' I was cross with myself for wanting to know.

'Well, her sister Marie was there and Anna May Reilly dressed to the nines, and two strange men who were maybe the bride's relations and a couple of others I didn't know.'

'No sign of her parents at all?'

Cissie snorted. 'No, they wouldn't be seen at it either. So you see, miss,' and she put on her know-it-all face, 'it's not just your lot who're upset at this coupling.'

Well, that bit of news astonished me a little for I'd imagined her family would be over the moon at another conversion. Ignoring my surprise, Cissie went on, 'Dolores looked beautiful, I have to say, though a wee bit pale, and your James? Well, you should have seen him. You'd have been so proud. He stood tall and calm as a statue, not a sign of nerves. The priest, I don't know his name, said a lovely Mass, and when the bride and groom, now husband and wife, knelt to receive the sacrament, you could have heard a pin drop.'

I felt ill then, stayed silent, and the line of a poem slid into my mind: 'When so sad, thou canst not sadder, cry . . .' and oh, I needed to cry, needed to take my sadness away to my bed.

CHAPTER 46

Sunnyside, 1982

Although many years have passed since that, I still remember how defeated I felt at the time. I lost interest in the house; the hens stopped laying, and I was glad to see the back of the calves. Whenever I went out to the garden I loved, the sky just fell around me in folds of grey. There was nothing. It was as if I'd been dropped down a well: no light, no Gospel, no hope. Before that my faith had always consoled me: God had been father, protector, redeemer and friend, but he was no longer like that, no longer close in the staring blank places I inhabited after James abandoned me and the Presbyterian Church and took the calamitous path to Rome. Little did Thomas know, the day he sat calmly taking his tea at the table, that he would prove to be the cause of bringing Rome into the heart of our family, and little did he know that the infant who played at his feet, baptized in Bally-mount Presbyterian, would one day be talking about 'Mary Queen of the Apostles' and 'Father This' and 'Brother That'. What a business my husband had started, and what devastation it had led to. But Thomas slept now in his neat Presbyterian grave out in the grassy spaces beside his own church, him at peace and me struggling with what he began. Oh, it's easy to give in when there seems no way forward. Yet even a worm will keep going, and the blackbird too that squints from the bush, so with an effort I pull myself up.

All has quieted down for the night now, but before lying down I'll fetch my stick and go to the window again. I'm always hoping for some kind of sign that I'm not alone with this heap of trouble. Drawing back the curtain, I look into the night, but there is nothing at all out there. Only a slice of moon and the dark girth of pine trees wedged in the stars, and I shout out to the dark in angry frustration, cry out so loudly that Bernadette comes running to see what's wrong. 'Oh my good woman,' she cries, 'what has you out of your bed?'

'I'm searching for God,' I tell her and I tremble all over. But she takes hold of my arm and steers me away. 'Well, I think you'll find him easier now if you just lie down, nice and quiet.'

I sigh and take out my hankie.

'God builds the back for the burden, petal, and he has given you a good strong back.' She straightens the covers. 'Go to sleep now, like a good woman.'

But I lie awake, feel the arthritis crunching my bones. Perhaps, after all, God is secretly testing me. 'But you know, God,' I whisper boldly into the pillow, 'I hardly believe in you any more . . . for all the years I spent in Ballymount singing Psalms and listening to sermons. Year in, year out, I attended to your Word – all my life I listened – but now I just don't know . . .'

Yet, in spite of myself, I am driven to pray: my pleas dribbling out in forlorn little bubbles of breath that somehow I may be delivered, that this wasteland of torturing trouble may vanish, and in its stead might open a plain . . . and sometimes, in truth, I can make out a plain . . . and someone running to meet me, small at first but growing and coming, desert-like dust clouding and hiding . . . but still someone coming.

CHAPTER 47

One evening just two months after the wedding my son came to see me himself, entered the back door without knocking. I was sitting by the window looking out unseeingly with the Bible on my knee, and he startled me. I shouldn't have been startled for it was the same way he'd always come from the time he was a child, and yet it wasn't the same at all. I hadn't seen him in a good while, didn't really know him any more; he was somewhat alien to me now.

He stood in the doorway, a dark tall figure silhouetted against the light, and he went on standing there, for ages it seemed. Then he took a step, what a long step it was, towards the place where I sat, and he stood there beside me, saying nothing at first. Then, 'Mother,' he said at last, his voice like crushed stones. 'Mother?'

The clock on the wall ticked away loudly, but the cuckoo inside was broken, and I turned my head away, not knowing how to respond to the tall stranger who yet was my own flesh and blood, and I could feel a pain twist through my gut and rise up to my throat so that at last words were forced from me: 'Yes, James?'

How strange my voice sounded. I hadn't used it for a long time now that neighbours had mostly stopped calling, uncomfortable, I supposed, about what had happened; indeed the whole community was hanging its head, Presbyterians for shame, the rest for embarrassment.

'Yes, James?' I repeated into the stillness.

He came closer, eager. 'I've brought you this, Mother . . . from Galway.' And he held out a packet.

'From Galway,' I echoed and took a deep breath. The honeymoon, I supposed. Herself with her beads and her missals and my son. Gone to Galway. And here he was now with a present no less, to make it all right. I had to laugh to myself at the very idea, and my laugh was bitter as gall. In disbelief I watched as with clumsy and trembling fingers he drew from a nest of tissue paper a silken purple shawl, shook it out to tempt me perhaps with its sparkle of jewelled peacocks. It was quite a large piece, I could see, almost sheer, and the weave so fine that when he held it out, the sunlight turned the purple to a rosy pink that flowed like water down to the tasselled ends. Through the warp and the weave of our lives together, he'd learned what pleased, and I recalled the little tweed suit he'd worn for his First Communion, for his first time to sit around the Lord's Table – couldn't wait to get into long trousers – and how that day I'd worn the hat he'd admired: blue with a spray of forget-me-nots.

But he was standing here before me now with his present, entreating. Yet I said not a word. Nor did I raise my eyes further than the thing he held out. No, I would have none of his peace.

'Mother,' he was saying again. 'Mother, I . . .' But he couldn't finish that sentence for what was there left to say? The time for making amends had passed. He went then, at a stride, to the kitchen table, where as a boy he'd studied the *Shorter Catechism* and done his homework, and, pushing aside the tea things I hadn't been bothered to clear away, he put his offering down, and he stood there wordless as if waiting for something, but the kitchen was silent except for the clock and the rose bush scraping the window.

When he was gone, I rose to my feet and just screwed up that shawl in my hands, twisted it, wrung it the way you'd wring the neck of a chicken and threw it aside.

CHAPTER 48

I tried to carry on as normal after that, but it was hard and sometimes I didn't feel very well. My heart wasn't the best, and my nerves were at me, tugging and straining – they'd pull me into a slump of despair if I yielded.

I hadn't gone to Meeting for a very long time, but I made one final determined effort. It could only be good if I were to renew my attendance in the place where I'd once enjoyed fellowship. So one Sabbath morning soon after that visit and just before Harvest Thanksgiving I picked up my courage and decided this was the day I'd return to Ballymount. A Sunday routine could only be wholesome. I carefully chose my outfit and looked at myself in the bedroom mirror. I was too thin and my face was well weathered, but the pale blue costume was nice and the shoes good. I was dressed up as I hadn't been for a very long time, yet already I feared them, felt their eyes accusing. But I wouldn't let them best me. I smiled at myself in the mirror as I pulled a wide-brimmed hat down on my forehead and told myself I'd do. Downstairs, I picked up my hymn book and Psalter, damp from sitting so long in the porch window, and snapped my handbag shut.

There was plenty of sunshine that morning, and I felt invigorated, reminding myself that although I hadn't been in the church for so long, it was still God's house from which no one could ever be turned away.

Sam Hanna and another elder, both a bit stooped now, were at either side of the door like a couple of guardian angels, and as I approached they seemed to be standing so close together that I almost had to squeeze in between them. They didn't speak more than a 'Nice morning'. Somewhat cross and unnerved, I headed up the narrow aisle with the strip of deep blue carpet, well faded – Presbyterian blue, we called it. I nodded a silent greeting to this one and that as had been the habit, but the people who sat at the end were praying, all their heads bowed, or else they were skimming through their Bibles. Women adjusted children's shoelaces and men stared blankly in the direction of the organ. None looked up, not one, and so I just lifted my chin and marched straight into the big boxy Campbell pew, which was now a refuge. In it I bowed my head, but instead of praying I was looking at my feet in their doughty bunion-shaped shoes, calming myself by recalling places they'd carried me in happier times: the lanes that ran past the gate of The Cairn, the Big Meadow waving all heavy with grass, the room where I'd cradled and sung. But I was making myself sad, so I raised my head and looked to the ladies in the choir. Molly herself was at the harmonium but she was busy, looking over some sheet music with Sarah and didn't seem to notice me, so I determined to look around no further.

The service that day was taken by the Reverend Boyd, who came down to greet me briefly before he entered the pulpit, but for the following hour of worship, as he preached the Word, I sat like a fire untended. The text that morning was Daniel 9:9: 'The Lord our God is merciful and forgiving, even though we have rebelled against him.' But I'm afraid I didn't attend to it much.

When the service was ended, I didn't stir, didn't want to be caught in the chilly tide, be embarrassed by abrupt greetings, so I just stayed breathing slow and deep, alone in the pew. As I sat I noticed how little had changed: the boards on the floor were still scrubbed to a whitish grey and the old red runner on the moth-eaten cushion had never been mended. I listened as the people behind me jostled and nudged their way to the door, and I waited, wanting to be last. I looked again at the walls: they were white and bare, colder than ever; the plaster bulged and crumbled, and outside the long lonely graveyard grasses seemed to rush right by the plain glass of the windows. At last I got to my feet and picked up my gloves. In the aisle ahead of me suited bodies shuffled, their backs fixed in a blur of blue serge and bright satin, and I was quite unnoticed. It was as if no one knew I was there. I felt my chest tighten, but it was only the old heartburn complaint again, I was sure, that I'd fix with a spoonful of baking soda.

Outside I pushed through the groups of people lingering around the door and went to get my bicycle. I had just pulled it out from the hedge when, looking up, I chanced to see someone I didn't know, a total stranger, come out the church door. He was a youngish man, about James's age, and all by himself. I screwed up my eyes and peered from under my hat. How had I missed seeing him, for I was the last out? Perhaps he'd tipped into the vestry for a word and was only now departing? If that was the case Mr Boyd would know who he was, but I'd never dare ask. Visitors were rare indeed in our part of the world so I took my time adjusting my bicycle saddle. He was tall with a well-cut face, unsmiling and thin, could do with a bit of feeding up. He didn't delay at the door for the customary fellowship either but strode out to the gravel, where, taking a few steps back, he stood and stared hard at the church as if he'd never seen one before. Maybe, I thought, he might be an architect, but by the cut of him he was more like a tourist: not a sign of a Sunday suit, only a raincoat and check trousers, if you wouldn't mind, and yellow suede shoes. All of the people stood back too, gawking and gaping, and Sam Hanna going after made as if to address him, but the fellow just turned on his toe, put on his hat and without speaking a word was gone down the path to the road before you could say 'Boo!' I shook my head. It took 'all sorts and conditions of men' to make up God's creatures.

At the gate I paused and looked back, saw the congregation slowly dispersing in twos and threes, making their way to their traps and carts at the back of the church, and I stood there alone for a minute: heard the crows scatter their broken calls over the ridge of the roof and over the parcelled graves, saw ragweed that should have been doused by the sexton still blooming bright yellow. And of a sudden I knew a great lonesomeness: Ballymount was become a cold dead thing in my chest.

CHAPTER 49

As one year and then another passed by, I knew I was all but cut off from the world, although Cissie still came and we'd go walking together on evenings the rain held off. And there was Anna May Reilly too, who it seemed would never leave off. Poor Anna May was half simple, I sometimes thought, but it's the simple ones, the ones who seem to lack the full shilling, that are often most cunning. I'd never welcome her, but I wouldn't send her away either for she brought news and plenty of harmless gossip: how Benny Maguire had been held overnight in the barracks and how a young one had got herself into trouble by staying out late. Anna May would have heard of course that I'd left Ballymount, but she knew more than that.

Anyway I wasn't long in from a walk in the woods one late September day, had just taken off my hat and replaced the pin, when I heard her familiar rattling at the door. Sabbath or no Sabbath, it was all the same to her and indeed to myself any more. Taking my time, I folded away my scarf before opening the door. There she stood holding out a porringer of blackberries, juice staining her fingers, running purple over her wrists. 'The hedges are full of them, missus.'

I let her in but reminded her she'd come at an ill-chosen time, and I'd things to be at, though in truth there was only the bite in the scullery safe to be eaten and the fields to be wandered alone.

'You could make a small jam tart with these, missus, maybe a bit to have in a tin when he brings her calling.'

Outraged, I turned my face to the wall and moved to stir up the range, heard her set the dribbling porringer down on the table behind me. My impulse then was to cast her and her berries into the yard, but I said not a word.

She gave her old cough. 'I hear his wife's expecting.'

At that the familiar sickness welled up in me once more and the clamminess and the smothering black futility; surely I could bear it no longer. But her eyes were a-glint like two little live things behind the thick glasses. 'And isn't that grand, God bless her! And what a good daddy himself will be!'

I pulled open the door of the press in the corner, fumbled and found a bit of crochet I was working at: it was a mat for the teapot to sit on. I untwisted the purple and yellow strands and pierced them firmly with my hook.

'Is any of this your business?'

'Well, missus, to be sure it's my business!' She leaned nearer to me, impertinent, cockier than ever before, 'Didn't I half rear the cratur when you were too busy to know? Taught him his first ABCs, I did, and gave him a love for Our Holy Mother.' She picked up the porringer then and wiped her fingers on the hem of her coat. 'And isn't it enough for you that he's a teacher now with the Brothers and herself a holy pillar in the Church of the Sacred Heart?'

Oh, the impudence! Yet what else could I expect from her? I swallowed the outrage that was smouldering in me. 'A bruised reed shall he not break, and the smoking flax shall he not quench.' That scripture rose up in my mind to restrain me yet it served only to cast me back to the fields and to Thomas, and my poor old hands all reddened and raw from pulling the stalks.

And she stood there still, stooped a bit yet brazen. 'But enough said, missus. Let the hare sit now. Let bygones be bygones.'

I laid the crochet down on my lap and twisted the strands around my fingers until they hurt, and my eyes grew warm and soft with tears as I watched her open the press and take down a bowl for the berries. 'Stay where you are, missus. I know my way round, and I'll just pull over the kettle now and make you a sup of tea, for you looks a bit pasty, if you don't mind me saying.' She spooned some tea out of the caddy. 'As your poor husband, God rest him, used to say, there's no use crying over milk that's spilled on the floor.' No, there was no use, no use at all. My son was going to father a child, a Roman child, and I could see them all lining up in a rage at my side: Thomas and his father Isaiah, and behind that again old Cromwell Campbell, Isaiah's father. But I wasn't crying; instead there was anger, spitting and sizzling on the stone in my heart. She poured the tea into a mug, but I pushed it away. With that she muttered something about 'helping out', picked up the porringer and went off, banging the door behind her.

It had grown very dark outside: the weather had changed, and rain poured down in a deluge over the yard, sheeting byre and haggart. In the gullet outside the back door, water spouted and foamed, and the drops on the kitchen window slid heavy and fat like slugs, but myself I hadn't a tear. And the kitchen too grew dark as night and it only four o'clock.

CHAPTER 50

Sunnyside, winter 1982

Sometimes when I can't sleep I go over in my head the old hymns we used to sing. I remember so many of them and this night it's the words 'change and decay in all around I see' that again ring through me. I know indeed that change can be a real blessing, lightening many a burden in unseen ways. On the haskiest day, for example, with a wind from the east and the fields turned to grey, change can come limping in through the night, and when we're all fast asleep the bud can turn and a leaf move, the shoot get greedy for light, and all be done so silently, so unfussily, just its own inspiration breathing the seed and the bud and the plant. That's how quietly change can come. And that's a good thing.

But it's easy to think like this, fall into step with God when the lights are dimmed and my pains damped down, but I have to face the fact that my anger refuses to yield to change, and the memory of those terrible days lies like rough salt on a wound. Almost weekly, from this one and that I heard of his doings: his visits to an RC chapel on Sundays . . . so on and so forth.

Reverend Boyd visits me often, tries to bring comfort, give me release, I suppose, from my pent-up emotion. He talks about faith and the weather, and sometimes, in the same hushed tones we always used when we mentioned Rome, he talks about things out there in the world: the IRA hunger strikes, the carry-on in the Dáil with Charlie Haughey and Garret FitzGerald and so on. Now I don't know what good any of that is to me, but the minister is kind and means well.

CHAPTER 51

I think they were married a good few years when she – I must call her his wife – entered my life again. It was strange to realize I hadn't seen her up close since that day long ago by the river. Life has a funny way of weaving people in and out of our years, some not seen for the longest time and then they turn up in the most startling of places. She stood on the step in front of me now in a bottle-green frock and well-polished shoes, trim and shy, a handbag over her wrist and her eyes shining, daring to smile. She was almost as I remembered her, though thinner in the face, tired-looking, and I sensed she was fearful the way she knocked at the front door instead of coming round the back. We seemed to stand a good while there on the step, looking at each other, and I waited for her to break the silence.

'Mrs Campbell.'

The cold air was sobering, discouraging. One Mrs Campbell to another. How nervous she was.

'I'm Dolores.'

Well, of course I knew who she was, her name and her breed. And, as I went on looking at her standing there in the blue arc of sky, I thought, *So this is the one who now comforts my son; this is the one who knows his secrets, the one who brings him to Mass.* I bit on my tongue as the familiar weakening pangs twisted in my stomach, but I rallied at length and invited her in.

We went together to the parlour, which was still a chilly room even in summer but apt enough for today, for the sorry scene that was taking place. I showed her to the horsehair sofa, and she sat down, drawing her skirt under her just as she'd done with her coat that day long ago by the river. I took my seat across from her in what had been Thomas's favourite chair. It had been handsome once in its red sateen but was now a bit frayed at the corners and, like so many of my things, in need of a patch. But the cushions were still good and the picture too of the stag hunt, and the scripture text I'd worked in cross stitch: BEHOLD, HOW GOOD AND HOW PLEASANT IT IS FOR BRETH- REN TO DWELL TOGETHER IN UNITY. PSALMS 133:1. And I wondered if she'd notice this text and if it would make her think, for I felt an urge to draw her out, reason with her some- how, but the impulse passed and I just sat, lacing my fingers together, looked at her fixedly. 'Why are you here?'

She wrung her handbag in her long thin fingers, wrung so tight that her knuckles whitened and I could have been moved to pity if I'd let myself.

'I came to ask if you'd be good enough to visit us some time, meet the children.'

So that was it. I stiffened. 'Did James send you?'

'No.'

'Why then?'

We sat away from each other, not looking, until in the end she faltered, 'He is deeply troubled.'

I breathed in as a tide of hopelessness welled up in me, sour- ing my throat.

'What can anyone do about that, pray tell?'

'I thought you might be able.'

I fixed my eyes on her now, felt hard as nails and thought

of all I had lost and of all that my son had lost. 'Able to do what?'

She sighed and looked away; her face was flushed as if she might cry but she didn't answer.

'What did you think I might do?' I asked, savouring the cruelty. 'Did you think I could undo what he has done?'

She shook her head. 'That can never be undone. But he loves you; you are his mother.' She was granting me that much.

'And he's troubled, you say?'

She nodded, her eyes brimming. 'My own parents are troubled too, both of them very upset. They didn't come to our wedding either.'

'Well,' and I stood up, ramrod straight, 'we'll all just have to get over this, won't we!'

Oh, how hard I felt and cold, for I knew I'd never really get over it. I could pretend to however, and something prompted me to say, 'All right then. Tell him I'll get a lift to the house some day soon. I've been told where you live, on the other side of Crockban.'

'It's quite a long way,' she faltered. 'I could come here and drive you . . .'

I thanked her but said I'd find my own way in my own time. When I'd shown her out, I stood looking after her as she hurried across the yard, watched as she started up a car, and I couldn't help thinking what a pity it was she was Catholic for there was something about her.

CHAPTER 52

A month later I kept my word. I booked Jim Brown's hackney car for half past three and asked him to call back for me at seven. This visit would be a grim ordeal, and I went only to perform my Christian duty just as I'd been taught all my life: 'Love your enemies, bless them that curse you, do good to them that hate you, and pray for them which despitefully use you, and persecute you.' But there was no love in me; it was all shrivelled up like dried ferns.

Marching up the tidy path to their house on an afternoon that was grey with a kind of a haar at only four o'clock, I noted the neat edges and the well-trimmed borders and guessed my son had been trying to recreate what he might wish to have known at The Cairn: a garden where a child might play and themselves sit in the cool of an evening, not that his father and I had ever done much sitting about in a garden. The gutters were in good shape too, and the paintwork, for he'd always had hands on him in spite of his soft ways with poetry and the like. Maybe he should have stayed on and worked the land, for he'd been given the chance, worked so hard that there'd have been no room for folly. I stood for a minute at the door looking around and about, but there wasn't as much as a field to be seen, only rows and rows of the same class of house with lace-curtained windows, and I imagined he'd be sitting inside nervously waiting. As I stood, I thought of the years I'd let slip since the last time we met, how many I couldn't now tell, but I knew that the last was the time he'd come with the shawl.

When I knocked, it was she who greeted me, all warmth and welcomes, but I resisted her overtures, smoothed down the leather of my handbag and straightened my scarf. He came himself next, hand out and smiling. But here was no suppliant, no docile person; here was a tall filled-out man in an Aran jumper and long tan shoes, standing and blocking the doorway. Talking and talking in the face of my silence, he laid a hand on my shoulder and drew me into the house, introduced me to their girls, aged about four or five, Mary and Bridie. They were well-mannered children and I was the grandmother they'd heard of, their daddy's mammy. They were very shy with me at first and I, in truth, with them, but when I asked them to tell me their names and their ages and so on and what class they were in at school, they slowly lost their reserve: stood at my knee, grew ready to chatter and laugh, and I felt my heart warm. But when they started to tell about Sister Josephine and her hard sums, they were hushed and sent out by their father. 'Go play,' he told them in the gentle voice I remembered.

So we went on sitting, the three of us, in that little room with its cheap green carpet and plastic-covered chairs. She kept a good house, I had to say, for there wasn't as much as a fleck of dust to be seen. Naturally I was on the lookout for signs of Rome, but found few, although the pale oblong shapes on the wallpaper where the holy pictures must have hung didn't escape my notice. They'd removed them for my visit no doubt but they needn't have bothered, for a stoup of holy water remained on the wall by the door and rosary beads lay curled on the windowsill.

In the squeaking uneasiness of that room which they called the lounge she poured tea, her hand shaking, while he talked and babbled some more about The Cairn and Ballymount and the harvest and Hanna and how great it was we had 'rural electrification' and all that had happened in the years since the war ended.

She passed a plate. 'It's kind of you to come, Mrs Campbell, in spite of the weather.' And then struggling on, 'I hope your journey here to Crockban was pleasant.'

But I just sat unpitying, gazed past the tea tray, past the rosary beads and the holy water, and thought of my hurt and the one who had hurt me. He sat across from me now with his head thrown back and hands clasped over a knee drawn up, full of seeming good humour as though the world went right with him. Yet now and again, as if forgetting, he'd untwist himself to crick and crack at his knuckles the way he used to when pressed. He looked pale, I thought, was a bit too thin for his height, and for a minute I felt myself wanting to take him home, wanting to rescue him. But in a flash I was casting the idea away. This big man here on the sofa beside me was no mere simpleton, just a great fool who'd sold his birthright to Rome.

When tea was over, he pulled out his pipe. I frowned, was preparing to censure, remind him his body was the temple of the Holy Spirit, when she chipped in with a little smile, 'The girls often say that everyone else has grannies, and they want their own.'

Then, putting his pipe down and tapping out the dottle, James looked at me full in the face, suddenly serious. 'The children do wonder why their granny doesn't visit us, you know.'

There was almost a dog-like plea in his eyes, but I shrugged my cardigan up on my shoulders for the room was like ice, and 'Hm' was all I could think further to say. She shifted in her chair, and I burned once more to think of that day long ago when she'd appeared with her sister.

When she spoke again, smiling still, her tone was shyly inviting: 'Mrs Campbell, the schools are all closed for the summer, and I believe my James has some time on his hands.'

She beamed over at him, and he responded right away as if grateful, 'Yes, Mother, I have plenty of time. Term is over and I've nothing at all to do beyond tend our wee bit of grass and coach a few fellows in Latin. Besides,' and he rubbed at his knuckles, 'the girls are more and more impatient to get to know their grandmother so maybe if I was to bring them over to The Cairn sometime . . . do a few turns . . .' He bent down to me then, still talking, and I felt his hand warm on my shoulder and noticed the bitten nails.

'They've heard their granny can tell a good story.'

'Hm.' I refused to smile.

'You could tell them the one about the elephant and the tailor?'

The two of them chuckled together at that, but I turned away for I didn't know what I was feeling.

'Oh Mrs Campbell,' she said then, composing herself, 'James could quite easily drive over and give you a hand now and then?'

'Of course I could.'

He jumped up at that, attentive again and lively. He'd really become such a vigorous man, Greek scholar gone, Ballymount gone, and he'd intimidate me now with his new fancy ways if I let him.

'And the girls would be only delighted – I'd show them the loft and the haggart, bring them out to the paddock, even show them the room I was born in.'

She laughed lightly at that. 'But would you believe it, Mrs Campbell, they've never once been to a farm.'

I twisted the ring on my finger and lifted my chin. 'Oh, there's not much left of a farm any more.'

Sitting cold as a flint and upright, I thought of the broken fencing and the moss growing over the cobbles, the cart rotting in the stable, and I couldn't help myself but I'd cool his heels for him now, bring him into the light of reality. I cleared my throat. 'Your father had hoped for better, James.' I looked down at the floor. 'He'd hoped there'd be someone to inherit the place, someone to take up the mantle. But,' and I bit my lip, looked at the ceiling, 'sadly, my son, that isn't to be. You dirtied your bib.'

Like the fog which was thickening outside, a swag of grey silence was slowly seeping into the room, curling about us, smudging my words, flattening them out on the walls, wooden and colourless. And I thought now of how surprised the little solicitor had looked when I told him neither my son nor his children would ever inherit the Campbell place, the place where his father and I had laboured year after year. But let that be as it might.

And the silence curled on, long and mean and malicious, broken only by the sighs of our breathing and the chatter of birds at a drainpipe outside near the window. To tell the truth, I didn't know what further to say after that and was greatly relieved to hear the children's voices drift in from outside. They were playing a game with a chant I remembered so well: 'Lavender's blue, dilly dilly. Lavender's green. When you are king, dilly dilly, I shall be queen.' And my heart softened somewhat so I said, in a kinder voice, 'You must know there's nothing to see at The Cairn any more, no turns to be done, but you can bring the girls if you like, though I'm seldom at home myself.'

Now he probably knew I was lying, but I wouldn't be there if they came, for it'd be more than I could bear to see any papists trample through Campbell land.

It began to look as if it might thunder, and she rose to flick on a light. He called the children in and they clamoured for him to read. I glanced at the well-filled bookcase and saw how eagerly he went, the children at his heels. 'What will I read?'

He turned to me with a wink. '*The Pilgrim's Progress*?'

'Oh no, Daddy, not that!' And the older one laughed. 'Go on with *The Selfish Giant*.'

'OK,' he agreed and turned to me. 'It's a little story by Oscar Wilde.'

And as I listened, he began to read, a child on each of his knees. On and on he read, his voice taking on a melancholy tone as if recalling something: '"'I cannot understand why the Spring is so late in coming,' said the Selfish Giant, as he sat at the window and looked out at his cold white garden; 'I hope there will be a change in the weather.' But the Spring never came, nor the Summer."'

I soon lost track of the story itself, heard only my son's pleasing tones and the strength in his voice, the firmness of purpose and the occasional crack when it broke for some reason. And I was taken back to the times when I was the one who had done the reading, to the times he could do nothing wrong in my eyes.

Now, as he read and turned a page, I studied his face, recalling the day long ago when in a fit of childish bad temper he'd kicked over the bucket of skim set aside for the calves, and his father had taken the cane as the milk pooled blue in the gutter, and it was I who cried and cried. He was my own precious boy then, my little companion and friend. Nor could I but think of the times when, with the jobs all done and his father away to the Lodge, the two of us dandered alone in the lanes where the blackthorn frothed white on the hedgerows and the broom burned orange, and how looking for nests we'd sometimes startle a rabbit.

But I came back to the story he was reading – about children who played in a giant's garden – and the girls, enraptured, hung on his words: ' "The Autumn gave golden fruit to every garden but to the Giant's garden she gave none. 'He is too selfish,' she said." ' He read as nicely as ever he read, but at this point he closed the book. 'Now, little ladies, it's getting late, and that's where we stop, so away you go.' Then, as if under orders, the children bade me farewell and I felt their young lips on my cheek like rose petals fallen, but I brushed them away as the last words he'd read still echoed: ' " 'too selfish,' she said".' Too selfish.

Not very long after that a car pulled up outside: Jim Brown was back. My son came with me to the door where we stood for a minute, just the two of us, lingering together on the step; for a second I thought he made as if to come close, as if there was something else to be done, some little forgotten thing to be said before I set off. But the time was short; the car couldn't wait, so I swiftly drew on my gloves, settled my bag on my arm and nodded to Jim.

Arriving home, I threw down my things in annoyance. I'd wasted my time. Nothing had changed.

CHAPTER 53

Sunnyside, winter 1982

That was the summer of 1951, and between that terrible visit and my own decline the years echoed hollow and sombre, and often I strain now to measure them out, the way you'd count buttons, one at a time. But they mostly come in a blur and pass swiftly away like a weaver's shuttle. I remember how, crossing the yard, I'd sometimes stop and look up to the loft where the rivers of prayer had flowed to the Heavenly Throne and I'd shake my head. Sometimes I endeavoured to speak about doubt to the Reverend Boyd when he called to The Cairn, mention my sense of futility, perhaps even open my heart, but I found no occasion for that, and so he continued, albeit kindly, to offer me Bible and prayer when Bible and prayer didn't work any more.

Summer passed after summer and then once more the end of a year. Now I never liked Christmas itself much and was always glad it was over, even though from the time I was left on my own Cissie and I had spent it together. I'd always found it a time of remembering, even more than November when we got out the poppies, and remembering never did me much good. Yet there were times when James was a child and Thomas still in the full of his health when the Christmas went over quite nicely. In the days leading up, I'd make a big cake full of raisins and cherries, and

Thomas would look in the woods for holly, and Santy would come through the snow to see James. It always felt jolly, yet no neighbours came to The Cairn that day, and aside from going to Ballymount to sing a few carols we didn't stir out ourselves. Then in the evening, the big dinner of roast beef and plum pudding over, Thomas would fodder the cattle before stretching out on the sofa and falling asleep. That night had a kind of holy quiet – something inexpressible hung in the air – and with the work all done, James and I would play one of his games – Ludo or Snakes and Ladders – but cards were strictly forbidden. Christmas lasted only the one day then, and when the new year came, we didn't mark that at all except once when I went on my own to the Methodist church in the town to attend a Watchnight Service at midnight. After Thomas's death, James and I tried our best to be festive at Christmas, cheery the rest of the time, but without much success; it was all really just more of the same: the McKinleys and Williamsons, Sam Hanna and Ballymount and sometimes a dance in the Lodge.

And so life lurched on, carrying me with it, albeit slower and slower, in house and in garden, each year getting shorter, a little bit rounder. My son drove over once or twice with his wife and his children, but I made sure to be always 'about to go out' when they came; never encouraged their visits. And my neighbours were very discreet: seldom mentioned his name to my face, just spoke on occasion of a gate left open. Even Cissie said nothing and she'd have known plenty, but Cissie and I only had words whenever she talked of 'forgive and forget', neither of which I could ever do. And when the doctor advised her against climbing even the smallest of hills, Anna May as good as took to her bed and died not long after. So the source of most of my news ran dry.

Of course 'the lad', as I'd begun to think of him, came on his own out of duty at Christmas, came on my birthdays too, never missed one all down the years, and latterly drove up the lane in a fancy red car, scattering the chickens. He went on honouring his mother just as he'd honoured his father, couldn't let go of the words he had learned as a Sabbath School child: 'Hearken unto thy father that begat thee, and despise not thy mother when she is old.' (Proverbs 23:22) This text had been well drummed in, and I'd often longed to erase it, rub it out of his being, for those visitations of his made twice in a year grew to be mutual torment. They were cold and tight, no room for either of us, and sometimes I thought he'd surely give up repeating them.

Yet life was manageable enough in those days on my own, although I grew into myself considerably over the years and I had to pray I wouldn't get odd. When I went for my monthly check-up, Dr McGettigan, a shrewd old man, well aware of the Campbell history, advised me to look after myself. Keep busy and active, he said, so I developed a system to keep myself right.

I just got along with things then and for a good while there was really nothing I couldn't handle. I was still in my fifties and fairly spry: knitting and sewing bootees and bonnets for impoverished babies; rubbing and scrubbing day in, day out, as if I was wiping away all my worries and woes, erasing time itself. And yet withal I was ever lonesome and sad, something paining my being, plaguing my nerves. And while dusting and sweeping that big empty house, I was most loath to enter the parlour for it was here that the visitations took place. Here's where he and I sat, when he came, among books and prizes, eyeing each other from opposite poles. Oh, I had to struggle so hard against misery and nerves and as my hair slowly turned white and my joints stiffened up, I clung fast to a wholesome routine of housework and garden, and tending to the chickens. I still went walking with Cissie, no longer through green leafy lanes, however, but on wide tarry roads that seemed to lead nowhere.

Once in a while, I went on my own as far as the river, but folk seldom fished there any longer with all the new licensing laws, yet here in the quiet I'd think I could hear the faint plop of a bait in the water, hear his soft voice through the drift of the wind in the trees, and I'd go back home, heavy of heart, to prepare for the Beginners' Pottery class I'd signed up for.

All in all, it was Cissie who kept me going those times: at her nudge I gave in and bought an electric washing machine – it was called a twin-tub – and an electric cooker and even an Electrolux to suck up the dust. The Cairn was so easy to manage then, compared with my early days: just the flick of a switch and lo! the rooms were all brightly lit up, it was goodbye to the paraffin smell and the weaving shadows that would ruin your eyes if you were trying to put in a few stitches. One year, I boldly added a telly as a Christmas box to myself and Cissie often came over 'to view'. There was only the BBC at first with Blue Peter *and* Dixon of Dock Green *and so on but on New Year's Eve 1961 we got our very own Teilifís Éireann, and it was wonderful to see Dev addressing us both from the end of the dresser, George Mitchell reading the news, then people dancing and twirling in the Gresham Hotel. That was a splendid occasion, and when the national anthem was over that night, Cissie slyly drew from her pocket a small wee bottle of whiskey and wished me a happy new year. Now of course I didn't drink any whiskey myself but she was my friend and I was glad to see her so merry.*

During all those years, I secretly pined to live in the town, get away from the wet and the muck, thought if only I could sell that old place I'd move to a 'semi-detached' with a neighbour over the wall like in Coronation Street, *and I'd never be lonely again or sick with my nerves. But the thought of a move and a selling-up made me sad, although I was thankful I'd made things secure. I was getting to be an old woman now, and when the time came the solicitor would seek out that distant cousin of Thomas's, and that would be the end of The Cairn.*

CHAPTER 54

Ballymount, July 1970

Every single fourth Tuesday in the month I went to visit
Thomas's grave, which lay in the church grounds near enough
to the front door. I was feeling the years a bit now, knew my
heart wasn't the best and that any visit could be my last before
I'd yield up the ghost, as they say, and 'lie down with my
ancestors'.

In all the years since Thomas's death I missed only a couple
of visits, like the time I took ill with bronchitis, so 'going to the
grave' had become a ritual. Here I'd lay a few flowers from
the garden and stand and think about Thomas and read again
the inscription on the headstone. Aside from his name and the
date of his death, the stone said only, THE ANCIENT OF DAYS.
It was actually old Mr McGoldrick's suggestion that these
words be used, and I'd listened carefully while he'd explained
their meaning. Yet, even as he was explaining, I couldn't but
hear the terrible words of the prophet Daniel: 'As I looked,
thrones were placed, and the Ancient of Days took his seat – the
court sat in judgment and the books were opened.' But Mr
McGoldrick was dead and gone and I wasn't now comforted.

That burial was such a long time ago and yet I regretted
those words each time I saw them. I read them on every visit

and stood reading them again this warm day. They no longer frightened me for what could this Ancient of Days have to do with me or my son, or even Thomas? I stooped as well as I could to scoop back some of the stones on the surface of the grave and gather up the mossy vase, which needed a wash. It was very quiet there: the church was locked up, no sermons being preached, no boots scuffling the gravel, and there was room for my thoughts, which weren't as sad that day as on many another. Here in the deep countryside the air was pure, the birdsong clear, and as I tipped out the old blooms and the sour green water, I sensed in myself something like a tremble of hope, the merest shiver.

I had just put the vase back in its place by the headstone when I heard a car engine thrumming behind the low wall that gave on to the road and I was annoyed at my peace being broken. A door slammed and boots crunched the gravel. I prayed it wouldn't be the sexton or even one of the elders. Glancing furtively through the headstones, I saw a man in a green shirt and at once recognized him. Funny the way you never forget the singular events of the past and yet can't remember what you had for your dinner. It was the man I'd seen linger that faraway lonesome day as we'd filed out of church at the close of Meeting. He looked older now, a bit stouter perhaps, and I watched him closely. He seemed a bit lost, looked all around him, made as if to go to the church door but then turned back. I made myself thin behind the headstone for I really wanted no intrusion and was hoping he'd go away, but he was continuing to search around as if expecting to find something, or someone.

Then the next minute I heard him call in a hearty voice, 'Oh, hello, there you are! Mrs Campbell, I think?' And it was as if he'd found me. I leaned back further into the stone, suspicious and alert.

'I hope I'm not disturbing your peace.'

His voice was brisk, energetic, and without waiting for me to respond he came over to where I was hunkered and, bending over, the way tall men do, he rubbed at his chin. 'Interesting inscription that! "The Ancient of Days".' And he went on standing as if deciding on something, and yet it was none of his business what we'd written on our headstone. He was putting me into a fluster, and my hands trembled as I separated the long green stalks and laid them out in a row by the coping. The lupins were poor enough that summer because of the rain, but the dog daisies were good and prolific, even the ditches were high with them.

At length, for I was no flower arranger, I managed to bundle most of them into some kind of posy and set them into the vase. It was very warm that afternoon – the wind had died and the birds grown silent – and I was eager to get done and be on my way to Cissie's, so I just couldn't believe my ears when his voice came on again, persistent. 'I think,' says he, standing back, his head to one side, 'those words are quite unfathomable.'

Quite taken aback at his interest, I stood up and folded my arms.

He was polite, a gentleman too, I supposed, with that finely shaped head, and he spoke like one who'd been educated, but what could those words possibly matter to him? He sat down on the kerb of a nearby grave and took out a paper bag and a flask. 'This is your church, I believe?' He nodded towards it, a sandwich in his hand. 'And you're still a faithful attender?'

I must say he wasn't slow with the questions but he'd a sincere and earnest manner and I was beginning to take to him.

'I think I've seen you before?' I parried. 'After Meeting one Sunday, many years back.'

He'd been loitering then too, much as he loitered now: hanging around, taking things in, sizing Ballymount up. As he bit into the sandwich, I couldn't help asking what took him here again to this back-of-beyond after such a long time. He said he'd just come back from abroad: he'd been living in New Zealand the past fourteen years and was glad to be home now for good. My curiosity was getting the better of me: 'Would you be a Presbyterian by any chance?'

'Yes and no. I was even a Presbyterian minister once.' He shook my hand: 'The name is Wilson McHenry.'

I scrutinized him as he went on lazily munching, his body stretched out and his tanned face turned to the sun. He looked like no Presbyterian minister I had ever known, and half of me didn't believe him. I eyed him warily and with a degree of reproach. 'Why not still?'

'Because I sinned once and fell short in my youth.' His words tumbled out on the grassy mounds and over my sleeping forefathers.

'What do you mean?' I spat out the question, but he just went on looking at me, smiling and eating, and I felt my face redden in anger. 'Why are you saying these things to me?'

'Oh, I'm from not too far away, you see, and I suppose it's because we're both Presbyterians that I don't need to explain how wary we are as a people, how guarded – you know all that. But I'll try to make myself clear.' He tugged at a shoelace, and I looked away, remembering.

Then he turned to me. 'You and I carry the baggage of our tradition, and while most of it's good stuff, it can be damn heavy.'

I fixed my eyes on the flowers that trembled in my hand, not liking the way he said 'damn'.

'Isn't that so, Mrs Campbell?' he persisted. Now he was finishing off the sandwich and screwing the top back on his flask. 'Oh, I don't mean the Bible's teaching or the Church's faith as such.' And he frowned. 'It's the rancour and divisiveness that religion breeds; that's the heavy stuff. And it's not only the Presbyterian Church, I might add, but all Churches, even the ones in New Zealand.'

I was finding it hard to follow him, but he went on talking almost as if I wasn't there. My hands shook as I took the flowers one at a time back out of the vase and began to rearrange them in earnest. His words were bringing me back to Ballymount, and I was hearing all over again the stern preaching and the spiteful murmurings in the sewing circle.

'I've heard about you and your son.' His eyes met mine. 'Like me, your son fell short.'

The softness had left his voice now, and instead there was something else. I could almost feel the edges of it, rasping and raw, like a drill. I pulled myself up and stood to face him while shadows of pain and discomfort fell across me once more and the leaves of the poplar nearby trembled silver.

'Did you turn too?'

He smiled. 'Not the way your son did. In another way.'

He looked into the sky then, his face all screwed up as if searching for what he might say.

'I fell in love with another man's wife.'

Oh! I breathed in. Well, here was scandal indeed for, in spite of my anger at Churches, I still held it firm that ministers should always be pure, free from lust and adultery. So I had nothing whatever to say to this. Here indeed was a double fault.

He looked me straight in the eye. 'I had to resign.'

'How long ago was that?'

'Nineteen forty-five.'

'My son was married that year.'

Ignoring this, he went on: 'I was then a very young man, had barely begun my ministry. But let me explain how I come to be here. You remember old McGoldrick, always a bit of a stickler, and how distraught he was and angry when your son went over to Rome?' He looked a bit sad now. 'But you hardly need me to remind you of that.'

No, I remembered it all very clearly: the manse and the sun pouring in and the books, all those books proclaiming against us.

'Well, on that occasion McGoldrick, who was in his seventies at the time, sought the support and advice of a younger colleague who had charge of the nearby congregation of Ballyturk, and this colleague, believe it or not, happened to be the Reverend Charles McHenry, my own late father.'

In spite of the hot afternoon, I was suddenly very alert, my attention fixed firm on his words.

'And I chanced to overhear their discussions . . . about your own son, as it later turned out.' He looked down at his shoes now, muddy brown shoes, and he cleared his throat. 'And although I didn't know the miscreant they spoke of, I was deeply interested, being in trouble myself.'

Now I was beginning to understand.

'But my father,' and he smiled at me, 'was more sympathetic to your case than McGoldrick was, and I'm sure he'd have told that gentleman as much. For my father was suffering greatly himself at the time, when I, his own son, had so foolishly erred.' He looked thoughtful again. 'But to give Father his due, he stood by me throughout all my trials, helped me move to New Zealand, where I have lived ever since, ministering in a more liberal branch of the Reformed Faith. I've never married.'

His voice was breaking over me coldly like water.

'So, you see I know at first hand how you suffered because of that marriage. Chastised, "with whips and scorpions", as the Bible says somewhere. One Church took your son and another rebuked you for it.'

I clung to the gravestone, protesting weakly that God was good in his providence, but my words sounded hollow even to myself. I couldn't in truth construct any bridge between God and those Churches: the Roman and Presbyterian.

He pulled at a tuft of grass between his shoes. 'And in my case? Well, they asked me to go, of course. Oh, in the nicest possible way: nothing public, just some well-intentioned advice along with a letter and a cheque. I don't think my father ever forgave the Church for its harshness, but he said not a word and continued in faithful ministry till the day he died.' He paused here to wipe his forehead. 'But you,' and his voice was almost a whisper, 'you got no letter or cheque.' He looked at me keenly now. 'Listen. I'm a young renegade no longer, but from the time I heard of your son's conversion and marriage, I pitied you and determined to locate you one day to offer encouragement, give you some kind of assurance that all was not lost, in fact much to be redeemed.'

Now I didn't know where all this was leading, and he was saying so much all at once that I felt a touch of the old dizzy feeling sweep through me again and hoped I wouldn't go into a faint as he talked away, oblivious of my discomfort.

'Yes, you did indeed see me that day in Ballymount Church. It was shortly before I went abroad. I considered talking to you then, but the time wasn't right for you; it was all too raw.' He cleared his throat again and looked away, hesitating. 'At first I wanted to rescue you, shield you from the deluge of incrimination that I knew would be falling on you as it had on me, but now,' and he looked at me closely, his eyes almost kind, 'it's your own self I want to rescue you from.'

And with that I felt of so little account, just a small thing tamped down, smothering in the smouldering greesha of old anger and pain, embers of a fire almost forgotten but not quite put out.

When he spoke again, it was in a voice that was curiously composed. 'You know,' he murmured, 'God has no Church and no religion.' And he laughed out loud as if he'd just discovered something amusing. 'God is not a Catholic or a Jew or a Muslim, not even a Presbyterian, and he's a hell of a sight more compassionate.'

I ignored this coarseness of speech, but I was still taking in what he said for I had never once thought of anything like that. All my life God had been 'Almighty', his name 'Jehovah, the most high over all the earth'. He'd been angry and wrathful even in times of dereliction. I sat down on the edge of the grave, looked at my shoes, then folded my arms and heard my words coming in strange little jerks, yet firm: 'Well, to tell you the truth, young sir, I've not seen much of his compassion.' And with that a great loneliness fell over the graveyard, and I gave in and started to cry. Of a sudden I was no longer in charge, no longer the one wielding sword and buckler. Weak as a newborn kitten, I felt shameful tears wash over my face, their watery saltiness scraping the back of my throat, and I did nothing to stop them as they poured out torrents of anger and grief.

And Wilson McHenry still stood. 'There is something

remaining, Harriet, something far more tormenting than grief, more destructive even than anger.'

I choked back my tears. How easily he spoke my name now as if we'd been friends for years.

'I'm not a pastor for nothing, you know.'

I could feel my eyes filling again, but I raised my head and looked at him querulously. He was standing astride the grave now, reminding me of a poem I'd learned by heart long ago in the Sixth Book about two vast legs standing alone in a desert. So like an elder he looked, poised and ready to pounce with the right answers. Yet he needed to say no more for I knew it was forgiveness he meant and hardness of heart, and I shook my head fiercely. I wasn't ready for any of that; it would take more than words to get me to open my heart, bound as it was the way I wanted, with steel, and hard.

Ignoring my confusion, he leaned towards me, his hands clasped together as if in a plea, as if he would say something more, make something perfectly plain perhaps, but I turned away. He could keep his soft preachings for others who needed a sermon; I wanted none of them, I who had crossed the gorges and gullies of life on my own. Crossly, I ground the heel of my shoe into the soft earth at the edge of the coping where an earwig was wriggling himself out from under a piece of slate and a spider carefully spinning. Then of a sudden I turned on him, fierce and undaunted, my flowers and soft-spoken ways laid by. 'There are certain things I must tell you, Mr McHenry, before you go any further.' His eyes widened at that and his jaw fell slack, but I drew myself up and, filled with new strength and a kind of fire, I spoke right into his face: 'For thirty-two years, since the death of my husband, I have knitted life for myself as well as I could. All on my own I have pulled it together piece by piece, the good and the bad, year in, year out, and I won't be spoken to now like this about what else I might do.'

He began to protest, opened his mouth, spread out his palms, but I wouldn't hear more.

'How dare you now speak of anger and grief to me, whose kindred they are?'

He looked truly dismayed, made again as if to protest, but all my ladylike habits were folded away and I continued standing before him, no longer a weakling.

'For you see, Mr McHenry, I am nurtured by anger; I make my bed with grief, and my waking hours are mottled with mourning.' I swallowed the tears that were coming again. 'When I rise in the mornings, I wish it was night, and the webs of my days hang long in their minutes.' I paused for breath, looked at the willow beyond the hedge and the calm in its delicate branches, but I had to go on: 'Oh, it's easy for you to talk like this, you who've got over your own little hurt, but mine is no little hurt, I can tell you. My son is lost and I'll never forgive him.'

After this I could say nothing more. Those long-fingered years were falling upon me again, vacant and pale like veins when the blood is stopt, and empty save for the steps-at-a-time, the waiting and watching for him to come back with the penitent word. And all the while a curse buried deep in my own heart. Nothing would ease that out, not even the slap and the suck of a spade.

And Wilson McHenry, seeming kind no longer, recoiled at the force of my anger. His face grew so dark I was suddenly frightened, fearing I'd gone too far, been carried away on the back of my troubles, taken a liberty with him who, although cast out from the Presbyterian Church, was still of the cloth and unused to being contested. Anxious, I looked to the ground and saw how the clay at my feet was all dried up, the mosses beginning to curl, and how even the earth was drawing a breath as if ready to thunder.

I drew back as he took a step closer. 'So I've got over my little hurt, you say? Well, be that as it may, rest assured there isn't a hurt in the world that's any way easy to heal. You must know that every impairment takes time to mend, time and a great deal of courage and patience.'

I shook my head again and went on looking down. This was none of his business. My affairs were my own, too deep to be aired with a stranger, and I regretted having spoken. He'd tricked me into disclosing what I'd always kept hidden away.

'Oh, believe me, it was no easy matter for me to recover myself,' he went on, 'and get fully back on my feet, and it won't be easy for you either as long as you're like that in your heart.' And now he stooped and abruptly picked up his things, stuffed the flask back into his pocket: it was as if he could take no more of me. But down at the gate he paused, looked back to where I still stood at the stone, and he called, 'Cheerio for now, Mrs Campbell. I'll be seeing you again. I'll keep in touch.'

And I heard myself calling back 'That would be nice' in a voice that was doubtful and thin as a wafer.

Quite shaken, I gathered my things together. It was getting late, and the magpies were screeching again in the tops of the pines. I looked to the heavens as I'd always done when searching for answers, saw the clouds forming in ashen loops, twisting and curling, cluttering the sky, but there wasn't a sound to be heard in the whole of the world except for a rooster crowing beyond in Hennigans' yard. Alone in Ballymount graveyard, I shivered although it was warm, with thunder rumbling and baying among the drumlins. Then I hoked the stones around the vase and, looking to the wee roundy hills, thought of the psalm so often sung in the church: 'I to the hills will lift mine eyes, from whence doth come mine aid.' But there wasn't as much as an echo from the hills; the land all about lay silent. Chilled, I buttoned my cardigan tight and headed down to the gate. Although the sun had lost its brightness, I'd still go over to see my old friend and wondered how much I would tell her.

I left the graveyard, carefully closing the gate behind me. The landscape was just as it ever had been: the hills were in place and the trees stood tall, yet something had shifted, disturbed the peace. Flustered still and disconcerted, I took my time going over to Cissie's, and to calm myself down I dandered along by way of the field and back lane. Around me, their chimneys quietly smoking, lay the prosperous farms of the Ballymount people, the Orrs, the McWhirters and Ingrams, and, stout in the distance, the square blue eaves of the church.

That strange encounter was gone from my mind.

CHAPTER 55

Sunnyside, January 1983

*Over the succeeding years, however, I grew more and more pleased
that Wilson McHenry had promised to keep in touch: my nerves
were still bad and I'd no one else in the world to speak good sense
to me any more, certainly no one else who could share my pain,
even a little, and he seemed very kind under all his preaching.
He'd settled down in a place not far from Ballymount and I gladly
encouraged his ever-more-frequent visits to The Cairn. A friend-
ship grew between us, just a flicker at first, then a sun bursting
through: he'd just be passing and would come in, drop his hat,
stay for some tea, or he'd a book to tell me about or a paper. I was
always glad of his presence. He'd just come to chat, see how I was
getting along, and I liked when he read to me out of a book, as he
often did, more relaxing for us both than talking, he said.*

*Usually, when he came, he'd turn off the telly and begin with a
verse from the Bible – the Gospels, of which he was fond, or maybe
the Psalms – and he'd follow this up with perhaps a poem or bits
from a book by someone called Emerson. I could never be sure of
what he'd read next, but it was always something with a moral or
meaning, something uplifting. And I learned so much, drew pleasure too, but he never reopened the topics of hardness of heart and
forgiveness, which was just as well for I wouldn't have wanted to*

hurt his feelings or let him see that his earlier preachings had been wasted time. Once, by pure chance, he called on my birthday, one of the days my son put in an appearance, and I saw him gravely shake James's hand, saw in some wonder how they were both of an age. That was a moment when I thought my heart would crack open, the ice in my core would melt, and tears would flow like a river . . . but the moment passed.

On the whole The Cairn was a happy enough place in those times, for along with Wilson there was Cissie of course – though now stiff with arthritis – and Sarah too. Now I hadn't seen Sarah for such a long time but she was a forgiving old soul and had never given up on me, in spite of all that had happened in Ballymount and in spite of my shameful neglect of her. Also the Reverend Boyd, who, being my pastor, would always continue to visit. Sometimes we turned on the TV and flinched at the bombings and shootings and kneecappings that went on in the North, and the brutal IRA murder of our neighbour Senator Billy Fox. Still, on many evenings that old kitchen was a very cheery place as we yarned and cracked around the fire, telling, over and over, our little humdrum stories often till late in the night.

Yet, when I'd seen the last of my friends out the door and turned off the lights, I often knew lonesome, long hours when angry thoughts buried deep would rise to the surface. Sometimes, preparing for bed, turning back the old quilt, I'd hearken back to the start of my son's downfall and how the little seeds sown in his childhood took root and were strangling me now like briars. I heard a man say on the wireless once that secret anger could strangle your life, tighten its grip like bindweed until you'd actually begin to find this anger a comfort, a blanket to be huddled into when you were all on your own: you'd be so naked and cold without it. And I think that was me.

*

I lie back in my bed now and think how the descent into real old age came upon me, took me so hasty, stole up unawares. The shadows of night came falling, silently creeping, and I began to slow down and down, the hours allotted me seeming too few and many things slipping my mind. Over the months, my spirits fell low and I slept a lot of the time, while my waking hours were tangled into a muddle with visits to doctors and chemists and the young woman who looked after my toes. Sometimes I was taken on an occasional outing by people from the town, but I wasn't able for Meeting and I never opened my Bible, which lay long untouched in the corner press.

CHAPTER 56

Coaxed by Cissie, I finally agreed I was no longer fit to live alone but would go to Sunnyside Home for the Aged and Indigent, with its nice view and the church handy. It was my last morning in The Cairn and Sam Hanna's son would be coming for me soon with his car.

Nervous and apprehensive, I'd risen too early and had to grope for my slippers in the half-light. I shuffled over to the window now and sat peering out, a hunted animal run to earth this cold January day in 1982. There wasn't much to be seen that hour, only a couple of magpies perched on the rotting hen house. There'd been a hard frost and I stood for a bit admiring traceries of ice on the pane: swirling hoary grasses, elegant ferns nestling in snowy feathers. I scraped at the glass with my nails, and before me lay stretches of Campbell fields all bandaged in white and irreverent black-fingered trees pointing skyward. Over in the Big Meadow itself, cow parsley and white-bearded elder stood frozen and stiff. Nothing stirred, not even the brush of a fox; only a solitary crow rattled its wings on the sagging roof of the byre and a couple of feral cats went mooching about the place keeping the rats down, everything blighted, the yard and the haggart in a mesh of decay. I drew a hand across my cheek. In the cold dawn the sky was sweeping itself clean, showing up shadows that slunk round the derelict stable, getting caught in the rusted thresher. Over the tops of the roundy hills I could just see the roof of Ballymount Church, and below me on a window ledge the remains of a broken cricket bat.

I went down to the kitchen then, where Cissie, kind soul, was making porridge on the Primus, for the unlit range sat cold and black. Thomas's chair was still in the corner but falling to pieces with woodworm in the legs and the back broken. Even the merciless clock was silent. We didn't speak at first, and I searched in my sleeve for a handkerchief. Around me curled the air of folk who'd gone, just for a minute it seemed, and would be back in a minute to wind up the clock, rinse out the mugs, take up a spade. Yet it wouldn't be the Campbells who'd ever return.

I looked at Cissie's broad back stooped over the pot. 'I can never thank you enough.'

'Hah!' She turned to look at me. 'It should be himself that's minding you now and here in your own place too.'

I lowered my eyes, closed the gates on the scars and crags of beetling memory. 'He's a married man, remember, with a wife to care for.'

'Well, if you hadn't fallen out with him, he'd be caring for you too.'

'You know I'd never have that.'

'Sweet Jesus!' She tore off her apron. 'You have no mercy in you and less sense. You sent that good boy away because he didn't marry to suit you.' She hesitated now. 'But there's still time to make it up. You don't want to be carrying this to the grave with you, do you?'

'It's hardly your affair what I take to my Maker.'

She shook a spoon at me, her face askew with emotion. 'Well, go ahead then. Just be the bitter, unforgiving old woman you are.' Her words stung, but I had a hardness in me like a china plate. The sun would turn to ice before I'd forgive. Then she banged down a dish on the table and took herself off out the door.

By midday the sun had shortened the shadows, and the sky was bald and hard and blue. A solitary hooded crow sat bold on a nearby fence, and I rapped the window at it, ugly scavenger, carrion-hunter, but it didn't budge, just settled its tarry black feathers and jerked its beady eyes. There were some chips of broken delft and rusty buckets lying around the yard, and if I'd been stronger I'd have gone to pick them up. No one had bothered much with picking up since Thomas died . . . how many years ago? How many since I'd fallen out with the other one so that he came back just twice in the year? And during those grey and empty diaphanous years the ivy had gone on choking the trees in the lane and the scutch had crept quietly over the lawn. How grand 'the lawn' had sounded, I thought, when first I came to The Cairn and had imagined it shaven and neat, ready for tennis perhaps. But of course no one had ever played there. And during the cast of those yawning years my heart stayed hard as a stone, supremely hard and alone, like a rock in the sea.

Relentlessly, after my two men went the spaces in my life closed down, click, click, one after the other, and finally, gradually, I drew the curtain on all outside activities, aside from keeping company with my few last friends. More and more I kept to the house, but even the stairs were a problem, so I ended up sitting most often in the kitchen among the dusty geraniums and the cactus plants with the King James Bible on my knee, and when I found it hard to read, I looked in the fire. Day by day, in the end Anna May's niece had been coming as paid help, to rake out the range, do a message and so on. She was a finer class of a person than her aunt and she called that last morning as if it was like any other.

All business, she opened my case that stood ready by the door. 'Mind if I take a look, Mrs Campbell? You can't go off to Sunnyside needing things.'

She was pert and a bit nosy, but that's how the young ones were these days, I supposed.

She looked through my things. 'Is that all you're bringing with you?'

'It's enough.'

'What about a hairnet and curlers? You'll want to look nice in there.' And then, 'Ah no! Would you look at your lovely shawl lying there on the chair! You're not going to leave that here, are you, for the mice to nest in?'

Well, you know, I could never fully forget about that shawl, and I'd thought of leaving it behind for Cissie. Yet now when it was shaken out again and held to the light, I saw once more how it flowed to silken tassels in wine-red waves. It had cost a lot, one way or another.

'Put it in then, but I'm sure I won't be using it.'

She folded it more carefully than I would have done, laid it on top of my Bible and snapped the locks fast just as the car pulled up outside.

I didn't feel too lonesome heading away through the gate and past the haggart for I knew that folk would visit: Cissie and Sarah and Wilson just as he'd promised, and of course the Reverend Boyd.

CHAPTER 57

Sunnyside, March 1983

Morning now and a pale light seeps into my room. The air is close as if I'd forgotten to open the window; the curtains don't flutter the way they should and the rooster's not crowing. It's only when I open my eyes that I see the worn-out pink eiderdown, frayed at the edges and a burn mark made by someone who'd smoked in bed. Reluctantly, I stir my legs, thin little sticks they are now, but I don't dally long for in a minute Bernadette will appear to help with my ablutions, an intrusion I deeply resent but yield to for the sake of peace. 'Needs must,' she always says, and I wonder how I ever managed at home on my own with a basin and a jug of hot water.

But she's late today so I take up my wrap. I can hear the others already swilling their tea in the dining room, shuffling about on their wee crooked feet, always shuffling as if there was someplace to get to. Take it slow, take it slow, I long to tell them, eke out your hours, for I've heard people say that when someone goes into a Home, they get contrary and foolish and last just a couple of years. I've been here myself well over a year already and know that the stream of my living grows thinner: minute by minute, it ticks away slow, like the old clock on the landing that Thomas kept meaning to wind and nearly always forgot. Oh, there's nothing amiss with my head any more, but I'm not as feisty and fit as I was and when the air seems so thick I can hardly breathe, they hurry to give me oxygen. To tell the truth, I don't feel a hundred per cent this morning: my hands tremble badly and my feet hurt, these useless knobbly things that carried me once to the town or out to the ditches to find where the pullets were laying. I do believe I could still draw a fair lap of hay and comb the hedges for berries, prune that old rose at the kitchen window, but the truth is I'm only a miserable lean-to protecting a haggle of bones. I resent being old. The years came on too fast – they relentlessly picked at my edges and never gave me a chance to undo them one at a time. Like a burned-out candle, I've no longer a flame to dance to and court me to life; there's only the slow-moving sludge of something not settled.

Now here's Bernadette, bustling and acting all coy. 'It's your son to see you again, petal. I told him before that you wouldn't always be ready, that we didn't have visits this time of the day, disrupting routine.' All flustered, she leaves, and I draw my wrap closer, uneasy. I'm at the mercy of everyone here, not like at home, where it was myself who took charge of the comings and goings. But in a minute, without as much as lifting my head, I know it's himself again by the way the feet shuffle. I tighten my face, grow excited and fiddle with the cloth of my wrap, my restless fingers fluttering like birds. He moves to stand before me. What a big man he is: used to play rugby for the Chartered School team, and often I worried in case he'd get injured. Now he limps on a stick and needs, he has said, a newfangled thing called a 'replacement hip'.

Outside the door Bernadette gets to work; I can hear the squeak-squeak of her mop as we regard each other, him unspeaking, me a floodplain while the morning sun slides into the room. I take a quick breath like a hiccup and point to a chair. It's a very long time since I sat in his house with him and herself, and his visits to The Cairn wearied us both. But he comes very frequently now that I'm here. Always he hovers and fidgets, seemingly wanting to spell something out, but I offer no help; just send him away when I'm tired. Standing beside me now, he looks with the same big eyes that used to follow me around the kitchen and out to the haggart and garden. I pinch my lips together, bite the words out: 'You're here again?' Then follows a silence like what'd lie under a stone. I listen to the beat of my heart; it is beating so busy, so noisy that I think it might break again. There are so many things I need to say if only I could reach a softness in me. I have a terrible secret need to unfold all the stuff that lies packed away like yellowing linen in an old trunk, unpleat it, shake it out like a wind-filled shirt to be cleansed, 'make a good Confession' as our mischievous Dr McGettigan suggested once. Yet 'my tongue cleaveth to my jaws' and I am dumb.

My son looks very old today, made so by the horn-rimmed glasses and that foolish bushy moustache he has started to wear, and I fill up with sorrow for the pale, lined face. He is sixty-two years old. Sixty-two years since that day in the bedroom and Thomas vouching one hundred pounds for his birth. Slipping off his gloves, he lays a hand briefly on mine. 'I'm compelled to come again, Mother, and I'll just keep on coming until—'

But I give the short barky cough I've developed. 'Forgiveness doesn't come cheap.' And the hardness of rock presses down in me, inflaming all of my parts so that, while I long to reach out to him, smother the smouldering fires, I'm held cold and stiff in a vice.

'Mother,' he pleads, 'we must let go of this quarrel. Time runs out.'

There's a burning edge to his voice, but he should have

reckoned with time long ago in the days of Sam Hanna and Mr McGoldrick. I lower my eyes, examine the tips of my new pink slippers.

'How can you bear to do this? Be like this?' He is pleading now. 'Can you never forget the past?'

'And can you not know that the past never goes away, that it's always tied up in the present?'

But he's quick with his answer: 'You mean of course the unshriven past.'

I smart at that: 'unshriven' is a word he's learned no doubt in the Roman Church, but I have no answer. I turn my head away to the bedside mirror and look in at my crumpled leathery face and I tell that face about the great love I really have for my son and about my need to forgive, but the slit-eyes squint back hard as nuts and the thin blue lips curl in contempt. Yet I persist in my telling, remind the wizened face about mercy, but it stays a blank, and my words sink into its creases.

And he goes on sitting beside me, twisting his cap in his hands until I can bear the tension no longer. 'James, I must ask you to leave. I am tired. Come back again tomorrow.'

He just nods at that in a worn-out way and makes to leave as he's left so often over the years with the same old hangdog look that he's had, I believe, from the time he got married.

The door hisses after him, and on his heels Bernadette comes busy and bustling. 'He's kept you late, darlin', but you'll still be on time for the breakfast.' But now my spirit is stanched and dry like the mossy old branches of a boortree and I tell her I won't get up after all. I lie back on a pillow while she tut-tuts, 'Visitors like him only upset us, isn't that right, petal? Never give a thought to how old ones might feel.' She swoops then to tidy the things on my table. 'Oh, we'd a phone call from Mr McHenry this morning and *he says he'll be here in the afternoon.' Well, of course I'd be glad to see Wilson for, with all his preaching that day long ago by the grave, he's turned out to be closer than any to grasping my trouble.*

Left alone at last, I lie listening to the humming in my ears, and I talk to myself in the darkness behind my eyes, say what I like, dispute both sides of a question. To forgive is a hard thing: it's like when you're hungry and chewing on stones. But I keep wanting to wrench something more from my son, screw some kind of penitence out of him, hear him plead for pardon, say how he wronged us all. For it's no longer the Catholic Church that inflames me or the Presbyterian either, but something else, something in me that I can't undo. Wretched, I turn my face to the wall. It's papered yellow and white like the daisies that grew around The Cairn, and the words of a distant psalm come to me slow and clear: 'Against thee, thee only, have I sinned, and done this evil in thy sight.'

'Against thee only' – I struggle to make out the meaning of that but think instead of the stream that ran by the meadow at home and how it flowed around the slippery stones in its bed, rinsing the weeds, all sleek and green. All clean. And I promise myself now I'll be open with James when he comes tomorrow, the way I was in the days when Thomas was alive and the hay getting done and the flute bands echoing round the hills. Maybe it's time I attempted to gather the shreds and scraps that still hang loose from my life, wind them up neat like wool on a skein and fold my long work piece away.

CHAPTER 58

Sunnyside, March 1983

When Wilson arrives, he slips quietly into the chair at the side of my bed. He has little to say and that pleases me well. He takes a book from his pocket, a little black book, and I expect he may read the Beatitudes, which I've known by heart since a child and could recite to him now if I chose. 'Blessed are the poor in spirit,' and so on. And I am suddenly back to Ballymount hearing these words read down from the pulpit by Mr McGoldrick himself. I know them so well already: the merciful and the peacemakers and the pure of heart, all blessed, but these words mean nothing to me any more; so common they are, they slide off like fishes. But I sit up and attend to his reading anyway if only because he cares and because he is kind.

I am still very tired, and as he reads, his gentle voice rises a little, barely filling the room's empty spaces, but it isn't the Beatitudes I hear after all; it is something totally new to me. Is it a piece of a poem perhaps or maybe a biblical text I've never been taught? But it makes me open my eyes, and I find myself drawn by the words to a place like a meadow, where I seem to be walking, calm and serene, through grasses brushing my knees. His reading goes on. It feels like the same words are streaming over and over, and it's as if I'm being taken by them to the banks of a river, where the

Reverend Charles McHenry is washing his son, a son like my own; and the cleansing water is flowing so clean and so free that I murmur aloud with the prophet Ezekiel, 'A new heart also will I give you, and a new spirit will I put within you.'

But then, startling and sudden, comes Wilson's own voice, and he asks what's that I was saying, so I tell him it was nothing at all. But I am wide awake now and alert, as if at the end of my days I've been born anew for the very first time. I ask him to write down the beautiful words he's just read, the ones he's repeated again and again, for they've borne me away to a lightsome place in my head. I'll need to read them another time, read them myself it may be. Wilson looks pleased to hear that, and when he has written, I see that he slips the paper into the back of my Bible.

I slept a long time after he left: in and out of warm-wrapping sandy waves that rose and fell. Sometimes I was in the Big Meadow at home, sometimes in the church. The sun shone, a gentle glow, and I passed, swift and silent, through scene after scene: the flax hole, the church and the bands marching, Anna May Reilly too and my own boy, reading again the lesson he'd read in the church at Meeting, and Wilson McHenry in the graveyard wanting to talk in the hazy sunshine, talk and talk as I knelt by the kerb and a new-dawning light that came streaming over the cold wintry stones.

But now I awake and see Mr Boyd is kindly wanting to pray with me as he often does, but I tell him no, there's something more urgent today: he must fetch my Bible. Then I finger its gritty black cover, press open the delicate whispering pages that have often breathed words of comfort and guidance and I draw out the paper inscribed by Wilson McHenry. I show it to Mr Boyd, and tell him I want to share this with my son when he comes again. 'Is it something really important?' the minister asks, and I tell him it is and there's so little time, to which he responds, 'There's an eternity of time in God's glory.' So I tell him that glory's no use at all now to me or James Campbell.

I'm coughing a lot today, and the choking rattle jolts my body, so I lie as still as I can, waiting, excited and longing for James's visit tomorrow. And here now again is that comforting light: it's hovering over the ceiling, calm and yellow, filling the spaces. Would my turning for home be like that some day, I wonder? Would it drop down gentle, unexpected, on a day when the leaves were falling to earth, curling and falling, the sycamore dropping its pendants, the chestnut its lanterns . . . ?

Now Bernadette comes hurrying in again to say I ought to be resting, so I'll fold my writing away. To tell the truth, I'm feeling done in a bit but not afraid or uneasy – in fact I'm a little buoyed up for when James comes back tomorrow, I'll tell him to pull up the chair and sit down – I can just see his face – and I'll read all these words to him; then who knows . . . well, you never can tell . . . and even as Bernadette straightens my blanket, I can see myself and my child together again: me pushing him on the swing, him reciting his psalm under the kitchen table, the two of us pedalling out to the manse on a morning in autumn with the leaves on the trees turning russet and red.

CHAPTER 59

St Mary's Secondary School for Boys, March 1983

Alone in the staffroom, James Campbell raised his head from the copies he was correcting. The phone was ringing. It would be Sunnyside again; they called whenever they took the notion, interrupting his work and often about the most trivial things: she needed soap or a new comb or whatever. They might have waited till school was finished, but she was low these days and they sounded urgent so he told them that yes, of course, he'd be there, in the blink of an eye, he said. He stacked his books, took a quick look in the mirror and frowned at the thin sandy-coloured hair, the florid face, the limp grey suit past its best, the untidy collar. He sighed. It was hard to be always on duty, but he'd go again and again to her, for you never could tell . . . unless she'd always refuse to be reconciled.

'Reconcile' was a word the Church used a lot, and he suspected his confessor might wish it for him, but he'd forgotten what it meant. It was something about waiting perhaps? Waiting alone on an indrawn breath. Yet his wife, her life wilting, had waited beside him, stayed with him under the cloud that perpetually filled and bellied between him and his mother.

As he buttoned his coat, he flinched: the old angina again. He stopped for a second, fumbled and slipped a capsule under

273

his tongue. He'd be fine. Perhaps he should give Dolores a call before he set out in case she worried or in case she needed the car, but it occurred to him that this was her day for cleaning the church. He was glad the girls had married, left home, for he'd found it hard to endure their continuous scolding advice about the granny they didn't know. It was Dolores who'd kept the peace in the house: explained when angry questions were asked and fielded the accusations. Even in the times of his own depression, when his stuck state all but paralysed him, she'd been there like a candle, gentle and calming. His love for her was true, 'constant as the northern star'.

He brushed the chalk dust off his trousers and snapped shut the handle of the briefcase, swearing quietly as he knocked over a pen holder. He had a right to feel hard done by, a right to pity himself, for as well as everything else he felt incomplete, knew that his teaching had suffered over the years and now retirement loomed. Reaching for his scarf, he recalled the day he'd taught that Langston Hughes poem, had even written the line on the board – 'The calm, cool face of the river asked me for a kiss' – a thing he should never have done but for his own despair coming through, seeping out to the surface, and he'd been surprised no parent complained.

Swinging the car through the school gates, his thoughts in a tumult, he braked suddenly, avoiding a child's ball. How would he find her today? Would he have the courage to stand up to her or would she say what he wanted to hear and let him breathe again? Grimly, he clenched the steering wheel, hardly aware of the road but knowing he was driving too fast. This woman, the mother he was going to see, had cast a long shadow, besmirching what should have been green and unspoiled. He went to see her each Tuesday in Sunnyside and always came home with a sea-surge of anger, black and mottled and deep, which in spite of his efforts to hide it spilled over his home like ink. He chewed on his moustache and reached for his cigarettes but knew he'd left them behind on the staffroom shelf.

Now he was passing the church and wondered if he'd time to drop by – Dolores would still be there tidying up after ten o'clock Mass – but he decided against it. When he'd given up going to Mass himself, she'd said nothing, never nagged or accused, but it saddened him still to see her slip quietly out on her own, morning by morning, with her missal and beads, her head bent. For many long years he'd refused to let her down, had learned by heart the workings of the Roman Church, its vowels and grammar, the bowing and kneeling, fast days, Confessions, novenas; he'd diligently made the sign of the cross and received the sacrament, had his children baptized and confirmed, and all in the face of Ballymount and her who continued to sit unmoved. Only in his heart did he confess that he missed the expounding of scripture, the singing of hymns and paraphrases. He still clung to his faith in God's free saving grace, and sometimes in the long silent nights he'd put himself over to sleep by reciting the portions of scripture he'd learned by heart in Sunday School: the Psalms and Isaiah, the healing prophet: 'As one whom his mother comforteth, so will I comfort you; and ye shall be comforted.' Yet when sleep did come it was often troubled by nightmare: tossed and rolled in waves of despair, he'd wait in a sweat for the two clerical creatures to come and lament by the rocks near The Cairn, their robes emblazoned with Rome's sacred hearts and Presbyterian burning bushes.

He relaxed his grip on the steering wheel, straightened his shoulders and shook himself out. This wouldn't do. He must slow down; he'd taken a corner too tight just now but there was a beast in his breast this morning. He'd bully her into speaking today. He changed gears, grinding them. Couldn't she just have pretended, the way he'd sometimes pretended? Couldn't she have joined him quietly as in a charade? Their lives would have been different then. But no, she hadn't been one to play games, was far too honest for that, and so now at the end of her days, at the end of the furrow, he was here to plead only for understanding.

When he'd seen her yesterday, he'd known again all the need of mothering comfort; the memory of it had swept over him, and he'd wanted to cry. She'd looked so frail, like the bits of Belleek in the parlour at home in The Cairn, looked so old and transparent that it came as a shock to find her still closed, tight and withholding, the thin blue mouth dropping hard little words like pebbles until he began to feel himself played with. *Could it be,* he wondered now, *that a person might actually forget how to forgive? Forget the mechanics of the thing? Forget how to untwist a snarl of censure?*

When he pulled up at the Home it was just gone eleven and he'd have no time now to look over that sixth-form sonnet or get to the chemist. Too sharply he pulled on the handbrake, and the wheels bit into the gravel where a nurse was already hurrying out to meet him. 'I'm so sorry,' she said, and he knew it of course, knew that this had to come, and he stayed there standing on the bare front step, looking and looking. Jackdaws reeled around the chimney pots, crows cawed from the pines, and in the lightening air the emptied-out sky came shawling around him.

Then over a sea of green lino that rose and swam on a corridor floor, he followed the nurse, who finally left him alone in the empty room. There was grass and mud on the toes of his shoes. She'd always been particular about mud on shoes, and he recalled the goatskin mats she'd made one time for the inside doors of The Cairn and how he and his father had teased her. Almost furtively now, he closed the door and stood washed by a silence that was full of her presence: she was still there, towering and hovering, as though she might suddenly say, 'Now we'll shut up the hens for fear of the fox.'

Soon the nurse was back, coy in the face of grief, but no, he wouldn't go to the mortuary yet, would stay for a while by the vacant bed and the vacant chair, where he noticed someone had neatly folded the purple shawl. He took it up in his hands, feeling its warmth, remembering the day he'd bought it. It was in Galway, a gift for her, a peace offering, and when he hadn't been able to decide on the colour, it was Dolores who'd chosen it, had shaken it out in the sun for him to admire, saying, 'That's a colour would warm the coldest heart.' And here, in this room, remembering, a surge of anger rose up in him, pure as fire annealing, to slough off the cast of shame that had chased and fashioned him. Breathing hoarsely, he grasped the shawl in his hands, twisted it, wrung it, his knuckles whitening. There was just nothing at all of shame in his life, nothing at all of blight, unless love be shame, love that caused him to toss off a harness and race off unbounded. And was that a sin? Was freedom a sin? And the longing for wholeness? A sin against her or the Church of his fathers? Because for that he'd been left with a sour curdle of guilt in his heart, scourged, even broken at times when the pills didn't work, when sometimes even his marriage was threatened.

And still he stood by the empty bed holding on to the shawl, hearing his voice come thick, gouged out like an echo, a regurgitation of something he'd heard before, heard it whisper now, vowels slow and deliberate: 'Mother, I'll never forgive you.' Appalled by his words, he took a step back from the bed and stared out the window, where the well-kept lawns were awash with the calm of crocus and snowdrop and the easy sweep of the sky. She'd wanted too much, his soul and his body, and all for her pride and her fear of Rome. He felt sick now, drained as a cup, yet purged and strangely clean, ready to go with the nurse, who led him to where she was laid. He looked at the undisturbed face, the firmly closed lips and the full-blooded veins gone pale in her folded hands. But Dolores was beside him now. Taking him into her arms, she drew him away. He must rest, prepare for the funeral.

CHAPTER 60

Seated in the front seat of the car behind the hearse, he hunched over the dashboard, twisting his gloves over and over, yet calmer now. Forty-five years ago he'd made this very journey along with Reverend McGoldrick, had bumped over those same potholed, gravelly roads. Now through the darkened windows he could see the roadside bushes tinged pink and yellow and red, and the rain slanting cold on the roundy hills and the scraggy, hummocky fields that were forever plugged with rushes and ragweed and thistles. If he strained, he could make out the gable end of The Cairn and beyond it the moorland, springy with stag's horn moss and rusty fern and the spiky undergrowth that could draw blood. No luxuriance of leaf there now or buds swollen with promise of life. *Was it possible to love and hate at the same time?* he wondered. *To plead for forgiveness and yet withhold its balm?*

The car swayed and rolled through the narrow roads, passing the streams and woods of his childhood and the desolate boggy acres that yielded to no horizon. He huddled into his collar. She who'd always been with him like God had left, had clanged a gate shut in his face so that like Cain he'd been banished. But oh – and he recited the psalm to himself, '*My sin is greater than I can bear . . .*' – could it be true that he'd killed her, soused her spirit with the oils of his Roman anointing, then cursed her? And must he now mourn the loss of the one who'd set a stone at the door of her heart, who'd turned and flicked like a lizard, changed so quickly from what she once had been, who'd asked for too much?

Behind him Dolores and his daughters whispered occasionally to themselves, soft little courteous murmurs, and it occurred to him that they'd never been here before, never heard God's Word ring out true in Ballymount Church or been uplifted by 'Praise', the congregational singing he'd loved, so part of every Presbyterian service. All this was only a legend to them, a shadow, darkly staining their lives. Their grandmother a legend too, save for the trouble she'd brought on the house, the cold visitations and them being told not to talk about Mass.

Now the hearse was swaying and crunching into the lay-by that stood for Ballymount's car park, and he straightened himself up. Dolores was out of the car before him, to help him, always at hand, but he brushed her hand away. 'Go ahead, the three of you. I'll be up in a minute. You'll be shown where to sit.'

He leaned on his stick by the limo, drew his scarf close, fearful of chills, and stood looking about. Most of the trees were still bare, just a grey mist combing their branches, and ahead, under poisonous green of cypress and yew, lay the church, crouched firm in the graveyard. Fifty years ago he used to come here, clinging to the hands of his parents, a proud little man coming to worship and be forewarned. The graves, he noticed, were still all over the place: some with copings, some without, many headstones crooked, pockmarked with lichen and green with moss, interspersed, here and there, with the gleaming white marble of several newer stones. And here, not far from the door, was the fresh-opened grave and the stone with the names of his forebears, his father's inscription too, majestic and stable: THE ANCIENT OF DAYS, foothold into a world beloved of him once, now lost awhile.

Nearby lay a vase, sullied, forlorn, a few withered stems still strewn on the scutch, and he guessed she'd come here often over the years, paying her dues, remembering. He picked up the vase, rubbed it clean with his thumb and, holding it close for a second, he placed it gently beside the fresh grave. Then he dusted away the green stuff staining his sleeve and took a step closer. This crumbly black earth was where they'd place her remains, stanch the wildflower fragrance that had webbed his young years, and here, in this place where the earthworms channelled and the cold air cringed unyielding, it would come to an end. She was gone forever and hadn't forgiven. And a limitless plain lay before him, stretching and stretching to places of healing he'd never be able to reach, not if he lived for a thousand years. Yet when he looked up from the hole in the earth and lifted his face to the wind and the sweetness of air, he could see her still coming: running and running towards him, her arms outstretched and apron flying, to tell him the news of the heifer's birthing or the price she was currently fetching for eggs.

Around the church door a few men were standing, waiting, but he knew none of them although they'd certainly know who he was: he was the 'one who'd betrayed them', 'let them all down', 'destroyed the mother', and, 'Here now's the boyo himself.' By the side of the door he saw a man linger alone, a man seen somewhere before? Who had greeted him once? But now someone else was approaching, quietly urging: he must take his place in the church. How small it was, how bare and how strange. The floorboards creaked as he trod the blue carpet, worn to threads, but the walls had been newly whited with wash – he could smell the lime – and the open Bible still sat on the lectern, its yellowing leaves curled at the edges. So different from the Church of the Sacred Heart, with the smoke of its waxy odours and flagrant disturbing colours.

Brushing by the coffin, he took his place with his wife and daughters in the same old echoing pew where he'd once started to scratch his initials before being caught and given a slap. The church was cold and dank, smelled slightly of mildew the way it had always done, and the velvet-clad pulpit sat moored like the bow of a ship becalmed, full of blessings and warnings but never, he mused, of curses. Wincing at the pain in his knees, he propped his stick against the pew in front, then glanced at Dolores, saw her look cold and pale, too thin. She'd endured so much: the bite of his mother's tongue and his own too on the days when he couldn't forget where he'd come from.

There was only a scattering of people present: Cissie Lynch, God bless her, sat in the back, and beside her that man who'd looked through him at the door. Sam Hanna of course was dead and gone, Florrie McKinley too, but he recognized Molly at once: small as a bird now, she sat bent over the harmonium keys and he wondered if she still gave testimony and if she'd ever married. He reached for Dolores's hand, chafed the cold fingers and then held them tight as the congregation stood up to sing, in doleful assurance, a hymn that called the Lodge to his mind.

> Yes, we will gather at the river,
> The beautiful, the beautiful river;
> Gather with the saints at the river
> That flows by the throne of God.

Ere we reach the shining river,
Lay we every burden down;
Grace our spirits will deliver,
And provide a robe and crown.

And he was glad that for her, in death, there'd be nothing of Purgatory, no period of purification.

Then, at the minister's beckon, he walked to the front and turned the heavily wadded pages of the great book until he found the passage he'd already chosen from the Book of Revelation. Clearing his throat, he grasped the wooden lectern to keep his hands from shaking and read firmly as he'd been taught to do in this very place. Looking at Dolores, he informed the world, directly and resolutely, that there would be no more of 'mourning or crying or pain' for the 'first things had passed away'. Yet he knew that, as she'd said, the past never went away, and even now the first things in his own life were all rising up to condemn him: the bedside prayers, the homely nurturings, the golden sheen of his new Orange sash. And there'd be no remittance: he'd always be the lost sheep she'd never reclaimed, always the prodigal son she would give neither bite nor sup to.

The burial was quick. All the right words were spoken, and then it was done. The few people who'd waited to shake his hand were gone home; only the minister remained, inviting him back to the vestry. Here in a streak of watery sunlight dust motes swam and the thick-piled carpets dizzied his head as the minister spoke, softly now, as if from a distance: 'James,' he was saying. 'James, very shortly before your dear mother passed, she said you must have this.' And he drew a paper from under his clerical gown.

'She'd planned to give it herself when you came again, but sadly she was called home before she could do that.'

'What is it?'

Numb as the granite and limestone around him, he reached for the folded paper, dreading to find there further entreaties and exhortations from scripture. Through the years of his childhood she'd told him so often the stories of Daniel and the Lions, Abraham and Isaac, Jacob and Esau, but now, it seemed, she was wanting to tell something more. He wiped his eyes, saw a few blurred words running, crooked like ants, across the thin paper, and then, fumbling with his glasses, he read in silence. Again and again he read, frowning and searching. *This was from her?*

At last he looked up and with a glance at Dolores he started to read aloud. Slowly, haltingly, the words stumbled out, his voice catching and holding on to each one, as though it might vanish: 'Never despise a man who has broken with the faith of his fathers.' He recognized the words at once: they were Elie Wiesel's, a Hungarian Jew the Nazis had tried to destroy. Was his sad and bitter old mother telling him now, through his tears, something she'd hoarded too tight in the folds of her ageing body, something she hadn't been able to name? And was she telling him now in the same old matter-of-fact way she'd told him once that a bogey man never haunted The Cairn in spite of Anna May's nonsense? All of a sudden his body was aching as if for the loss of something, he didn't know what, but he continued to read, the words coming careful and wary as if crossing a barbed-wire fence: 'It is a man's duty to make a free choice and to push back walls.' *Duty? Free choice? What nonsense was this to Ballymount! What heresy to Rome!* Yet it would seem that someone wise must have given these very words to his mother, someone wanting to tell her a new and different story.

He set the paper aside, and in the cramped little room stuffy with Bibles and gowns and clerical robes he grew cold in a drenching sweat. He made a rush for the door, the minister and Dolores calling after, but he wanted to be alone, wanted to head into the wind, feel the air flood over his face as when they'd swung together in the garden under the berry bushes before his father died, before the Hebrew and the Orange Order, before the rebuke of the Churches.

A few fields over, a lone tractor followed by gulls was ploughing the first furrow. The driver, small as a toy, had his head down in the bite of the wind, powering on, zigzagging and lurching but always on. When the tractor struck the furthest ditch and seemed almost upended, it turned with grace and made its way back. Up and down it went, again and again, preparing for seed to be scattered, the good with the bad and the 'bud that would yield no meal'. It was laying the ground. James wiped some earth from his shoes with a dock leaf and, giving himself up to the sky and the clean-pouring air, he threw his head back. There was a wonderful purity everywhere, lying like fresh-fallen snow, sensed in the white of the gravestones, in the green of the grass, in the blazing whins. An almost palpable wholeness was knitting together the hedges and ditches on Ballymount's cradling hills. It was all of a piece. There'd been a coming together in the darkest of places, a labouring and a birth.

Acknowledgements

I wish to thank the following people without whom this book would never have seen the light: my daughter Gwyneth for her unwavering support of me; my late husband who offered frequent, and sometimes bemused, critique; Brian Langan, my patient and meticulous editor, to whom this book owes so very much; Eoin McHugh; agent Susan Feldstein; and Josh Benn at Transworld. I am grateful also to Pauline O'Hare for her judicious and kindly reading of the manuscript and for her dogged belief in this book; to Eileen Casey, who got me over 'writer's block'; and to the Ardgillan Writers' Group, where it was Verena who first whispered the word 'publish'. I am deeply indebted to my earliest readers for their sustaining encouragement: Patrick Rudden, David Jameson, Hugh Fitzgerald Ryan, Denis Campbell and William Marshall. I also thank Moyra Smyth, my lifelong friend, and Eithne Lannon who kept my spirits from flagging.

Author's Note

This book, while drawn out of my own life experience, is entirely fictional (aside from points of historical fact) and the likeness of any of the characters to real people is purely coincidental.